Winter Jacket

ELIZA LENTZSKI

ISBN: 1483908771
ISBN-13: 978-1483908779

Other Works by Eliza Lentzski

Date Night

Second Chances

Love, Lust, & Other Mistakes

Diary of a Human

CONTENTS

DEDICATION

To Troian and Nikole

PROLOGUE

It's funny how seemingly unconnected events can come together like a perfect storm and change the entire trajectory of one's life. In my case, none of this would have happened if not for a broken space heater.

It was winter in the upper Midwest, and I was starting a new semester of teaching academic writing at a university where I'd been hired a few years prior. I liked the school; it was similar to the university where I'd received my own undergraduate degree not that long ago – a small, intimate, private, liberal arts teaching college. I liked teaching at these kinds of schools because the students always seemed so bright, polite, and hard working. This school was no exception. I taught the core writing class in the English Department and sections were capped at a dozen and a half students. It made for a congenial environment where you got to know the students well and they you in return. Students didn't have the luxury of hiding in the anonymity of a large lecture hall, but that was part of the attraction of the college.

Despite the small classroom size, students could still fly under the radar if they really wanted to. Being absent from class or never making eye contact were a few ways to do so. I had a handful of students who regularly participated in each section, and during the 50-minute class period my attention was divided amongst the more active students. I certainly knew and was friendly with the other,

1

more silent students, but not to the extent of those who eagerly and regularly participated. And if not for a broken in-room heater, I probably wouldn't have even noticed her.

Her name was Hunter. And she was lovely.

I knew from introductions on the first day of the new semester that she was a student in the nursing program and that she'd grown up in a nearby suburb. Her name was a bit of a misnomer. I had learned years ago during grad school not to make any preconceived judgments about students based on their names, but I still found myself doing it at the beginning of each semester. Hunter could either be a male student with shaggy hair and a star on the university baseball team, or one of those undergraduate women who predictably wear UGGs every day and pink sweatpants with something equally obnoxious scrawled across their ass. The Hunter enrolled in my class, however, was neither of these people.

She was one of the more quiet students, reticent to volunteer an answer in class discussion, but I was struck by how when I *did* call on her, even if she didn't have her hand raised, she was ready with a thoughtful answer and spoke in a confident, even tone that surprised me. Most undergraduates stumbled over themselves if they weren't voluntarily participating, too nervous or too shy to put themselves out there for fear of being wrong in front of their peers. But not Hunter. It was as if she knew what question I was going to ask even before I asked it. As if she knew I was going to call on her, and was thusly prepared, even before I knew myself that I was going to ask her to participate.

But these were all things that I only took stock of after the heater in the classroom broke.

We'd been having typical Midwestern, winter weather – snowy, cold, and blustery. I was born in this part of the country, so the harsh weather was certainly no stranger. The building where I taught was one of the oldest on campus and hadn't been updated in decades. There was no central heating or cooling in the building either, so each room was equipped with its own wall unit that controlled the temperature in each individual classroom. Unfortunately, the units were never that reliable and had the tendency to break, either leaving us to deal with the cold or suffer through excessive heat. The windows were painted shut, too, not affording the opportunity to at least regulate the temperature with outside air if the heater was on the fritz again.

On this particular winter day, we were dealing with a hot, muggy, sauna-like classroom. As soon as I walked into the small room, I was hit by the stifling heat wave. The students who had arrived early to class were already seated in the U-shaped table configuration, each stripped down to t-shirts and tank tops and fanning themselves with the homework for that day. They looked at me forlornly, their eyes collective begging that I *do something*. But we all knew that I was powerless to the University Physical Plant. Numerous calls and work orders to the college's maintenance department had gone unanswered. We'd all have to suffer.

I pulled my wool jacket off and silently cursed that I'd chosen to wear a sweater that day. I could have stripped down to the tank top that I wore beneath it like all the students, but that felt unprofessional. As a junior academic, I always did my best to put on a professional front since I was only a handful of years older, and in some cases younger, than my students.

I started the lesson for that day, my face feeling flushed from the unsavory heat. But as I looked around the room, I knew that I was in good company. We were *all* suffering. We were *all* miserable together. Except for her. Except for Hunter.

While everyone else was down to their last clothing layer possible without becoming indecent, she sat in the far corner of the room, *right* next to the broken heater, still wearing her winter jacket. It was one of those puffy down jackets that practically reach your knees. They're especially popular around this part of the country because of our brisk, winter winds. I remember taking note of the jacket earlier in the week because my ex-girlfriend had had the same coat. Instead of being a dripping, sweaty mess like the rest of us, Hunter looked amazingly comfortable.

The unexpected sight nearly caused me to forget what I was even lecturing about. I couldn't fathom how she could sit in the back corner of the room, looking anything but distracted by the heat, calmly taking notes in her spiral notebook, all while wearing her heavy winter jacket. I mentally shook myself, perplexed, but didn't put too much thought into it and continued on with the lesson.

The next day the heater still wasn't fixed, and Hunter was still wearing her jacket. At no point during the class session did she make a move to take off her coat. And it wasn't that she'd come to class late and needed to hustle into her seat and immediately start taking notes; she was always early to class with ample time to get settled and take off her jacket. The classroom was slightly cramped, but not so packed that there wasn't room for her to hang up her jacket on the back of her chair like everyone else.

This persisted over the next few class periods, and as a result of this funny quirk, I took more of an interest in her. I even mentioned her and the jacket in passing to a few friends – my funny student who never took off her winter coat. I made up scenarios in my head why she couldn't take off her jacket: she'd woken up late and hadn't had time to put on a shirt, or it was laundry day and everything else was dirty. The scenario reminded me of a ghost story I'd heard told around the campfire when I was young. The story was about a girl who always wore a scarf, even in the summer. She was horribly taunted and teased because she refused to take it off. One day some bullies stole the scarf from her, and her head fell off. My friends and I joked, not unkindly, about what would happen to Hunter if she took off her jacket. Would her arms fall off? Did she even *have* arms?

Because I had started to take more of a keen interest in perpetually coat-clad Hunter, I began to notice a lot more about this usually silent student. Since it was an English composition course, my students had to do a lot of writing in class. At the beginning of a new period, I'd ask them to reflect and write on a question about a contemporary event, a memory, or something from one of the assigned readings. It wasn't anything they had to turn in; it was simply meant to get their brains ready to actively participate in class that day.

Hunter, still in her winter jacket, seemed to take these writing prompts very seriously. She'd hunch her body over her desk, her face just inches from her notebook, and she'd scribble furiously on the page; she wrote with a purpose. I couldn't tell if her unusual posture was to keep others from peeking at her page, but it turned into another one of her quirks that caught and kept my attention.

Because I observed how frantically her pen worked along the lined pages of her college-ruled notebook, I also noticed her hands – long, feminine, tapered fingers with short polished fingernails. Most of the time she wore a clear coat of nail polish, but sometimes she'd come to class with a dark blue polish that coincidentally matched the color of her winter jacket.

Over the span of a few class periods, Hunter transformed for me. She went from being a quiet student who would have easily slipped under the radar to something akin to an obsession. Firstly, she was beautiful – traditionally so – blonde, fair skin, tall, long-limbed, and angular. Her mouth was wide, but not unattractively so. Her facial features on their own could have been described as "too large," but for some reason everything seemed to fit proportionately on her face.

Unlike the other undergraduates who stumbled into the morning class still in their pajamas with their hair hastily thrown in a ponytail or covered beneath a baseball cap, Hunter always came to class looking polished and put-together. It wasn't that she dressed up (not that I could see much of her clothes with her jacket on), but even her jeans looked crisply fitted and not baggy from multiple uses without having been laundered. Her natural blonde hair was always meticulously flat-ironed and perfectly parted to one side. Even when she wore it up in a ponytail, her hair was smooth and the part was immaculate.

Day after day, as she walked in and out of the classroom, I came to appreciate the gracefulness and poise that seemed to come without much effort and how she possessed a quiet maturity beyond her years. I noticed the way her grey-blue eyes crinkled at the corners when she made small talk before class with the people who sat near her. Other students would flop into their chairs and loudly announce how hung-over they were or how much they hated a particular professor. Hunter, while still being friendly and cordial with her classmates, seemed uninterested in contributing to those kinds of conversations. She appeared content to set out her homework and get a page ready in her notebook for that day's class.

But even more so than this grace and poise and maturity, what really drew me in was her silent intensity. In a sea of laptops and smart phones and tablets, a plethora of devices students brought to class that distracted them from the content of my class, Hunter's eyes followed me around the classroom. I could practically *feel* them on me as I paced the room and talked about Thesis Statements and Quote Sandwiches. It was my Achilles' Heel – women who make unwavering eye contact.

And damn me if I couldn't stop wondering what she looked like beneath that puffy jacket.

+++++

CHAPTER ONE

"No need to thank me, but I found your future wife." My friend Troian threw her messenger bag onto my desk with her usual, dramatic flair.

I looked up from my grading with a bemused look. "Is that so?"

She sat down in the chair on the other side of my desk, the one usually reserved for my students. "Yup. I think she's a keeper," she confirmed with a crisp nod. Her eyes scanned around my sparsely decorated faculty office. I had been hired as an Assistant Professor nearly three years prior, but you'd never know it from the empty walls and bookshelves. The office still felt unsettled; I suppose I was superstitious – as if putting my personal mark on the space might jinx my good luck to have landed the tenure-track position.

"I appreciate the effort," I started, not bothering to set down the paper I was grading. I had too much grading to let Troian suck me into this conversation. Finding me a "future wife" had recently become a self-appointed duty for my friend. "Cady and I haven't even been separated for three months," I pointed out. "Isn't there supposed to be a longer grieving process before I start dating again?"

Troian waved a dismissive hand. "No offense, but you and the Cat Lady were emotionally separated long before the official break up. And for how much you used to whine about it, *physically* you'd both gone your separate ways a long, long time ago."

I audibly sighed. Her words weren't untrue, but that didn't make it any better.

"Also, it's totally weird that you still hang out with her as

7

'friends.'" She used air-quotes and everything. "That doesn't seem healthy."

"You can't judge me about that; you've never had an ex-girlfriend before. Exes can totally be friends."

"It's weird," Troian said, wrinkling her nose. "And Nikole agrees. Are you and Cady broken up or not?"

"We're broken up," I insisted. "We just hang out sometimes. And it's not even like we talk everyday. I see *you* more often than I see her. So does that mean that you and I are dating?"

Troian snorted. "You wish, Bookworm."

I tossed my pen onto the daunting stack of ungraded papers on my desk. Experience told me I'd never get anything done until Troian had had her peace. "So tell me about my future wife."

The smile on Troian's face broadened. She loved getting her way. She rubbed her hands together, looking eager. "So I don't actually know her name, but she's the new bartender at Peggy's."

Peggy's was the name of a horrible little gay bar across the train tracks that I sometimes frequented with Troian and her long-time girlfriend, Nikole. Of the pair, I had met Troian first, but I couldn't remember a time when she and her other-half hadn't been together.

"You don't know her name, but apparently she's my perfect woman?" I could feel my eyebrows lift toward the ceiling.

"Perfect for you, yes," Troian nodded. She leaned forward in the chair. "Just think of all the free beer!" she chirped.

"But you don't even drink," I pointed out. "You get all red."

Troian sighed and rolled her eyes. "Which is why she's the perfect woman for *you*, not me."

"So my soul mate is a beer slinger," I deadpanned. "You must really think I'm an alcoholic."

Troian shrugged, unaffected. "Well, you are from Wisconsin."

"Using that logic, my soul mate could also be a cow."

Troian wiggled her eyebrows. "You said it. Not me."

"Well as enlightening as this conversation has been, I need to get back to these papers." I picked up the discarded pen and tapped at the unwieldy pile. Spring Break was on the horizon, but I still had a stack of grading to wade through until I could mentally check out for a week.

"Is that a paper for your English comp class?" Troian asked.

"Yep."

"Have you gotten to Winter Jacket's paper yet?"

I didn't know what had possessed me to tell Troian about my quirky, yet attractive, student. I suppose it was the novelty of the situation that had compelled me. I'd never before had such an acute crush on a student. I frowned and shook my head. "Not yet. But our meeting isn't for a few days."

Students had to meet with me in my faculty office throughout the semester to discuss how the class was going and talk about whatever upcoming paper they were working on for my class. During these meetings, I gave back their rough drafts and provided guidance on how to improve the essays for the final version. I found that students were grateful for the one-on-one time and the personal feedback on their writing. It was a small campus with an equally small student-to-faculty ratio that fostered that kind of personal attention; most students had chosen the school for exactly that reason. This wasn't a diploma factory like other schools where I'd worked previously.

In our initial meeting, I'd found Hunter surprisingly easy to talk to. She was polite and earnest; it was clear her parents had done a good job raising her. Her genuine interest was paired with that intense, almost unnerving eye contact. The intensity was muted when the span of a classroom separated us, but with only my desk between us, I had felt myself mentally squirming beneath her gaze. I was equally looking forward to and dreading this second one-on-one meeting.

"You interested in going to Peggy's tonight?" Troian asked.

I smirked. "So you can set me up with the hot new bartender?"

She smiled innocently.

"I could be convinced to go out tonight," I nodded. "For a drink," I was quick to add, "not to hit on the new bartender."

Her face lit up and she pulled out her phone. "Awesome. I'll let Nik know," she said as she began to text her girlfriend. "What time are you off today?"

I glanced at the clock in the bottom corner of my computer screen. "A couple hours," I noted. "I don't have any more classes to teach today, but I've got student meetings about these papers," I said, tapping my fingers against the top of the stack.

Troian leaned back in her chair and yawned exaggeratedly. "That sounds horribly boring. I don't know how you do it."

"Well, we can't all be fancy screenwriters like you."

Troian held up her hands. "Hey, don't look at me; I offered to put in a good word for you at my studio. You could be a hot, new writer for some TV show. Nothing makes panties drop like saying you work for Hollywood."

I rolled my eyes; Troian was a paradox. She talked a big game and her word choice often made me blush, but she was the biggest monogamist I'd ever met. She was that rare breed of dedicated girlfriend who felt guilty if she even had a sex dream about a woman other than Nikole.

"And I've told you before that I'd rather be a teacher than a writer," I said with conviction.

She nodded sagely. "I can see why – the wacked-out hours, bottom of the barrel pay, and bad Departmental coffee." She wrinkled her nose and pointed at my nearly empty coffee cup. "I don't know how you stomach that stuff, woman."

"I'm educating the future generation," I retorted. I crossed my arms across my chest as if daring her to defy me.

"Ah, that's right. Young, impressionable minds just waiting for you to mold them." Troian's eyes took on a faraway look. "Ripe for the taking."

I shook my head. "You make it sound so sordid."

"Hey, I'm just proud of you for hanging out with undergrads all day and keeping it in your pants," she smirked. "You should win a prize."

"How do you always manage to paint me in such an unflattering way?" I complained.

"What can I say?" she grinned. "I've got a knack."

We both looked towards the open office door when someone knocked. My chest seized slightly, worried that someone who shouldn't have been overhearing had just been witness to Troian's unorthodox compliments.

One of my students, Mike Bobeli, a sophomore on the football team, stood in the doorway looking awkward. "I can come back," he said, not making eye contact. He shifted his weight from one foot to the next. "I just had a quick question."

I waved the student in, hoping my face hadn't turned a telling shade of red. "No, no. You're not interrupting anything, Mike," I said with an exaggerated grin. "My friend was just leaving."

Troian's eyebrows rose on her forehead. "I was?"

"Uh huh," I confirmed, shooing her out. "I'll meet up with you later."

+++++

After my last student meeting of the day, I met up with Troian at Peggy's, an understated lesbian dive-bar with a small dance floor. Troian, Nikole, and I weren't regulars, but we went enough to have become familiar with some of the tenured bartenders. I'd never met Peggy, however. I wasn't even sure there *was* a Peggy though.

"You're wasting a perfectly good opportunity," Troian complained. The two of us sat at a table for four a few feet from the main bar. She demolished a peanut shell between her thumb and forefinger and brushed the crumbs onto the floor. She rubbed her fingers together, now dusty and salty from the peanut shell, and made a disgusted face.

Tonight was some kind of cowboy or ranch-themed event, which meant the DJ was playing country music and every table had a bowl of peanuts. Lately management had been experimenting with themed evenings to drum up business mid-week. For a Thursday night the bar was relatively empty, despite the drink specials and complimentary nuts. The place was usually packed on the weekends with local college women, so when I did frequent here, it was usually on a weekday night. I didn't hide my sexuality from the University or students; I just wasn't about to rent out space on a billboard to announce it. The school was small and a little on the conservative side.

I ran my own fingertips over the rim of my beer glass. "I told you I'm not ready to date again. It's too soon."

Troian rolled her eyes and made a frustrated noise. "You're single for the first time in over a year, Bookworm. If I were in your situation, I'd be getting *so* much random pussy."

"Why do you have to be so crude?" I said, wrinkling my nose.

"Oh, please," she scoffed. "Don't pretend to be a prude. I know you too well for that."

"Well it's easy for you to sound so cavalier about one-night stands," I countered. "You've only ever had sex with Nikole. You're a shiny gold star, my friend."

Troian stuck out her chin defiantly. It was so easy to get her worked up; it had become one of my favorite hobbies over the years. She was great at dishing out the hits, but pouted like a professional when she felt attacked. "Yeah, well I bet you wouldn't have objections to a one-night-stand with Hunter."

I choked as some of my beer went down the wrong tube. By now I was used to Troian's taunting and off-color comments about my quirky student, but like me, she'd always called her "Winter Jacket." Hearing Hunter's name out of Troian's mouth made me uncomfortable. Using her actual name seemed too taboo, even for us.

I couldn't meet Troian's smug stare. She knew she'd gotten to me. "When is your girlfriend getting here?" I asked as I shredded a cocktail napkin. It was a habit of mine, to tear at things whenever I felt uncomfortable, needing something to do with my hands.

"Why? You need someone to protect you?" she smirked. She loved winning.

"Maybe," I grumbled.

I watched her dark eyes light up and a broad smile spread across her face. That look could only mean one of two things – free cake or Nikole had arrived. Troian hopped up from her seat to greet her girlfriend. "Hey, babe," she said, still smiling.

The look on her face was enviable. Troian and Nikole had been together forever, while I had whipped through a rapid succession of insignificant significant others. It wasn't that I had anything against monogamy; I just wasn't very good at it. But I wanted it. I wanted to find that one person who could still make me smile after nearly a decade of being together, who the anticipation of meeting up with after so many years still gave me butterflies. I was 30-years-old. I'd done enough sowing wild oats for one lifetime.

"I'll get you something to drink," Troian offered without having to be asked. She gave Nikole a quick kiss – quick for my benefit knowing how much their public endearments made me sick. It was unnatural to be that happy.

While Troian bounced off in the direction of the bar, I stood to give Nikole a quick hug in greeting. I could tell she'd come straight from work because she smelled like dirt. It wasn't an unpleasant scent –

on the contrary, it was comforting like warm sunshine and fresh air. Her long dark hair was pulled back in a ponytail and she'd changed out of the company logoed clothes in favor of dark jeans, a v-neck shirt, and a fitted leather jacket.

Nikole owned a small landscaping firm that mostly contracted with private residences, designing and planting flower gardens for some of the town's wealthiest families. Even though the ground was currently frozen and covered in at least a foot of snow, she was still busy with her small staff, planting seedlings in small pots and getting ready for Spring. When the snow melted, she'd have her full staff back again during the growing seasons. I often steered students her way who were looking for part-time or summer jobs. Troian made more than enough money from her writing to comfortably support them both, but Nikole wasn't the "kept-woman" type, no matter how much her partner insisted on doting on her.

"So I hear Troi is trying to hook you up with Peggy's new bartender," Nikole said as she sat down.

I returned to my seat and looked in the direction where Troian had literally skipped off to get her girlfriend something to drink. She was leaning against the bar and looked to be engaged in a serious conversation with the newest bar employee. As if sensing my gaze, they both looked in our direction. Troian waved in an exaggerated manner while the dark-haired bartender simply smiled.

I quickly looked away before I got sucked into one of Troian's set-ups. "She may already be designing the wedding invites," I groaned.

Nikole smirked and shook her head. "You know she means well; she just wants to see you happy. And for Troi, happiness is a committed relationship."

I sighed, but nodded. "I know, I know." I took a quick sip from my pint glass. "I just always thought I'd get to choose my future wife."

Nikole chuckled, deep and throaty. "Not if my girlfriend has her way."

"I'm really not into arranged marriages. How do I distract Troi from this latest quest of hers?"

"You could always find yourself a new girlfriend before she does it for you," Nikole pragmatically suggested.

"Yeah. That's not happening. But enough about my lack of dating life," I deflected. "How is work these days?"

She took the bait. "It's going well," Nikole nodded. "Kind of the calm before the storm. Once the snow melts, things will pick up. I've got to hire some new staff before that happens though."

"I'll look through my rosters and see if there's any local kids who might do a good job," I offered.

Nikole grinned. "Excellent. I knew I could count on you."

Troian took that moment to skip back to our table. She grandly set a double shot of something ominously amber near my hand. "What's this?" I asked, looking down at the miniature drink. "You didn't order this for me, did you? You know I don't do shots."

The proud grin on Troian's face was unmistakable. "It would appear you've attracted a fan." She nodded in the direction of the bar.

I swiveled in my chair to see who had bought me the drink. Our eyes met, and Peggy's new bartender gave me a quick wave; apparently she was my not-so-secret admirer. She smiled and of course there were dimples – there were always dimples.

I turned back to Nikole and Troian, who had sat down beside her girlfriend. "What do I do?" I hissed in a panic.

"Go talk to her," Troian urged, grinning ear to ear. She practically bounced in her seat with mildly contained energy.

"Or just drink up," Nikole shrugged. "Free booze." Whereas Troian typically behaved like she'd ingested one too many pixie sticks, Nikole had a calming energy about her. They seemed to balance each other out.

Taking Nikole's more reasonable advice, I tossed back the shot and sputtered a bit when the liquid burned down my throat. "Is she still looking over here?" I whispered. I could feel the tears pricking at the corners of my eyes. I fucking hated shots.

"Even better," Troian whispered back. "She's walking over."

Oh, no.

I stared hard at my hands, hoping for an exit strategy to be written on my palms. *Why* had I agreed to come to Peggy's tonight? I could be at home right now, in my pajamas, watching public access television, and drinking a nice glass of pinot noir. *And slowly becoming a spinster* my brain unhelpfully supplied.

I could sense movement in the shape of a slender woman stopping near my elbow, but I didn't dare look up. "Hey," a feminine voice greeted. "I'm Megan."

I snapped my eyes up to her smiling, waiting face. Troian had been right – she *was* cute. I gave her a thorough appraisal from my seat. Her porcelain skin was like a china doll. Her wiry arms were peppered with tattoos – not enough to call them sleeves, but enough to see she'd spent a good amount of time under a tattooist's needle. Her hair was long and dark with some of those trendy feather things woven into her wavy locks. She was tall, but not too tall, with legs that went on for miles encased in black skinny jeans. A black belt hung on a narrow waist, small breasts beneath a loose, maroon v-neck that looked touchably soft – the t-shirt, not her breasts. Okay, so her breasts looked touchable, too.

Yes, she was definitely cute. The cuteness, in fact, was kind of startling. Someone with so many tattoos shouldn't have been able to be labeled as "cute."

"She's Elle," Nikole supplied for me. I felt someone, probably Troian, kick my shin beneath the table.

"Do you play pool, Elle?" Megan questioned. I was surprised she was still talking to me. I hadn't said a word so far. I'd only been staring, slack jawed, like a mouth-breather.

I glanced towards the back of the bar where I knew there were two pool tables and a dartboard. Two women played at one of the tables and the other remained unoccupied. Near the billiard tables was a misused jukebox that was filled mostly with Ani DiFranco and Indigo Girls albums. Peggy's was a certified dive, but it was the only gay bar in this small town.

I turned back to the new bartender. "Not very well," I admitted, finally finding my voice. I knew how to play, but I wasn't any good at the game. I was much better at the international lesbian sport of foosball.

"That's perfect," she smiled broadly. Damn those dimples. "Now I can teach you something, and afterwards you won't be able to resist my charms. I read that somewhere," she added with a wink. She jerked her head toward the vacant pool table. "So how about it? Can I drag you away from your friends for a quick game? I'm on break."

I hesitated, but felt Nikole's elbow sharply poking me in the small of my back. What was with these two and their need to poke me? Oh, who was I kidding? I hadn't had a good poke in months.

"Go," Nikole whispered for only my ears. "It'll be good for you."

I took a deep breath and gazed into Megan's caramel-colored eyes.

"Okay," I conceded. "One game."

+++++

Hello, hangover. Nice to see you, too.

I looked at my bleary reflection in the bathroom mirror and made a face at what I saw. My mascara was smeared and my eyeliner was smudged, forming dark circles beneath my eyes. I peered closer and tugged at my skin. At least those had better be makeup circles and not just the natural, sickly pallor of my skin.

I couldn't believe I let Troian and Nikole keep me out so late the previous night. I couldn't even remember how or when I'd made it back to my house. I was just thankful that I'd woken up safe in my bed – minus the throbbing in my head.

I rummaged around the medicine cabinet for the Excedrin I could have sworn I'd purchased a few weeks ago. I thankfully found the white and green bottle after a little more searching and popped two pills into my mouth. I turned the bathroom faucet on, leaned over, and with my hands, brought cool water to my mouth. I drank greedily. My thirst was insatiable; it was like I'd slept with cotton balls in my mouth. To add insult to injury, my body ached all over like I'd been run over by a car. Fuck. I hated getting old.

Luckily I didn't teach on Fridays, so I could go back to bed and sleep off this hangover. Teaching the writing seminars four times a week gave me an unusual teaching schedule because most classes in the undergraduate catalogue met twice or three times a week. The university's administrators wanted students to end the semester having the ability to write an academic paper. I'm not sure how much one extra day a week helped with that goal though, but at least I had my Fridays off.

When I wasn't teaching, I typically worked on my own personal writing. I was fortunate that in my discipline tenure was determined not just by published works of nonfiction, but also the poems, short stories, and novels that you wrote. So instead of publishing a close reading of Shakespeare or Chaucer or something similarly mundane, I could write fiction.

These days I was assembling a collection of short stories – obtuse vignettes about people with unusual powers. It wasn't the stuff comic books were made of though; my characters weren't superheroes, and their special abilities weren't necessarily helpful or a hindrance, they were just odd.

I thought about writing a story based on Hunter. Lately she'd been on my mind so frequently, she'd become a kind of Muse. But I couldn't decide what her superhuman special power would be. Eye contact that if left unchecked literally bored holes into solid surfaces? Shoulder blades so delicate and sharp they could cut through anything, making her the perfect thief? The ability to make her English professor weak in the knees?

I was still thirsty, so I plundered from the bathroom upstairs to the kitchen downstairs to get a proper glass of water. I gulped down another pint-full before refilling my glass from the sink and padding back upstairs to return to my bedroom.

By this time it was close to 11 o'clock. A few rays of early afternoon sunshine poked through the semi-closed blinds in my bedroom and fell on the body lying in my bed.

Wait a minute.

The body in my bed?

"Oh shit."

I froze in the doorway. There was definitely a body in my bed. I could just make out the shape beneath my duvet. How had I not noticed that before I went to the bathroom? If I didn't already have a hangover, I'd think I was still drunk.

I swallowed hard. There was an unruly mane of dark brown hair obscuring the face of my bedmate. Well, at least it looked like girl hair. That was some relief. I was still going to kill Troian and Nikole though. How could they let me bring someone home from the bar? I didn't do one-night-stands. I was a serial monogamist with a tendency for infidelity, but even my indiscretions were with women I knew well.

The figure in my bed stirred. The movement startled me so much that I dropped my glass of water. The pint glass fell to the hardwood floor, and while it didn't shatter, the sound of impact echoed loudly in my bedroom.

The noise jarred the woman in my bed awake, and she sat up abruptly. "What was that?" Her voice revealed her alarm, and her face showed that sleepy confusion that comes from being yanked out of a deep sleep.

"I dropped a glass of water," I said in a calm, even tone that surprised my ears. Water puddled and crept at my bare toes. I'd have to do something about that, but first I had to do something about the stranger in my bed.

Her sleepy face scrunched up. "Oh. You need help cleaning it up?" She sat up a little higher in my bed, and I was relieved to see she was wearing a tank top. Well, not relieved that I didn't get to see her naked, but relieved because that probably meant I didn't have blackout sex with her.

"Uh...Megan." Points to me for having remembered her name. "Hi. Um, morning."

"Morning," she grumbled, rubbing her eyes with her hands.

My brain lurched into overdrive, trying to piece together the hazy memories from the previous night out. I remembered her buying me a shot of something gross. And then there was a game of pool, followed by more gross shots when I'd lost. And then there was dancing. Lots of dancing with lots of faceless girls. Not that they didn't have faces, I just couldn't quite remember them right now. And then had come even more drinks. All of this I could somewhat remember. But one glaring and important hole remained. Namely, why was Megan in my bed?

She pulled back the sheets a little to reveal more of her lithe figure. She wore black, lacy undergarments that made her pale skin look even more powder white. "Wanna come back to bed?"

I felt the blush creep up on my cheeks, and I averted my gaze from her half-naked form. "This might be a really stupid question, but what happened last night?"

I looked back up and saw something that resembled regret and guilt mirrored in her eyes. "Don't remember much, huh?"

I sighed. Stupid alcohol. Stupid lack of control. "I'm sorry. No."

"Well firstly, we didn't do anything," she reassured me. "I mean, hell yeah I want to have a go with you, but not when you're blasted. Call me old-fashioned," she grinned.

"That's sweet of you," I said with an embarrassed smile.

"I have an idea," she proposed. "Let me make you breakfast, and I can catch you up." She smiled warmly and I nearly forgot my discomfort. "I make a mean frittata."

"That's really nice of you to offer, but it's really not necessary."

She raised a painted eyebrow. Huh. I never noticed in the bar that she didn't actually have eyebrows – they were just makeup. Weird.

"Not necessary because you're not hungry," she asked for clarification, "or not necessary because this was just an almost one-night-stand that's not going to go any further?"

I had to give this woman some credit. She didn't mess around. It was kind of refreshing actually. And because of her directness, I knew I owed it to her to be explicit as well. "Megan, you seem like a really nice girl..."

She held up her hands. "Whoa. Let me stop you right there." She climbed out of my bed and gathered a few discarded pieces of clothing from the floor.

"Really?" I asked, blinking in disbelief. "Just like that?"

She grunted, pulling on her skinny jeans. "I get it," she stated as she hopped around and slid into her painted-on pants. "I don't need an elaborate speech. Last night was fun. But I get it – that's all it was."

It felt like a giant weight had been lifted from my shoulders, but I was still skeptical. "You're being surprisingly cool about this." I inspected her face, looking for some kind of hidden emotion. "Where's the U-Haul?"

She picked her jacket off the ground and gave me a quick peck on the cheek as she made for the bedroom door. "No U-Haul," she chuckled. "Lucky for you, I'm not a lesbian."

The floorboards creaked as she descended the stairs, followed by the sound of the deadbolt unlocking and the front door opening. "See you around, Dr. Elle," I heard her call out.

I heard the door close again, and I was suddenly alone as if the previous night had never happened. But the cold water still tickling at my toes reminded me that it hadn't been a dream.

+++++

19

CHAPTER TWO

"I still can't believe you," I said, shaking my head. "How could you let me drink so much, *and* how could you let me bring that girl home?"

Troian gave me a skeptical look. "When did I become your babysitter? You're a grown ass woman."

"You don't drink alcohol though," I pointed out, still frustrated with myself, but taking it out on my friend. "I thought you'd have my back when Megan bought all those shots."

I had met up with Troian at a coffee shop near campus. We hadn't spoken since our night out at Peggy's, a little over a week ago when I'd unintentionally brought home the new bartender. I wasn't purposely avoiding my friend though; I wasn't even really that mad anymore. But I'd been out of town on a research trip over Spring Break, so I hadn't had the opportunity to see her since that night.

Troian was appalled that I hadn't taken advantage of the situation, while I was equally horrified that I'd gotten myself into that situation in the first place. I normally had a pretty high tolerance for alcohol and knew my limit, but when it came to hard liquor, I tended to overdue it.

"I *do* have your back," Troian replied. "Which is why I let you have fun." She pursed her lips in disappointment. "I can't believe you didn't tap that when you had the chance. That girl is seriously cute."

"How can you tell?" I snorted. "You've never looked at another girl since you and Nik started dating, back at the Beginning of Time."

My best friend shrugged. "I don't feel so guilty when Nik looks, too."

"I'm trying to be a better person," I sighed. "We all know I haven't had the best track record when it comes to women." I paused and took a sip of my coffee. I was trying to cut back, but like my students, my caffeine consumption steadily skyrocketed the closer the semester came to a close. "I'm like a bull in a china shop when it comes to emotions."

"I can appreciate you wanting to do things right in your next relationship, but what I don't understand is why *now*?" Troian asked over her oversized mug. Everything was oversized in comparison to her. "Are you having a mid-life crisis? Is this what I have to look forward to when I'm old like you?"

I made a face. Troian was younger than me, but only by a few years. She liked to tease me about my advanced age as much as I liked to taunt her about her diminutive stature.

"If I was having a mid-life crisis I'd be buying a red sports car and dating a girl half my age."

"Ohhhh." Troian nodded her head sagely. "So *that* explains your crush on Winter Jacket."

"That's not it at all!" I hushed, feeling an involuntarily blush creep onto my cheeks.

Troian smirked. "I don't know why you don't just ask her out."

"Are we still talking about Megan?"

"Or Hunter." Troian leaned back in her chair and smiled even wider than before. "You seem to have some options, lucky girl."

I took a final drink from my mug before standing up. "I have to go," I said, ignoring her blatant teasing. "I have student meetings."

I pulled on my jacket to prepare for the Winter that refused to go away. The Ground Hog had said only six more weeks of Winter. This season, however, was further proof that you should never trust a rodent with the weather forecast. It was nearly April, and we still had a few feet of snow on the ground.

"Is one of those meetings with Winter Jacket?"

I made an uncomfortable noise in the back of my throat. "Maybe."

Troian grinned. "Awesome. I wanna hear all about it when she's gone."

I slung my messenger bag over my shoulder. "Maybe."

+++++

I rushed up the stairs to the fourth floor of the campus building that housed the English and Writing Department. I had overextended myself by meeting up with Troian off-campus and was now running short on time before I had to meet with my first student of the afternoon. I hated being late. I hated feeling rushed. I liked having ample time before commitments so I could mentally prepare for my next responsibility.

When I pushed through the stairwell door, I bumped into someone on the other side. I immediately blurted out a sincere apology when I saw papers scatter in the air. Thad Darwin, an Associate Professor in my department, stooped to pick up the student papers I'd made him drop.

I crouched down to the floor to help him collect the discarded assignments. "I'm so sorry, Thad," I apologized again. "I never should have had that extra cup of coffee; I knew it was going to make me late."

"Don't worry about it, Elle," he said as he continued grabbing papers and re-arranging them into a neat pile. "But you may owe me a cup of coffee now." He smiled charmingly, and I wasn't sure if he was serious or not.

Thad was cute, in that hipster-glasses, tweed jacket with leather patches at the elbows without irony kind of way, but apparently he'd never gotten the memo that he wasn't my type. He was a leading scholar in Medieval Literature and I respected his scholarship, but I routinely found myself cornered in the mailroom by him and having to make up excuses why I couldn't have dinner with him at a quaint, new restaurant or why I was too busy to check out a must-see band at the local theater.

When I saw where his eyes had landed, I stood up and self-consciously straightened the neckline of my top. He stood as well and raked his fingers through boyishly shaggy blond hair. I knew our undergraduate women thought it was adorable; I thought it made him look like a surfer. I hoped he wasn't growing it out so he could wear it in a ponytail. There were enough tragic clichés in our department already without that addition. "So, uh, I hear you're hosting the party for the graduating seniors again this year?"

"Uh huh," I nodded, mindful that the longer I stood in the

hallway with my colleague, the greater the chances I'd be late for my first student meeting. I didn't want to be rude and dash off after colliding into him, but I hated being late. It was practically a phobia.

"Do you need any help?" he offered.

"That's nice of you to offer," I said, genuinely touched that he'd offered, even if he had ulterior motives, "but I think everything is already taken care of. Tricia is taking care of food and drinks with the campus catering services, but you could ask her if she needs help. Hosting is actually pretty easy; I just make sure my house is clean enough for undergrads."

Thad laughed, dark blue eyes crinkling at the corners. "So what you're saying is, you don't have to clean."

I nodded. "Exactly."

I could tell he was gearing up for Round Two of the conversation, so I cut him off before he could delay me any longer. "I hate to hit and run," I said, already moving, "but I've probably got a line of students waiting outside my office door right now."

He closed his mouth and knowingly nodded. "Some other time then."

I gave him a quick smile that I hoped didn't look too forced or too flirty before hustling around the corner to where my office was located.

When I unlocked my office door and hurried into the room, my phone buzzed with a text message. I paused long enough to produce the phone from my bag and read the note from Troian: *Have a great meeting with Winter Jacket today. Try not to stare at her tits too much.*

I threw my phone back into my workbag and sat down. I rested my elbows on my desk and rubbed at my temples. I really needed the semester to end.

I loved teaching writing because I was providing students with concrete skills. Unlike the other Humanities, we in the English Department didn't have to scramble to justify our existence to the Board of Trustees when budget cuts loomed every year. Plus I didn't have to lecture too often. I'd throw in the occasional presentation about thesis statements, MLA style formatting, or the importance of the Oxford comma, but classes were generally seminar style and discussion based.

On the class periods leading up to a paper being due I didn't have to teach at all. Instead, students used the class period for Peer Reviews. During those sessions, I divided the class into small groups, and they used the period to give feedback on each other's papers. I chose the groups for them so I could pair weaker writers with stronger students.

Lately I found myself being especially mindful of the groups I put Hunter in. I didn't give her an unfair advantage over students, but I made sure no cute boys were in her group. I knew it was totally inappropriate and unnecessary, but I also knew it would drive me crazy watching some frat boy with questionable hygiene flirt with her.

She seemed the type to listen politely and laugh at the appropriate times even if she wasn't interested. I also worried that perhaps her reticence to actively participate in class was due to a lack of self-esteem. I felt protective and didn't want her to fall trap to an undergraduate boy with ulterior motives being nice to her.

I also found myself avoiding looking in the corner of the room where she habitually sat. If I did dare look in that area, I simply passed my gaze above the heads of the students in that vicinity. I actually felt guilty looking at her. It was a small classroom though; I *had* to look at every student.

At one level I recognized my paranoid guilt was unwarranted. I wasn't giving her any kind of advantage over the others. In fact, she might have thought I didn't like her because I now refused to look in her direction. Troian had been the one to point out that detail, but I didn't know how to deal with this. The best I could do was soldier through the rest of the semester. I'd suffered through worse, I told myself. I could handle a little student crush.

My head snapped up at the sound of knuckles rapping against my open office door.

"Professor Graft?" Hunter stood in the threshold, wearing her unmistakable blue winter jacket and looking charmingly concerned. I realized she'd probably just caught me looking sullen and miserable. I banished the sour look from my face and forced a smile there instead.

"Hi," I greeted. "How are you?" I gathered whatever papers were on my desk and stored them inside the top drawer to give her my undivided attention. When I was a student, it had always annoyed me when my own professors had tried to multitask during a scheduled meeting.

"I'm good," she confirmed. "And you?" I was still amazed by how polite the students were at this school.

And then she did something so unexpected, I think my eyes literally bulged out of my head – she began to take off her coat.

The simple act made me immediately lose my train of thought. Our meeting was only scheduled to last 15 minutes, but she was hanging her jacket on the back of the chair as if settling in for an extended amount of time. It struck me as peculiar – why would she take off her jacket in my office when she never took it off during a 50-minute class period in a significantly warmer room?

Beneath her coat she wore a half-zip running top, the kind whose material clings to curves for aerodynamics. It was an immaculate white as if she'd worn it straight off the rack. She wore it unzipped and it fluttered open near her neck, showing a hint of a pale, defined collarbone. She tugged at her sleeves, pulling them up to a three-quarter length, revealing delicate wrists and more of that porcelain skin.

I pulled myself together, but dedicated the details to memory knowing that Troian would bug me about them later and be disappointed if I failed to entertain her with a vivid retelling of how my meeting with Winter Jacket went.

"Good, good," I confirmed, bobbing my head. "Busy," I unnecessarily noted, "but that's to be expected with the semester coming to an end."

She nodded solemnly, that penetrating gaze making me instantly uncomfortable. "I don't know how you grade so many papers. I have a hard enough time completing a 5-page paper."

"Oh, don't sell yourself short," I said. "You do very well writing 5-page papers."

She ducked her head demurely and her cheeks flushed attractively. I always tried to be warm and approachable as a teacher, and that included giving students positive feedback. But anytime I said something remotely encouraging to Hunter, it felt unprofessional.

"Any plans for summer?" I found myself asking. With any other student, I would have just thrown myself into the paper corrections after exchanging surface pleasantries.

She shook her head. "Not really. Just going back home to spend some time with my parents."

"Do they live close?" I already knew the answer from the first day of class, but she didn't need to know that. She wasn't a special circumstance this time though; I remembered where all of my students were from originally.

She nodded and fanned her fingers out on my desk. "Yeah. Out in the suburbs. I thought about going to school further away, but this is a good college," she said with a graceful shrug, "so why not?"

"I couldn't do it," I said, shaking my head. "I had to go to school in a different state to get away from my family."

I watched her take her lower lip between the top and bottom row of white, straight teeth. I wasn't sure if my admission made her uncomfortable, so after clearing my throat, I moved the conversation in the direction it should have gone from the beginning. "So, let's talk about your rough draft."

+++++

I threw my jacket over my head and walked briskly from my campus building to my waiting car in the faculty parking lot. The rain had made that morning's dusting of snow turn into slush, and I could feel the cold seep into my boots as I dodged one puddle after the next. I only lived a few blocks from campus, and normally I walked to campus even in the snowy months, but I'd had the foresight to drive today knowing I had a mountain of student papers to lug home. I had always dreamed of buying a house steps from whatever campus I worked at. Some girls dreamed of Barbie weddings; I dreamed of real estate.

Once in the shelter of my car, I took a moment to inspect myself in the rearview window to make sure my mascara wasn't streaking down my face. It had been a long day filled with committee meetings and student conferences, and I was looking forward to the weekend. I had a pile of student drafts to sludge through, but at least I could do that in my pajamas.

Nikole and Troian had invited me over for dinner later that night, but I was considering making up an excuse to get out of it. I loved my friends and Nikole was actually a pretty good cook, but when I spent a lot of time with them, especially in their home, I couldn't help but feel sorry for myself and resent them and their happiness.

It was my own fault for being single though – I had a nasty habit of self-sabotage just when things were starting to go well. I'd done it in practically every long-term relationship I'd been in. It was like I couldn't let myself be happy. I continually found faults in my partners, petty or otherwise, and incessantly picked fights over paltry, unimportant things.

The worst part was, I was completely self-aware. I *knew* when I was poisoning my relationships, even in the moment. But for whatever reason, I just couldn't stop myself.

As I continued to sit in my car, it started to rain harder. I watched the giant droplets spatter on the windshield until everything beyond the glass blurred. I was in a funk and the weather wasn't helping. Normally by this time Winter had broken, the snow had melted, and new green life was poking up amongst the mud. But this had been a relentless Winter, the cold refused to lift, and a blanket of clouds permanently choked out the sun. I was feeling verbose. Moody. The best kind of mood to get writing done, but not grade papers. If I graded with this murky attitude clinging to me like a damp towel, they'd all be getting C-'s.

I started the car and pulled out of the parking lot. The rain continued to steadily fall. I turned off the radio and listened to the soothing patter hitting against the car roof.

When I stopped at the intersection around the corner from my house, I saw a familiar blue jacket. I peered past the rapidly swiping wipers and through the rain. I rolled down the passenger-side window.

"Hunter?"

She whirled her head around. Grey-blue eyes peered back at me from under the hood of her jacket.

"Can I give you a ride?"

"I'm fine, thanks," I heard her say. As if mocking her, the rain immediately picked up.

"Get in," I implored.

I could see her hesitate only briefly. She ducked her head and immediately trotted over to the passenger side door. She tried the handle, but found it locked. I mentally berated myself – I always forgot my car automatically locked itself as though it was paranoid I'd be tossed from the vehicle while driving, Grand Theft Auto style.

I released the locks and as soon as Hunter heard the telltale click, she yanked the handle up and pulled the door wide open before slipping into the passenger seat. Once in the car, now sheltered from the rain, I heard her sigh in relief. She pulled her hood back and ruffled at her loose hair, droplets splattering against the inside of my vehicle.

I tried not to gawk too much. With her hair thoroughly wet, she looked like she'd just stepped out of the shower, which of course meant my head went to an inappropriate place. My nostrils were invaded by the scent of her shampoo, re-awoken by the rain – rosemary and lemon.

She swung around in her seat to face me. "Thank you, Professor Graft," she breathed. "I wasn't expecting the rain; otherwise I would have brought an umbrella." That detail didn't surprise me. She seemed to me the type of person who religiously kept track of the weather, always prepared. I was thankful that for at least one day, the weather had taken her by surprise.

"Don't worry about it. This weather has been ridiculous lately. It can't decide if it wants to be Winter or Spring." I hated myself for running with the weather topic. Nothing like regurgitating the weather report to make you sound prehistoric. I might as well have popped an 8-trak tape into the dashboard of my car and started talking about the economy.

I wanted to say something funny, like I'd take her anywhere as long as it wasn't across state lines, but that sounded creepy. So instead of letting my mouth betray me, I kept it simple: "Where can I give you a ride to?"

"My apartment. It's on the corner of Marshall and Water."

I nodded, mentally picturing the intersection. It was near campus, normally within walking distance except for the current monsoon.

We drove in silence with the soothing swish of mechanized wipers and the sound of rain spattering against the roof of my car filling the void. I was tempted to turn on the radio, but I worried something embarrassingly Top 40 would start playing. I was a college professor. I was supposed to listen to a steady diet of jazz and NPR. I did those things, but I also had a soft spot for ridiculously catchy pop songs and hip-hop.

When we reached the intersection of Marshall and Water a few minutes later, I pulled my car to a stop. To my left was a redbrick building that looked to be about 4-stories high. I ducked my head to appraise the apartment complex. "Don't most students live on campus?" Nearly 95% or something like that. Students needed to get special permission from the Dean of Students, in fact, to be allowed to live off campus.

Hunter nodded and tucked a chunk of damp hair behind her ear. "My parents are…" She frowned, as if searching for the right word. "Funny," she settled on. "I mean, they named me Hunter."

"I didn't want to ask."

"Weird for a girl, right?"

"Not weird, per say, just unique." Truth be told it was a strange name for a girl in such a small, conservative town – it was too gender neutral and too progressive even for the 21st century. Maybe it would have made more sense on the West Coast, but in the Midwest where everyone was named after his or her great-grandparents, it stuck out. I wondered if her parents were transplants.

"My parents wanted me to get more of a sense of independence when I came to college," she continued, "so they insisted I get an apartment instead of living in the dorms." Her lips twisted into a wry smile. "But they also insist on paying my rent for me, so it's not as though I'm *actually* independent of them."

"It sounds like they have your best intentions in mind though," I noted.

Hunter smiled suddenly. It was a playful grin I wasn't used to seeing on her wide, expressive mouth. "Yeah, but shouldn't I get to experience a kegger once in a while? Hide alcohol from the Resident Assistant on duty or something? Isn't that all part of the college experience, too?"

I laughed despite my misgivings to be chatting so familiarly with a student. Especially *this* student. "You're not missing much," I said.

She smiled wistfully. "I guess I'll just have to take your word for it." She looked up at her apartment building. The rooms in the front of the building were lit up, casting an eerie yellow light into the dark, stormy sky. "Thank you for the ride," she said politely, switching from playful back to demure.

I smiled to let her know it wasn't a big deal. "Have a nice weekend."

She got out of the car and raced up to the front entrance of her apartment complex. She bobbed from one side to the next as if running between the raindrops. I watched her pull a ring of keys out of her jacket pocket and, after briefly fumbling, she found the right one and opened the front door.

My hand felt for the shifter to pull the car into reverse, but my eyes stayed trained on her. She surprised me by spinning around and waving in my direction. I held up my hand in a similar gesture even though I was sure she probably couldn't see me through the rain and my steamed up windows.

When the door to her apartment complex closed, I pulled the car out of park. Even though I wanted nothing more than to go home and change into sweatpants, I drove in the direction of Troian and Nikole's. I needed to see my best friends to clear my head.

+++++

I plastered a smile on my face when Nikole answered the front door. My smile felt as plastered to my face as my wet hair.

The smirk on her face came all-too easily. "You look like a soggy rag."

"Hi to you, too." My teeth were practically chattering. It had been a miserable, wet walk from the parking lot to their condo. "Let me in, woman. I'm freezing my balls off."

Nikole grinned and stepped back to let me in. "I guess we'll have to find a way to warm you up." I loved that Nikole was a shameless flirt. It was nice to have a friend I could flirt back with without it getting either of us in trouble. Flirting to me was like breathing; I couldn't survive without it. Perhaps it's why I made for such a horrible girlfriend.

I stepped beyond the threshold and was greeted with the scent of something spicy – Thai or Indian, I guessed. Troian came bouncing into the front foyer. She wore a white apron splashed with an unidentifiable orange sauce. The sight of her made me pause. "Oh, no. Don't tell me *you* made dinner."

Her nose wrinkled and she stomped a foot. "Hey. I can cook just fine."

"So Mac and Cheese tonight?" I playfully teased. Being around these two instantly lifted my bleak mood.

"Keep it up and I'll send you back out into the rain," Troian said, shaking a wooden spoon at me.

I took off my jacket and shook it out. "I can't be too mad at the weather," I casually commented. "Thanks to this rain, I got to give Winter Jacket a ride home."

"Oh, I bet you gave her a ride," Troian said reflexively. "Wait," she paused, blinking. "Are you *serious*?"

I nodded. "It's not a big deal," I said, even though I started grinning like a Cheshire Cat. "I only did what any other Good Samaritan would have done."

"Sure, any Good Samaritan who wants to get in her pants," Troian shot back with a snort. "I'm surprised your head didn't pop off with her in the close-confines of your car."

I made a face. "I'm not an animal."

"Why don't we move this conversation into the kitchen," Nikole, always the voice of reason, suggested. "I don't want to let Troi's hard work in there burn."

"Would I be able to taste the difference?" I teased.

Troian might have been small, but she sure had sharp elbows.

I followed my friends into their kitchen, which was currently the center of a food hurricane. Pots of various sizes steamed on gas burners. Two cutting boards, one piled high with various vegetables and the other with deboned chicken, covered the island countertop.

"What prompted this little food experiment?" I asked, taking in the view. When they hosted me for dinner, rarely was the meal such a production. Burgers and oven baked fries were the typical fare – grilled chicken breast and vegetables when we wanted to count calories. I felt guilty for not bringing something like a salad or a bottle of wine.

Troian went back to the stovetop and stirred a saucepan filled with the same orange-yellow sauce that was splashed on her apron. "Just flexing my culinary muscles," she remarked. "I hope you like butter chicken and naan bread cause I'm not making you anything else."

I leaned against the counter and watched Troian do her thing. Nikole handed me a glass of red wine, which I gladly accepted. "Look at this service," I approved, taking a small sip. "Wine *and* a delicious home-cooked dinner? Who needs a girlfriend when I've got you two?"

Troian wrinkled her nose. "Ain't no way you're getting in our bed, Bookworm. I don't care if Nik keeps having those sex dreams."

Nikole made a noise beside me and looked like she was choking on her wine. I thumped her soundly on the back as tears sprang in the corners of her eyes.

"After all this time, and her mouth still surprises you?" I asked.

Nikole laughed and wiped at her eyes, mindful of her eye makeup. "I have no comment."

Troian snorted and twirled her wooden spoon like a baton. "You really make it too easy, Elle."

Dinner tasted just as delicious as it had smelled. Troian had outdone herself with rich butter chicken, piles of fragrant basmati rice, and warm, chewy naan. The three of us sat around the dining room table after the meal with empty plates, satisfied stomachs, and half-filled wine glasses. As dinner dwindled, our conversation had somehow turned to my recent dating adventures, or rather *lack* of.

"What about Internet dating?" Nikole asked. She swirled her wine glass around by the glass's stem. "Would you be open to that?"

I shook my head. "That's just asking for trouble. Posting a public profile and having a student stumble upon it?"

"You really think your students are browsing 30-year-old, women-seeking-women?" Troian pragmatically asked.

"Stranger things have happened. I'm not hiding being gay," I clarified, "but I don't want to be that clueless professor who's so awkward she can only get dates online. This school is too small, you guys," I sighed. "It's like high school all over again. And the faculty and staff gossip just as bad as the students."

"Don't get mad at me for asking," Nikole tentatively started, "but do you think you haven't actively been looking for a girlfriend because of Hunter?"

"What?" I nearly choked on my wine.

"Just hear me out." Nikole held up her hands in peace. "I just mean that maybe this crush is holding you back. It's safe to daydream and think about the What Ifs; you don't have to put yourself out there and risk getting emotionally hurt."

"Do you really think so?" My mouth twisted. There rang some truth to my good friend's words.

"Has this ever happen before?" Nikole asked. "I mean, you've been teaching for a while. This can't be your first student crush."

I shook my head. I swear I could feel my brain rattle around. Maybe that was my problem. My brain had become detached with all this obsessing. "Never. I mean, I can appreciate when students are attractive."

"You've got eyes, after all," Troian jumped in.

"It's never been to the point of distraction," I noted, choosing to ignore Troian's unhelpful interruption. "I get tongue-tied. I get nervous talking to her one-on-one. Even now," I exclaimed, my voice pitching higher, "I'm getting sweaty just thinking about it."

"Why this girl?" Nikole asked.

"Yeah, what does this girl do that makes you wet?" Troian grinned eagerly and leaned forward in her chair.

I rolled my eyes. Nikole at least had some sense of decorum. Troian was unexpectedly crude. As much time as we spent together, her mouth never failed to amaze me. How someone so tiny and innocent looking could be so crude was disorienting.

"She's beautiful," I noted.

"Boring." Troian rolled her eyes. "I could pick up a dozen chicks down at Peggy's tonight hotter than her."

Nikole scoffed.

"Not one hotter than you, babe." Troian batted her eyelashes at her girlfriend.

"You've never even seen Hunter," I pointed out. "Nor are you ever going to."

Troian stuck out her bottom lip and pouted. "You're no fun, you know that?"

"I've gotta agree with Troi here, Elle," Nikole noted, swirling the liquid around in the bottom of her wine glass. "You gotta let us see a picture of this girl."

"It's not like I carry a picture of her in my wallet."

They both raised their eyebrows at me.

"I mean it, you guys!" I defended myself. "I'm not *that* creepy."

Nikole looked thoughtful. "I suppose there are degrees to ones creepiness."

Troian pounded a fist on the table. "We all know that Elle is a perv, but let's get back to talking about this girl," she ordered.

"So besides the fact that she's allegedly pretty," Nikole said.

"Beautiful," I corrected.

"Right. *Beautiful,*" Nikole echoed, smirking.

I fanned out my fingers on the tabletop. "I just don't know. And it's so incredibly cliché, but there's just something about her."

A kind of uneasy silence settled on our group. I really didn't want to talk anymore about Hunter, but my friends seemed determined to press me about her.

After a while, Nikole broke the quiet. "I don't want to be rude," she said, stifling a yawn. "but I'm gonna let you two hash this out," she said as she stood from the table. "I've got seedlings to tend to in the morning." She kissed Troian and her hand lingered on her girlfriend's cheek. "Not too late, okay?"

I knew that if I stayed too much longer I'd be over-staying my welcome. And the way Troian gazed after her girlfriend as she sauntered off in the direction of the bedroom told me that me still sitting here might already be pushing it.

"I've got to get over her, right?"

Troian's eyes left her girlfriend's backside and snapped back to me. "Why?"

"She's my student." What about that was so hard for Troian to understand?

"I think you're allowed to have crushes," Troian reasoned. "I mean, look at me and my irrational obsession with nearly every brunette Hollywood actress."

"That's different," I countered. "Celebrity crushes are allowed. Everyone knows what."

"But I work with some of these women *and* I've got a girlfriend," she pointed out. "You're single, Bookie. Crush away."

"So you're condoning this?"

"It's harmless fun," Troian shrugged. "Besides, you freaking out about Winter Jacket has been one of the most entertaining things you've done in a while."

"Thanks," I deadpanned.

"As long as you don't start being anti-social or turn down dates because you're too busy scrapbooking every piece of paper she's ever touched, I think you're fine."

I tried to remember the most recent date I'd been on. I'd basically taken a break from romance after Cady and I split up. I wondered if the almost one-night-stand with Megan counted as a date. I decided to keep that question to myself. Troian didn't need to be reminded that I'd brought home the bartender to whom she'd betrothed me.

"Are you guys ever going to have a House Warming party?"

Troian shrugged. "What for? Isn't that just a lame excuse to demand presents from your friends? Like a wedding or a baby shower?"

I shook my head. "You're such a sentimental." I finished the rest of the wine in my glass. "How's work?" I asked, thankful for the opportunity to change the topic. "What are you working on right now?"

"Well, I just finished edits to my screenplay." Troian was an amazing science fiction author who had a singular talent for creating new worlds and original creatures. No vampire and werewolf love-triangles for this girl. She'd recently sold the rights to one of her novels to be made into a movie and had been charged with writing the screenplay as well. "My agent wants me to strike while the iron is still hot, so I'm working on a concept for a new TV show."

Her ambition and success made me feel like an underachiever sometimes, even though I was a published author, too. "How did I luck out and get such a glamorous best friend?"

Troian grinned. "Traffic jams and hot ass cars."

Troian and I had met through a happy coincidence. I had just started teaching at my university and was running terribly late. I didn't yet live in my house within walking distance from campus, and I was supposed to be attending a guest lecture that day by an alum who'd recently made it big as a screenwriter in Hollywood. The department was bringing in Troian Smith to campus to talk about her experiences to our undergraduate English composition and creative writer majors.

Because I was still a new hire, I was frantic about being so late. I'm not normally an aggressive driver or prone to road rage, but on that particular afternoon, stuck in a traffic jam due to road construction with minutes to spare before the presentation, I was honking my horn and uselessly slapping my palm against the steering wheel in frustration.

A woman stuck next to me in a custom Acura TSX started to laugh at my despair. I could hear her because it was a rare, hot Spring day and we both had our windows opened. I remembered her words: "You need to calm down," she'd told me, shaking her head and grinning broadly. "It's called a traffic jam for a reason."

I'd barked something back at her about being late and in a hurry and minding her own business, but she'd just smirked and turned her car radio up even louder. The bass pouring from the vehicle had practically rattled my teeth in their sockets. She had looked as if she was actually *enjoying* the delay.

When I had finally made it to campus, I had circled around the faculty parking lot, looking for a parking spot and unabashedly cursing my bad luck. It was nearly impossible to find a vacant spot in the early afternoon. It was one of the reasons living close to campus had appealed to me later when I bought my house.

I ended up having to park in a student lot. I had momentarily worried about getting a ticket or being towed because I didn't have the right parking stickers for that lot, but paying a fine had seemed more attractive at the time than missing Troian Smith's talk altogether. I was still insecure about having procured my job, feeling like a fraud despite my advanced degrees, and was kissing as much ass as necessary to stay in the Department's good graces.

I had walked at a brisk pace across the parking lots, not willing to break into a full sprint and draw unnecessary attention to myself. When I yanked open the door to the academic building where the talk was being held, the woman from the traffic jam was in the building lobby. I was in such a hurry, I had nearly collided into her. In my defense, Troian is short and easily run-over-able. If my clumsiness had startled or annoyed her, she didn't let on.

I had blindly apologized and was about to rush off to the auditorium when she called me out: "You seriously need to chill out. You're going to give yourself an aneurism."

"I'm sorry," I'd barked back, not really meaning it. "I'm terribly late."

She had pointed to a poster announcing Troian Smith's talk. "To the screenwriter's talk?"

I had been surprised she knew. Even though I was relatively new to campus, I didn't recognized her as a fellow faculty member and her car was far too nice to belong to an undergraduate. As a private school we had our share of undergraduates who came from wealthy families, but the student parking lot was filled with reasonable compact cars – not that flashy thing I'd seen this woman driving on the highway.

She had given me that same maddeningly cocky grin from before as if she hadn't had a care in the world. "You're fine. They can't start the talk if the guest of honor isn't there yet."

"How do you know she's not here yet?" I had shot back, forgetting my manners in my mild panic.

The woman had stuck her hand out in greeting. "Troian Smith. Pleased to make your acquaintance."

It was a nice feeling – being able to laugh at the memories of a day that at the time had caused me so much anxiety. I had significantly calmed down since then. More confidence in my teaching abilities and Troian's bad influence were partly to credit.

"You were a cocky shit back then," I snickered not unkindly. "I can't believe I put up with your giant ego."

"Whatever," she scoffed. "You wouldn't love me half as much if I didn't have major swagger."

"Speaking of which, I'm glad you got rid of that horrible car."

Troian looked appropriately appalled. "Hey, that car was awesome."

"Yeah and totally impractical," I said, making a face. "You could drive it two months out of the year because of the weather."

She shrugged, not affected by my teasing. "I'd just gotten my first big check for writing. You can't blame me for wanting a sweet ass ride. It's in my DNA."

"Why are you two still up?" Nikole had appeared in the hallway. Her hair was a little wild and her eyes squinted into the overhead lights. "Troi, you have a Skype meeting in the morning with your producer, and Professor Graft, I'm sure you have work to do in the morning, too."

"Yes, mom," I cracked, although I did feel guilty for keeping her up. With her landscaping business, Nikole kept some horribly early hours, often getting up before the sun.

I hopped up from my seat. "I'll let myself out," I called over my shoulder as I walked to the front foyer. I grabbed my still-damp jacket and pulled it on. "Hey, are we still on for lunch on next Friday?"

"Last Day of School Lunch?" Nikole asked.

"Yup. Although I may need more than just a congratulatory panini after this semester," I grumbled.

"Maybe Hunter will give you something," Troian giggled.

I rolled my eyes, but gave my friends a quick wave. "Thanks for dinner and for the chat. I'll see you guy later."

+++++

CHAPTER THREE

I looked up from my grading when I heard a knock on my open office door. Hunter stood in the doorway, her face impassive. She wore a fitted tank top and a cotton skirt that fell just below her knees. Conspicuously absent was her trademark winter jacket.

"Hi, Hunter." I finished making a correction on the sentence I was currently working on. My days lately consisted of grading one paper after another. "Come on in," I said, distracted by a misplaced modifier. "Let me just finish this paper, and I'll be right with you."

Hunter remained silent and closed the office door behind her. I looked up questioningly when I heard the sound of the latch. "You can leave that open if you want," I noted. We weren't supposed to meet with students behind closed doors for obvious reasons.

Hunter leaned her back against the door. Her hands were hidden behind her, clutching at the doorknob. She shook her head. "I don't like audiences," she stated throatily, still leaning against the closed door.

I set my pen and the partially graded paper down. I rolled my office chair away from my desk, backing up about a foot. "Is everything okay?"

She bit her lower lip and nodded. Her body language, however, indicated that she was the opposite of fine.

I stood from my chair. "Why don't you have a seat and you can tell me what's on your mind?"

"It's you," Hunter blurted out in a voice far less reserved than I was accustomed to hearing from her.

I was startled by the outburst. "Me?"

"You. *You're* on my mind, Professor."

I shook my head feeling perplexed. "I don't...I don't understand."

Hunter pushed herself off the door and lunged in my direction. I jumped backwards and nearly fell over the wheeled chair situated behind me. Instead of continuing forward, she braced an arm on my desk and released a shuddering sob. "I'm *so* sorry," she cried. "I just don't know how to do this anymore." She brought her hands to her face and her shoulders caved and shook with emotion.

I tried to collect myself, but my heart still raced in my chest. I wasn't entirely sure what had just happened. Had she tried to *attack* me?

"Hunter," I stated in what I hoped was a soothing voice. "What's wrong?" I stood back awkwardly, not sure what to do. I'd had plenty of students break down in tears in my office over the years, but it had always been on account of a bad grade. Hunter was a solid B+ student, so it couldn't have been that. "Hunter?" I tried again, slowly inching closer.

She remained with her hands covering her face. She wasn't audibly crying, but her shoulders were visibly tense and quivering.

"Hey," I tried again, dropping my voice to a lower register. "I'm sure everything will be okay."

Her hands slipped from her face. Her features were flushed and tear stains trailed down her normally pale complexion. Without really thinking, I reached out and swept away a few straggling tears on her cheekbone with the pad of my thumb. She visibly shuddered. "I shouldn't have come here," she whimpered.

"Hunter," I said, softer this time. I tentatively brought my hand up to her shoulder and gave it a brief squeeze. "Tell me what's wrong."

She looked down to where my hand rested on her shoulder. She leaned her head closer and my eyes widened when she pressed her lips against the back of my hand. Her eyes shut and she lessened the pressure until her soft lips just barely grazed the top of my hand.

From there, my body reacted on its own accord. It was as if her tentative but brave kiss had awoken something and I now had no control over my right hand. I trailed my fingertips across her exposed collarbone. She pushed out a sharp breath through her nose and her eyes fluttered shut.

I leaned closer and unabashedly inhaled. My nostrils filled with the light perfume that tormented me for hours after she would leave our one-on-one meetings. She smelled *so* good. I wanted to sink my teeth into her flesh. I wanted to make my beautiful student squirm on my desk. I wanted her spread open for me, panting to be touched.

I slipped my arm around her waist and I maneuvered her until she was perched on the edge of my desk. She eagerly submitted to me, her body giving no resistance to my advances. I held onto her hips, pinning her in place before dipping my head and pressing my mouth against her exposed breastplate. Her pale skin became more and more flushed the longer she sat perched on my desk. Her skin was warm and soft beneath my slightly parted lips.

I pressed my mouth harder against her. She filled her lungs with air and her soft breasts rose up, swelling beneath her tank top and providing me with an eyeful of tantalizing cleavage. I dipped my tongue in the v-shaped valley between her pert breasts. She sighed contentedly and arched her back, pushing her breasts more fully into my face.

A low growl bubbled up in my throat. I tightened my grip on her hips, pulling a quiet gasp from her. I could feel her quiver beneath me. I traveled my hands up naked thighs, bunching up the material of her skirt as I went. My breath caught in my throat when Hunter's underwear came into view, teal and lacy. I ran my fingertips along the elastic band that hugged her right hipbone. I hadn't even kissed her mouth yet.

A small noise, a discernable whimper, spilled from her tense mouth. "Professor," she panted. "Please."

I dipped further beneath the delicate material and my fingertips ran over warm, smooth skin that contrasted deliciously with the stability of her jutting hipbone. My fingers curled around the elastic edge, and I began to pull down.

I jolted upright in bed. My body was damp with sweat and my legs were tangled up in the sheets. It had only been a dream. I rolled over in bed to reach for the water glass I kept on the bedside table. The glass was drained, however. With a disgruntled sigh, I flipped the comforter off and stormed towards the kitchen downstairs.

My preoccupation with Hunter had become so overwhelming in waking hours that it now infiltrated my sleep as well. I was fortunate that the semester was nearly over. I could only hope that I wouldn't think about her so much when I didn't see her four times a week for class.

I didn't bother turning on the overhead lights. Just enough moonlight spilled in through the windows that I was able to make my way downstairs. I filled a glass with water from the tap and stared out the window over the sink.

The leaves on the maple tree in my backyard had just started to fill out. I made a mental note for Nikole to get me a quote for some new landscaping. The previous homeowners had planted hostas in the backyard, and they'd grown so much since I'd first moved in that they were starting to take over the yard. I didn't mind the plant, but I'd always wanted a flower garden of my own.

I didn't have a green thumb, but with practice I'd managed to keep some houseplants alive. I found that when I named them I was more invested in keeping them alive. It hadn't gotten to the point where I talked to them or confided in them, but that kind of craziness wasn't above me.

I made another mental note to drop by the Humane Society in the morning. Maybe it was because I'd just woken up from an unconventional dream, but it suddenly felt very lonely in my two-story home. I was a serial monogamist, never feeling quite whole without being part of a couple. Maybe it was time for me to branch out and get a proper pet that wasn't a spider plant. Or maybe I was finally ready to start dating again.

+++++

On the last day of the semester, I was in my faculty office waiting for students to pick up their final graded analysis. Because I taught writing, my students rarely had final exams. Instead, they wrote research papers and reflection essays on how their skills had improved (or not) over the duration of the semester. I often joked with colleagues that teaching writing would have been the perfect job if not for having to actually grade student writing.

As one student after the next stopped by my office to pick up their paper, time passed quickly between the goodbyes, and soon it was almost time to go. 11:57am. I had told students I'd only be around until noon; after that I had plans to meet up with Nikole for lunch. Normally Troian joined us to help me celebrate the end of another semester, but she was currently busy working on revising her screenplay and had a hard deadline to meet. I rarely saw her during these stretches; she'd bury herself in work and emerge a few weeks later, bleary eyed and blinking at the sun.

I stared at the clock display in the corner of my computer monitor and frowned. 11:59am. I hadn't wanted to hold out hope that Hunter would be one of the few students who showed up to pick up their final paper, but every time I heard footsteps in the hallway outside of my office, my heart had leapt into my throat. Few students ever came to pick up their final paper. As soon as exams were over most bolted off campus as fast as they could to start enjoying their summers. I had a few more obligations to attend to, but soon enough I would be enjoying summer as well. I knew it had been foolish to hope that I would see her one last time.

I started to pack up, putting some library books I needed to return into my book bag. I paused, however, when I heard shoes pounding up stairs and running down the corridor outside my office door.

Hunter's face appeared inside my doorway. "Am I too late?" Her normally alabaster skin looked flushed and she was breathing heavier than usual as if she'd just run a great distance.

Her sudden appearance startled me. Normally I needed time to mentally prepare for her; I'd all but given up hope that I'd see her one last time. To add insult to injury, the last time I'd seen her was in my dreams, seated on top of my desk, with me between her thighs.

"You made it just in time," I greeted without stumbling over my words too obviously. I handed her the folder that contained her final paper and her reflection letter. Unlike most of my other students, she didn't immediately tear into the folder in front of me like a savage animal to look at her grade.

"I'm so sorry if I made you wait," she apologized, still looking slightly disheveled. "I wanted to get here earlier, but time got away from me this morning." If possible, her flushed features made her look even more attractive than usual. She always looked so put-together. It reminded me of the day she forgot her umbrella and I had given her a ride home. When she was fallible, she became more

43

real. She wasn't just the quirky student who sat in the left corner of the classroom. She wasn't just some taboo teacher-student fantasy.

I watched a delicate line of sweat trickle down the hollow of her throat and disappear beneath the neckline of her t-shirt. She must have literally ran all the way here. I'd never seen her sweat, not even in the classroom when she'd kept her jacket on. My heart hammered loudly in my head, and her next words muffled in my ears.

"Hmmm?"

The world came rushing back into sharp focus. Her grey-blue eyes inspected me. "I asked if you're all done for the day now?"

"Oh, right. Yeah, I am," I managed to get out. "I'm getting lunch after this. If I don't eat something soon, my stomach will sound like a disgruntled dinosaur." I found myself avoiding her eye contact more than usual. Also, it had become inexplicitly warm. If I didn't get away soon, pretty soon *I* would be the one sweating.

She continued standing in the doorway. She hadn't really ever fully come inside the office this whole time. She just stayed there, hovering and twisting her folder into a tight coil. "I'm on my way to the cafeteria, too. I could walk with you?"

"Oh, actually I'm meeting up with a friend for lunch off-campus. It's kind of our end-of-the-semester tradition." I cast my eyes back to my workbag and continued putting things inside it for something to do. By now I'd run out of papers and library books and had moved on to office supplies.

"Oh, well, have a nice summer, Professor Graft. And thank you. I really liked your class."

When I looked back to the doorway to return the nicety, she was gone. I exhaled deeply, partly in relief, partly in disappointment.

+++++

Half an hour later I was at a quaint little restaurant a few blocks from campus. They were known for their sandwiches, homemade soups, and specialty sodas. When I entered and let my eyes adjust to the dim lights, I spotted Nikole sitting by herself at a table near the front of the restaurant. I waved at the hostess to let her know I didn't need to be seated.

Nikole looked up from her laminated lunch menu when I sat down at the empty seat across from her. "You made it. I was starting to think I was getting stood up."

"Sorry." I pulled my sunglasses free of my hair and set them on the table by my water glass. "Hunter showed up at the very last minute and we talked a little bit."

Nikole's eyebrows rose on her unlined forehead. "Oh really?" She set her menu down. "And what did you talk about?"

"Nothing really. She picked up her paper." I grabbed an extra menu and scanned down the list of sandwiches. "She asked what I was doing the rest of the day."

"And you said?"

"Getting lunch." Maybe I would splurge and get the chicken salad and cranberry on whole wheat even though it probably had just as many calories as a fast food burger.

"Does Troian have as much trouble prying details from you or are you just being difficult for me?" Nikole huffed.

I set my menu back down on the table. "I honestly don't have much to tell you. I could hardly look at her without blushing."

My friend arched an eyebrow. "Was she showing off a lot of skin or something?"

I shook my head. I honestly couldn't recall much about her outfit. I remembered the bead of sweat that trickled down her clavicle. I remembered the deep v-cut of her t-shirt and the slight swell of her breasts beneath the top, but I couldn't even remember the color of her shirt. Pink? Green? Orange? Had she been wearing shorts or jeans or a skirt?

"It wasn't a long conversation," I shrugged, not wanting to turn every interaction with Hunter into a dramatic event. "I said I was going to lunch, and she offered to walk with me. I told her I wasn't going to the cafeteria, and she left."

Nikole's eyes shut and she shook her head. "I can't believe you."

"What?" I asked, feeling mildly self-conscious. "What did I do?"

"Oh, Bookworm," she said with a disappointed sigh. "She asked you out, and you blew her off."

I nearly choked on my complimentary tap water. "She did not! I did not!"

"You're just lucky Troian isn't here for this. She'd be so disappointed in you. The Great Elle Graft is oblivious again to women's advances."

I felt a heat creep onto my cheeks. "You're wrong. She wasn't asking me out."

Nikole smirked, recognizing my embarrassment. "Let's think about this." She started to tick off on her fingers. "Imagine the two of you walk over to the cafeteria together. Once you're there she asks if you'd like some lunch company so neither of you has to eat by yourself. The two of you make casual conversation as you go down the lines with your blue plastic trays. You get to the cashier and you offer to pay for her meal because you're generous that way. She protests at first, but you insist. She reluctantly agrees, but only if you'll allow her to buy you a coffee after lunch."

"You're crazy. Why would she do that?"

"Because she obviously wants you to see her as an equal," Nikole said as if it were the most obvious explanation. "Anyway," she said, continuing, "after lunch she reminds you about her offer of coffee. You suggest going off-campus instead of getting coffee at that horrid cafe in the student center. You tell her about this adorable little place where you often go to grade papers."

"Del Sol?" I supplied, letting myself become complicit in Nikole's fantasy tale. If I'd thought only her girlfriend was the talented storyteller, I was mistaken.

She nodded and continued. "And you say your car is close by in the faculty lot and that you could drive. But Hunter points out how nice the weather is and that she doesn't mind walking if you don't. And the sunshine bounces off her hair and you can't help but think about how lovely and carefree she looks."

I cleared my throat. "So we walk to Del Sol and then what?"

"And you talk. And you drink coffee. And you talk some more. And before you know it, it's late and Hunter needs to get home, but you're too nice to let her walk home by herself. So you walk the short distance back to her apartment together. And when you reach her apartment, you both realize what a perfectly lovely afternoon you've shared together. And she worries she's being too forward when she asks you if you want to meet again for coffee at Del Sol's next week."

"She does?"

Nikole nodded. "But she's not being too forward, and you do make plans to have coffee together again."

I whistled lowly. "You've got it all figured out."

A satisfied, smug grin settled on her lips. "And just think. All you would have had to do was postpone lunch with me and have gone to the cafeteria instead."

If Nikole had cautioned me earlier about putting too much emotional stock into daydreams and What-If scenarios, she'd just given me ammunition for the entire summer. When our waitress came by the table to take our drink orders I was thankful for the distraction.

+++++

CHAPTER FOUR

The doorbell rang just as I finished wiping down the kitchen countertops. I smoothed down the front of my dress, a little black cocktail dress I was wearing for the first time, paired with a long string of pearls and black pumps. I felt more at home in a pencil skirt and blouse, my typical teaching outfit, but tonight was a special occasion. At the close of every Spring semester, I opened my home to graduating seniors and my faculty colleagues in the English Department. Because I taught at such a small school, I typically had the same students in my upper-level classes for English majors, and we got to know each other fairly well. It was nice to be able to host the event, and it was the faculty's final opportunity to send off the graduates before the actual ceremony later that week. Plus, it gave us faculty a moment to unwind before our summertime responsibilities kicked in.

When I opened the front door, a platter of cold cuts was thrust under my nose. "Sorry I'm late."

I took the serving tray, and Tricia, the Departmental Secretary, hustled into my house. She was one of those people who look perpetually harried. Her hair was always a little disheveled, her cheeks flushed. If I didn't know any better, I would have guessed she was rushing from one sexual adventure to the next. Actually, maybe she was. I didn't know much about her even though she sent me about 10 emails a day.

"Where should I put all this?" she asked, looking expectedly unhinged.

I pointed to the kitchen island. "Food can go in the kitchen. I thought we could put the drinks on the buffet in the dining room so not everyone hovers in the kitchen like usual."

"Good idea," she remarked, nodding her head like a bobble-doll. "Space the crowds out."

Before I could give her any further instructions she hustled away, looking more frazzled than usual.

The first students started showing up soon after Tricia arrived with the food. They said their brief hellos to me before immediately descending on the food spread in the kitchen like sharks in open water. It never failed to amaze me how one only needed to post "Free Food!" and students came running. I knew there would be no leftovers by the end of the night. Even the chip dip bowl would be licked clean. It wasn't long before the front of my house was filled with bodies, a collection of students along with my fellow faculty members.

From time to time I'd catch a glimpse of a familiar shade of blonde near the vegetable tray or by the window overlooking my backyard or by the television, and each time my breath caught in my throat. This girl was seriously haunting me, not only in my dreams, but in the flesh as well. But there was no reason why Hunter would be at this event. She wasn't a graduating senior, and she wasn't an English major. It was simply wishful thinking on my part – wishful thinking that seeing her in my office a few days ago wouldn't actually be the last time I ever saw her.

I made my way over to the dining room table where Tricia had arranged an assortment of wine bottles and soda. I gave a knowing smile to some students hovering around the drinks. I recognized them as seniors, all of legal drinking age, but it was clear they were unsure if they were allowed to drink in front of their professors. I filled my own glass with a merlot and left them, still warily eyeballing the alcohol.

More people had arrived when I made it back to the front of the house and the living room. Most of the English Department had shown up. I smiled and made eye contact with them all as I continued making the rounds. I really didn't care for small talk, but if I kept circling, if I kept moving from one room to the next, I wouldn't be stuck talking to any one person for too long.

I had to laugh to myself when I spotted my colleague Thad in the kitchen by the sink, surrounded by a horde of female undergraduates and one male student whom I suspected was gay. Thad looked like a natural, holding court among the students – their star-struck admiration was apparent in their faces. I must have been staring for too long though, because Thad looked up from his entourage and caught my eye. His eyes crinkled at the corners and he raised his glass to me in mock salute. Despite my misgivings about him – I must have been feeling collegial – I raised my glass in return. I immediately regretted it though when his grin widened and it looked like he was excusing himself to come over in my direction.

I spun away and cursed under my breath. I didn't want to encourage Thad. He was annoying and aggressive enough without me smiling at him. I went back to the dining room, hoping to discover we needed more ice or clean glasses or that someone had spilled red wine on my white rug so I'd have something to do other than chat with my clueless coworker.

On my way to the dining room, a woman sidled up next to me and bumped her hip against mine. She leaned in conspiratorially. "Nice party, Dr. Graft."

"Emily." I grinned, recognizing my teaching mentor with the infectious personality. "I'm so glad you were able to make it." She'd been on sabbatical for the semester and I hadn't seen much of her besides a few isolated times on the department floor.

"You look great, Elle." She gave me a quick hug with the arm not attached to her wine glass. "And your dress is so cute," she approved.

I looked down at my little black dress. "Thanks," I said, self-consciously running my palms down the front of the skirt. "I thought I'd try something different tonight from my typical school attire."

Emily twisted her wine glass by its stem. "Well from the way Thad keeps looking over here, I have a feeling he wouldn't mind seeing you without *any* attire."

"Emily!" I said, genuinely shocked. I wondered how much wine she'd had that night. She was a sharp-witted, sharp-tongued woman, but I'd never heard her talk like that before.

"I'm sorry," she chuckled. "I should feel badly for that guy. He strikes out with you more than the baseball team." Our university team was pretty horrible, and so was Thad when it came to flirting with me.

"How was your semester?" she smiled, abruptly changing topics on me.

"Really good," I said, bobbing my head. "I lucked out and had a really good group of students."

"Oh, don't give them so much credit," she huffed with a dismissive wave of her hand. "It helps that you're a great teacher."

"Why can't you be my entire tenure committee?" I laughed.

She gave my shoulder a squeeze. "You're going to be fine. Besides, you've got some time before you need to freak out about that."

"I'll try to keep that in mind." I spotted another familiar face in the dining room—the Chair of my Department, Bob Birken. "Speaking of which," I said to my mentor and friend, "there's Bob. I'd better go do some sucking up."

"Just think, Elle, one more year, and you'll never have to kiss ass again."

I grinned at Emily. "That's the dream, isn't it?" I excused myself from her presence and made my way through the student crowds in the direction of Bob. When he spotted me and we made eye contact, he lifted his drink in salute.

"Thank you for hosting this event again, Elle."

Bob Birken was a heavyset man with a bald head and a full beard. He was fond of argyle-printed sweaters and corduroy pants, and was just about the most talented poet I'd ever met.

"It's not a problem at all, Bob," I said cordially. "I'm just glad that we can do this for our graduates every Spring."

Bob rocked on the soles of his dress shoes. "How are those revisions going?" He was referring to an academic journal article I was working on. It had been accepted for publication with the caveat that I make a few edits.

"Really well. Slow," I admitted with a chuckle, "but well." I paused long enough to sip my red wine. "Once the semester is totally over and final grades are submitted, I'll be able to dedicate more energy to the revisions. Then it's just a matter of time before the editorial board finds something else wrong with it." Publishing in academia was a headache. I much preferred the world of fiction, but I knew I needed to have a balance of both in my discipline. At least until I secured tenure. Then I could do whatever the hell I wanted.

"Oh, I know all-too-well how that is," Bob nodded. "My latest book seems perpetually stuck in the copyedit stage."

I was about to continue talking about my latest project with my colleague, when I spotted an unexpected face near the front entrance. My throat constricted and I was rendered speechless. What was *Hunter* doing here?

I stared a little harder, unblinking, making sure that my imagination wasn't playing tricks on me. But she was really there. She was in my *house*. But *why*? I continued to stare at the blonde who had, only a few days before, made an unexpected appearance in my dreams.

Sometimes the seniors brought friends or family members to the party, but I certainly hadn't expected her to be here. She was standing in a small group of students, some of whom I recognized. She wore a dark purple, spaghetti-strap camisole whose color looked even richer contrasted against the porcelain hue of her skin. It was the first time I'd seen her in a tank top (outside of my dreams), and the view certainly didn't disappoint. Her collarbone was well-defined protruding from pale, alabaster skin that led up to a long, graceful neck. Her hair was down, parted to one side, and it cascaded past her bare shoulders. Our eyes connected, and I immediately looked away, embarrassed that she'd caught me staring at her.

My hand went to the pocket of my dress where I kept my cell phone. I had an impulse to call Troian to come save me from my own party, but I knew she'd only tease me about my inability to have a conversation with attractive women. I had a PhD in English; you'd think words would come easily to me. But beautiful women who made unwavering eye contact were my kryptonite.

As I stood there, ignoring the party happening around me, I gave myself a pep talk. It would be rude to not at least acknowledge her presence. I could go over there and say hi. I could handle that.

"Excuse me, Bob," I said as I started to separate myself from the conversation. "I've got to make the rounds. I don't want to be a poor hostess." He apologized for monopolizing my time, and I flashed him a reassuring smile. I didn't bother telling him there was someone else at the party monopolizing my attention.

I breathed in deeply, summoning my courage, and began to walk in her direction. Our eyes met again, and this time I didn't look away. A ghost of a smile played on her lips, and I felt my confidence bolster.

A hand at my elbow brought me to a stop. "Wonderful party, Dr. Graft." It was my boss, Dean Krauss, the Dean of the College of Arts & Sciences. He wasn't my direct supervisor; that was Bob, Chair of the English Department. Dean Krauss was much higher up the food chain.

"Thank you, Dean." My heart hammered in my chest. I sincerely hoped he hadn't witnessed me eyeballing up a student. "And please call me Elle." I glanced once in Hunter's direction and I swear I saw her look at me sympathetically and with a little bit of disappointment that I'd been sidelined by the Dean.

"You have a lovely home, Elle," he continued, casting his gaze around the open-floor plan. I loved the openness of the first floor. It was what had originally attracted me to the house. "Have you lived here long?"

"About two years," I told him. When I'd first been hired, I rented an apartment. I hadn't wanted to rush into a major commitment like buying a house in case the school didn't work out.

"Your Tenure Review is coming up soon, isn't it?"

I made a humming noise. "Soon," I confirmed. "Next Fall."

When the doorbell rang again, indicating I had more guests, I had an excuse to wiggle away from Dean Kraus. "I should probably get that."

The man nodded. "Well, keep up the good work. I hear good things."

I hustled away from the Dean and welcomed more students into my home. When I closed the door, I looked in the direction where Hunter had previously been standing. I saw the same group of students in that corner of the living room, but she was no longer with them. I frowned, realizing she'd probably come and gone and that I'd missed my opportunity to talk with her one last time. The semester had ended and as a nursing student I doubted she'd have any reason or time in her schedule to take another English class. There was always the possibility of randomly running into her on campus at the library or cafeteria, but I knew that most of the pre-professional disciplines had their students interning off-campus during their senior year.

The realization that I'd probably never see her again hit me, and suddenly I didn't feel like such a gracious hostess anymore. It was late in the evening and I wanted my house back. I wanted to trade my heels for slippers and my dress for pajama pants. But instead of being rude and immediately shooing everyone out, I plastered on a fake smile and tried to fight through the rest of the evening.

+++++

Around nine o'clock, the party finally started to die down. I was surprised that people had stayed for so long. Normally students stayed for half an hour, ate the food and drank the free alcohol, and then left for some other pre-graduation party. But for whatever reason, the crowds had lingered a little longer than usual tonight, well after the last celery stick and piece of cubed cheese had been consumed.

When my house emptied, I looked at the mess in the kitchen and sighed. I tossed some serving spoons into the kitchen sink. I might not have had to set up for the party, but the clean up was far more arduous.

Before I could start to give my kitchen a thorough cleaning, I noticed a light on down the hallway, coming from the direction of my study. I couldn't remember leaving a light on in the back half of my house. I'd planned on keeping that part of my house closed off to students and had kept the lights off to avoid encouraging too much exploration. Curious, I wandered down the hallway. By this time, I'd abandoned my high heels, and in my stocking feet, I padded soundlessly against the wood floor.

I couldn't have been more surprised by what I found – *who* I found – bent over my desk in my personal office, rifling through a stack of graded student papers. Hunter.

I stood, unnoticed, in the doorway until I cleared my throat.

Hunter seemed to jump out of her skin at the sound. She grabbed onto her shirt over the space where her heart resided. "You scared me!" she exclaimed.

My hand curled around the wooden threshold. Normally I'd feel guilty for startling someone so badly, but she'd wandered off to my home office and was digging through other students' papers like it was the most natural thing in the world. I felt violated, like someone had read my diary.

Her grey-blue eyes were wider than I'd ever seen them. "I know this looks really bad." The color had drained from her cheeks. "But

54

it's not what it looks like."

"What it looks like is you're looking through the final papers for grades." My tone was unexpectedly cold, but I was upset. I had opened my home to my students, but that didn't mean they were free to explore and rifle through my things. "But that couldn't be it because you picked up your paper," I said, thinking out loud. "You already know what your grade is. Unless you're stealing papers to sell to some student essay mill."

Her eyes bulged and she dropped the papers as if they'd burned her. "No!" she exclaimed. "I wasn't, I—."

Her panicked exclamation was interrupted when my new cat Sylvia, who had yet to warm up to me, jumped up on my desk with a grunt.

"I hope you've had your tetanus shots," I said, leaning against the doorjamb. "She hates everyone."

Hunter stroked her hand down the center of Sylvia's back and that damn little grey-fuzzed traitor actually arched her back. Hunter picked up the cat and sat down with her on my red couch. Sylvia made a small half-circle with her body and kneaded her paws into Hunter's thigh before settling down onto her lap.

"Are you the cat whisperer?" I asked, mouth surely agape. I'd never seen that devil-cat warm up to anyone. Hell, she barely tolerated me. I likened her to a refugee, still acclimating to her new environment.

"I like cats," she said simply. She seemed to have recovered from the initial shock and looked entirely at ease sitting on my red couch with Sylvia curled up on her lap. She scratched the cantankerous creature between the ears, and I swear I could see the cat's eyes roll back in pleasure.

"So do you always just make yourself at home in your teachers' offices?" The memory of her taking off her jacket in my campus office months ago came to mind. Maybe she did.

Hunter looked suitably shamed, but she didn't stand up. I didn't blame her; making sudden movements around my cat was generally a bad idea.

"I'm not normally this nosey. I was petting your cat out in the hallway and it wandered away. Then I heard some crashing noises later, so I followed the sounds to make sure the cat was okay. When I came in here, your cat was on your desk, knocking things over. I was just trying to pick up after her."

Sylvia had proven herself to be a housekeeping nightmare. She jumped on surfaces on which she didn't belong and knocked things onto the floor to make more room for herself. I'd already found a pair of reading glasses in the bathroom garbage and my favorite grading pens were often rolling around on the floor in the office.

"Don't worry about Sylvia," I said, waving a dismissive hand. "She can take care of herself." I continued leaning against the doorjamb. I didn't really know what to do with myself, but this felt safe.

"As long as she stays away from gas ovens," Hunter grinned.

"My, my," I murmured approvingly, standing up straight. That she knew of Sylvia's namesake was a surprise, and I was impressed. "You've been holding back."

Maybe it was because of the semester's end and that grades were submitted, but I didn't feel so restricted anymore around her. And maybe it was the comfortable way my pet and Hunter were curled up with each other, but I didn't feel so upset and violated anymore.

"I haven't actually read anything by Sylvia Plath," Hunter said, suddenly a little shy. "I just really liked the movie about her life." Her eyes, which I now noticed were almost the identical blue-grey as my cat's, dropped demurely. If I had subconsciously picked out that bastard cat because it reminded me of Hunter, I was officially a lost cause.

"You haven't read Plath?" I declared, sufficiently horrified. I immediately crossed the length of the room and walked to one of my bookcases. I thumbed over the bindings of several titles. Everything was alphabetical by author, of course. I pulled out the thin novel from its place between Parker and Plato. *The Bell Jar* was one of my favorite books. The copy I now held had been well-loved over the years. The binding was creased and worn, the top corner of the paperback cover rounded, and the inner pages were the rich goldenrod color of mass-produced pulp that's sat too long in direct sunlight.

I stuck the book in Hunter's direction, just within her reach. She stopped giving attention to Sylvia long enough to take the book in both hands. Her brow was furrowed in concentration, maddeningly adorable, as she read the back cover information.

"*The Bell Jar* is a masterpiece," I explained, geeking out. "I'm letting you borrow my copy."

Hunter looked up, eyes large and blinking. "Really?"

I never let people borrow books. I wasn't a public library, after all. I also didn't appreciate getting books back in worse condition than when I'd lent them. But I selfishly realized that if I let her borrow the book, I'd have a reason to see her again. I didn't have to give it a second thought. "Really."

The tick-tock of the grandfather clock in my study filled the silence. "Did everyone leave?" she asked. "Am I the only one left?"

I scratched at the back of my neck, once again aware of my awkwardness. At least when I was gushing about literature I hadn't remembered that we were alone. "Yeah."

"I'm sorry," Hunter genuinely apologized. "Not only does it look like I've been snooping, now I've overstayed my welcome."

My instinct was to tell her she could stay as long as she wanted. I smiled instead.

Hunter scratched between Sylvia's ears again. "I'm sorry, sweetie," she murmured, "but I've got to go."

If I had been smoother, I would have found a way to convince her to stay longer. 'Don't go. It'll break her kitty heart,' I would say. She'd admit she had no other plans that night and I'd suggest we take our conversation to the kitchen where I would brew a pot of late-night coffee. We could bring our filled cups to the front porch and we'd sit in the Adirondack chairs I'd recently purchased. I'd light a few candles—to keep the mosquitoes away, I'd explain—and I'd admire her profile, warmed by the glow of candlelight.

We'd start out with innocent remarks about the strange weather patterns. It had recently gone from Winter to Spring overnight. I'd hear about her plans for the summer and her relationship with her family. When the coffee ran out, she'd notice the late hour. She'd thank me for the coffee and conversation, and when she handed me her now-empty cup, our fingers would brush against each other's.

But I wasn't that smooth and I wasn't a moral-free zone. Instead, I'd have to be satisfied with the prospect of seeing her again when she finished reading the book. Maybe she'd be so impressed she'd ask me for other book recommendations. Maybe I'd see her periodically over the summer because of it. And maybe this would turn into a regular thing, and we'd meet for coffee to discuss the current book we couldn't put down. I wondered how she liked her coffee.

"Off you go," Hunter coaxed Sylvia. With a disgruntled noise, my cat stood from her lap. It made a big show of stretching before hopping to the floor. I felt ridiculous for envying that ball of fur.

Hunter stood from my study couch, the very place I'd graded several of her papers, and she brushed at the front of her jeans. Sylvia had a talent for getting her hair all over everything, and it was currently all over the front of her pants.

"Second-guessing making friends with my cat?" I posed teasingly.

She looked up and met my gaze. Her eye contact was relentless. "I got a book out of the deal, didn't I?"

This girl's mood-swings were hard to keep up with. One minute she was bashful and unsure, and the next, staring me down with an unstated challenge and a charming smile. I wanted to know her better. I needed to figure her out.

I walked her from the office to the front door. She had brought a light jacket, but even though dusk had turned to night, it was still warm enough outside to render it unnecessary. She hung it over her arm instead.

"Thank you for hosting a lovely evening," she smiled graciously. "I had a nice time." It was like a switch had been flipped and she was back to being a Stepford wife.

"Did you drive?" I looked out the front to the cars parallel parked outside, lining either side of the street.

She shook her head and tucked some hair behind her right ear. "No. I walked here."

"It's late," I noted. "Are you okay to walk back alone?" Even though it was a very safe neighborhood, I still worried.

She bobbed her head. "I'll be fine. My apartment isn't that far away."

I nodded, remembering the walk-up apartment where I'd given her a ride to once.

She clutched *The Bell Jar* against her chest. "Thanks again for the book." A small look of concern troubled her features. "How should I get it back to you once I've finished?"

I hadn't really thought that far in advance. "Um, just email me when you're done," I said. "We can figure it out then."

She ducked her head again. "Okay. Have a good night,

Professor."

She gave a short wave before leaving out the front door. I stood in the doorway and watched her make her way down the four wooden steps and the concrete sidewalk that led up to my house. She looked back at the house when she reached the street. Noticing that I still stood in the doorway, she gave me a brilliant smile. I felt my pulse quicken at the sight, and I quickly shut the door.

+++++

CHAPTER FIVE

I loved summer. For as much as I enjoyed the winter months and the way the sun's rays sparkled against snow that clung to naked tree branches, there was something about the scent of charcoal grills, the sensation of sunshine warm on my skin, and the feeling of gritty beach sand between my toes that never failed to put a smile on my face. In my part of the Midwest, summer was brief and mild, but I didn't mind that temperatures rarely crept past 80 degrees Fahrenheit. I'd probably melt like a snowman otherwise.

During the summer months when I didn't have to teach, I liked to get out of the house every now and again during "work hours," to shake myself out of routines. When I worked from home everyday, my cat Sylvia was usually the only interaction I had. I refused to allow myself to become another sad, lesbian cliché.

Today, I had relocated to Del Sol, my favorite coffee shop in the city. Decades ago the building had been part of a factory of some kind, but after the industry had been pushed out of the area and the structure had remained vacated for some time, a locally-grown coffee chain had reclaimed the space and transformed it into a two-story coffee shop with a lofted seating area that overlooked the main floor.

The staff prided themselves on the designs they crafted on top of wide-mouthed mugs of mochas and lattes and the limited menu was organic, sprinkled with local products. It was trendy to be sure, and over the lunch rush things got a little chaotic, but on this particular Tuesday morning at just after 9:30am, I had scored myself a prime spot where I was guaranteed to be productive as long as the refills kept coming.

After carefully placing my ceramic mug and blueberry muffin on the table, I methodically pulled out a hardcover book and legal-sized notepad from my bag and set them on the table as well. I was a little old-fashioned when it came to researching and writing. Whereas most everyone I knew took notes on a laptop, I preferred the comfort of pen and paper. Admittedly it took longer, but I was a creature of habit and not the least bit superstitious. I'd published a number of journal articles over my young career, each of them having manifested from careful notes I'd taken by hand. I didn't see the necessity of breaking up my routine.

I pulled out my phone and found a playlist conducive to working. I only put in one ear bud, however; the faint background music in my left ear was just enough to keep me focused. I had hardly submerged myself into my work when I heard a familiar voice.

"Professor?"

I looked up from my book and was surprised to see a former student standing next to my table.

"Hunter," I greeted, pulling my wits about me. I tugged the solo ear bud out of my ear so quickly that it hurt. "How are you?" I asked, biting back a painful wince.

"I'm good, thanks," she affirmed, bobbing her head slightly. "And you?"

I pushed the hair out of my face. Normally when I read for research I pulled my hair back in a bun, but that morning I'd decided to leave it down. "Busy," I admitted. "Always busy. There's this myth about teachers getting their summers off."

She touched the corner of the open book splayed on the table and twisted it clockwise to better examine the text. I thought it was a rather bold move to be so familiarly touching my things, but I pushed that observation to the side. "What are you working on?"

I stared at her long, feminine fingers. Her nails were short, the cuticles manicured and pushed back, and a clear glossy polish coated the nails. "Just a paper for a conference I'm presenting at in the Fall."

"Oh, that's all," she laughed, mocking my modesty.

Charming. That's the word that instantly came to mind when I interacted with Hunter. She had never been overly participatory in class, but in a one-on-one setting, she exuded a practiced confidence and sociability that comes from being raised by parents who treated you as an equal, as a peer. I'd had plenty of polite students before – it was the Midwest, after all. But those had always been a deferential politeness. This was something different and altogether unnerving. This was unwavering eye contact and an easy laugh that reminded me of weekending at the Hamptons and croquet. If laughter could have a socioeconomic status, Hunter's laugh was Old Money.

I couldn't help taking an indulgent moment to really look at her. Her skin was lightly tanned and her shoulder-length hair, now pulled back into a tight ponytail, was a shade lighter blonde from the sun. She wore a short white tennis skirt, revealing an alarming amount of toned skin that was, because of my seated position, unfortunately right at my eye-level. Her form-fitting light blue polo shirt made her grey-blue eyes even brighter, and the narrow sleeves hugged at the slight curve of feminine biceps.

"You play tennis?" I asked stupidly when nothing else came to mind.

She looked confused.

"Your outfit?" I clarified, pointing to the ensemble.

She looked down at her clothes and laughed. "Right." She self-consciously wiped at her forehead and re-adjusted her thin hair band. "I just finished playing a few sets with my dad at the courts around the corner. Hence the sweaty mess."

I thought she looked perfect, but wisely kept that thought to myself. "Having a good summer so far?" I asked, finding myself uncharacteristically making small talk with a former student. I hated small talk. If it had been anyone else I would have skillfully dismissed him or her after exchanging a few pleasantries, put my ear bud back in, and continued reading my book.

Hunter nodded. "So far. I'm back home with my parents in the suburbs, so that's always a challenge."

I laughed. "I can only handle my own parents a few days at a time before we're at each other's throats."

"My family is pretty close, I guess, but it takes a while to re-adjust to living under their roof after being on my own all school year." She fidgeted as she stood, touching the bottom hem of her mid-thigh skirt, and unknowingly pulled my attention from her face to slender, unblemished thighs.

I felt my face redden as explicit images smashed against my brain of those thighs spread open for me on my office desk, and I threw my gaze to the tabletop instead. "Did you get into all the classes you wanted for next semester?"

Hunter sighed. "No. There's a waitlist for one of my biology classes."

"You're in the nursing program, right?"

Her frown turned into a broad smile and she nodded. "You have a really good memory."

I shrugged. She didn't need to know I'd memorized various other details about her. "It's what I get paid the big bucks for."

"I really like the book, by the way."

I knew exactly what she was talking about, but for some reason I feigned ignorance. "Which book?"

"The one you let me borrow," she supplied. "*The Bell Jar*?"

"Oh, right. I'd nearly forgotten about that." Lie. I'd been checking my email obsessively since she'd left my house weeks ago with the promise to email me when she'd finished.

Her smile was so big, it threatened to cleave her face in half. "I really like Esther. She's a little dark, but I think she's funny."

"I'm glad you're enjoying it so far," I returned in the most professional voice I could muster.

"When I'm finished, maybe we could meet and talk about it? If you're not too busy, I mean."

Yes!

I nodded, holding back the enthusiasm that was bubbling just beneath my surface. I mentally gave myself a high five.

Hunter fidgeted again. "I'm sorry to run off, but I have to go; my dad's waiting out front in the car. I'm just supposed to be grabbing a pound of coffee." She held up a bag of ground beans that I hadn't noticed until now. I blamed it on the distraction of her tennis skirt. "He's addicted to their breakfast blend."

"I might have to go to a 12-step program myself." I tapped my own ceramic mug.

"It was really great running into you, Professor Graft." She started walking backwards, inching her way towards the exit.

I smiled and mock saluted her with two fingers to my temple. *God, could I be anymore awkward?* I mentally chastised. "Have a nice summer, Hunter."

She nodded her head as she continued walking backwards toward the main exit. "You too."

Her elbow caught a young man coming through the front door. She bobbled her dad's bag of coffee beans, nearly dropping it, before retaining her composure. I watched her apologize profusely to the man overdressed in a suit in the summer. I covered my mouth with my hand, hiding an amused grin. Hunter turned and rushed out of the coffee shop without looking back.

Charming, indeed.

When she left, I grabbed my phone and texted Troian: *She likes the book!*

My friend's response was immediate. *What are you talking about?*

I realized I hadn't told Troian about Hunter showing up at the English department's party and her lingering in my home office with my cat Sylvia and *The Bell Jar*. I'd decided to keep it to myself knowing she would have found a way to turn Hunter petting my cat into a million and one perverted euphemisms.

In that moment, I decided to continue keeping it to myself.

Sorry, that text wasn't for you, I lied.

I stored my phone out of sight on the off-chance that Troian would keep texting and pestering me. I typically didn't keep things like this from my best friend, but I felt that just this once I might keep this private. I didn't need her making conversations about good literature into an illicit act. And it's not like I'd let Hunter borrow D.H. Lawrence or any of my 1950s lesbian pulp fiction collection. There was nothing improper about an English professor lending a good book to a student for some summer reading. I'd just have to keep telling myself that.

+++++

Even though I didn't teach summer classes (one of the perks of working at a small school), I still managed to keep myself busy over the next few months. I had plenty of school-related work to do between getting materials ready for Fall semester, working on my paper for an academic conference I was presenting at in mid-September, and making revisions to my collection of short stories. I'd also managed to spend valuable time with friends, mostly Troian and Nikole, and a few coffee get-togethers with my ex-girlfriend, Cady, but I had also made the trip to my home state of Wisconsin to visit old friends and family.

I hadn't thought much about a particular blonde former student of mine, but every once in a while something happened that reminded me of her. Mostly it was just flashes of a familiar shade of hair color, which was exacerbated because in summer everyone goes blonde. But I also found myself going to Del Sol's more often than usual hoping I might bump into her again. But her dad must have quit his coffee fix or she was avoiding the place because I didn't see her there the rest of the summer.

It was late into the summer, just weeks before the start of Fall semester, when I finally heard back from Hunter. I'd nearly given up on ever hearing from her again or getting my book back. Bitterly I'd considered it a proper punishment for breaking my "No Book Lending" policy.

The email she'd sent me was brief, if not a little rambling, far too polite, and overall very Hunter-like. When I read it to myself, I could practically hear her voice and see her blushing and ducking her head:

Hi Professor Graft,

I just finished your book, and I wanted to know how you wanted me to give it back to you. I won't be on campus much this semester because it's my senior year and I have an internship at the hospital, but I could drop it off at your house or bring it by your campus office.

I'm sorry it's taken me so long—I'm really not this slow of a reader. I'm hoping you're still interested in talking with me about The Bell Jar *when you have some time. I really enjoyed it. Thank you for the recommendation.*

I hope your summer went well – even if you had work to do.

- Hunter Dyson

I snapped each knuckle separately as I read and re-read the email and thought about my reply. My mom had once told me I would get arthritis if I kept cracking my knuckles. I was sure it was an Old Wives' tale meant to scare like if a toad peed on you, you'd get warts. Or how masturbation gave you hairy palms.

What was an appropriate, professional response? How should we meet so she could give me back my book? Troian's voice popped into my head: *"Oh, I know how she can give it to you."*

I thought about Hunter's offer to drop the book off at my house. It was an unnecessary and out-of-the-way gesture; she could just as easily put the book in my faculty mailbox, and she'd never have to actually see me. It reminded me of other unnecessary acts – taking her jacket off in my faculty office for a 15-minute meeting, checking on Sylvia when she heard a crash in the back of my house, touching and turning my book at the coffee shop. They were all small gestures and I'd unnecessarily fixated on them as meaning something.

I knew what I had to do. I needed to stop this ridiculous, fantasy relationship with a student nearly 10-years my junior, who was most definitely straight. I moved my fingers over the track-pad on my laptop. I watched the little arrow scrawl across the screen, and I clicked Delete.

+++++

CHAPTER SIX

"Another pale ale?" the blonde behind the bar at Peggy's asked me. I vaguely remembered her name as being Leah and that she had her Masters in French Literature. We'd struck up a conversation once upon a time about *Madame Bovary*, one of my favorite works of French literature. Troian had scolded me after we'd left the bar that night for being too nerdy.

I nodded. I'd finished off my first pint quickly, but planned on pacing myself with the second. Peggy's was busy tonight, but the bar area was relatively vacant. I'd claimed a barstool without much effort. Most of the other bar patrons were on the dance floor or occupying the tables along the perimeter of the bar.

Leah removed my empty pint glass and placed a fresh cocktail napkin in front of me. As she poured me another pint, I twisted on my stool and glanced around the bar. I wondered if Megan still worked here, but I wasn't about to ask Leah. I hadn't been back to Peggy's since that night, months ago. I'd been absent partly because work had gotten busy, but mostly because I was too embarrassed to show my face. One-night-stands weren't my typical fare and almost-one-night-stands were altogether embarrassing.

I'd come to Peggy's tonight though because it was a new semester, and I was frustrated with one of my writing seminars. No matter how many in-class workshops I facilitated, they couldn't seem to figure out how to write a 5-paragraph essay. Normally after a challenging day I'd go home to Sylvia and run myself a warm bath, light a few scented candles, and read a novel in the bathtub. But tonight, after marking up one horrible essay after the next, I needed something a little stronger than a vanilla candle and warm sugar bath scrub. I'd left a message on Troian's voicemail to see if she wanted to meet up so I didn't have to drink by myself, but so far my phone was silent. I vaguely remembered her mentioning a date night with Nikole, but I couldn't recall if she'd said it was tonight or not. This was one of the drawbacks of being an extra-wheel. I desperately needed to find a wheel to call my own. Or just a girlfriend. That would work, too.

I'd thought about calling Cady to see if she wanted to meet up with me tonight. But I knew from the last time we'd briefly talked on the phone that she'd just started dating someone exclusively. I didn't want to complicate things and the way I was feeling tonight, lonely and self-depreciating, I was sure to do that. Cady was familiar and comfortable and that was dangerous. I wanted her to move on without me continually dragging her back down. I wanted her to be happy because I doubted she could ever be that with me.

"You guys are busy tonight," I said to Leah, conversationally.

She set another pint of beer in front of me. "The start of a new school year is always good for business. A whole new crop of freshmen." She grinned mischievously. "Or fresh *meat*."

"Now you sound like Troian," I said, shaking my head but smiling. She was always teasing me that freshmen were the only reason I never took her up on the offer to work with her in Hollywood.

"Where is that pocket-lesbian tonight?"

I shrugged and twisted my glass on the bar top. I played with the condensation on the outside of the pint glass and drew patterns with my fingertips. "Date night with Nik, I think."

"Gross," Leah said, echoing my cynical thoughts. "Those two are so sweet, it makes my teeth rot."

As she walked away to attend to another thirsty lesbian, I took a moment to appraise the friendly bartender. Leah was nice. She had a good sense of humor, was educated, and had a nice ass. I could do much worse. I *had* done much worse.

I grabbed my beer and twisted back around on my stool to watch the people out on the dance floor. Peggy's always drew a mixed crowd on weekend nights and tonight was no exception. It was the only gay bar in about a 50-mile radius and it pulled patrons from all over. Tonight's dance floor was packed with an assortment of co-ed women, no doubt from my school and other area universities, a few skinny-jeaned men, and a handful of older lesbians who, after a few beers, danced unapologetically with little rhythm.

It had always amazed me that such a supposedly conservative area could boast such a large, vibrant queer community. When I'd first been hired I'd been concerned that I'd have to stay Closeted until I found a job at a different, more liberal school. So far my sexuality had been a nonfactor, especially in the English Department. It made me feel more confident about my decision to pursue tenure at this school. Tenure went both ways; the school needed to commit to you to stay on permanently, but you also needed to commit to the school as well.

The crowd on the dance floor seemed to part, affording me an unobstructed view of a tall blonde on the dance floor. My approving gaze immediately went to the woman. I had a type and tall blondes were certainly it. My pint glass nearly slipped out of my hand when I realized I knew the tall blonde.

Hunter.

What was Hunter Dyson doing in a gay bar?

The slightly elevated dance floor was crowded, but Hunter was tall and her blonde head of hair poked up among the masses. Under the shroud of dimmed lights and flashing neon strobes, I allowed myself the indulgence of really looking at her, something my guilt-complex hadn't allowed me to do in a while. The music was a remix of some Top 40 song I've heard overplayed on the radio. Her eyes were bright and she threw back her head, laughing. She wasn't the most provocative dancer I'd ever seen. Actually, she danced just like I imagined she would. Her movements were hesitant, contained, like she was afraid to break out of her comfort zone. I didn't recognize the other girls who danced with her in a loose circle, their strategic formation challenging only the bravest souls to try and infiltrate their group, but they all looked to be about Hunter's age so I suspected they were also students, maybe fellow classmates from the nursing program.

There was a very real possibility that she wasn't gay. I was sure that a number of straight co-eds from my campus came to Peggy's because there wasn't a bouncer outside checking IDs, and I couldn't really recall having seen any of the bartenders ask patrons for proof of their age, either. Even Troian had boasted proudly about not having her ID checked and she looked about 12. That was part of the reason I typically avoided this place on the weekends during the school year. Besides the alcohol angle, I'm sure a few co-ed women came to Peggy's either to experiment with their sexuality or to go slumming – to see Real Life Lesbians in their natural habitat.

I knew I should probably leave. I didn't care if students knew I was gay – I didn't hide my sexuality – but I didn't like putting myself in situations where I might possibly observe an underage student drinking alcohol. I gave serious consideration to leaving, but I still had a full beer, and I'd be lying if I didn't admit to being curious as to which of those categories my former student belonged. Was she gay? Or was she just here to dance?

I thought about texting Troian to tell her about this recent development, but I knew she'd interrupt her date night with Nikole to message me back. I didn't want to do that to either of them, so I resisted the urge to reach for my phone.

I intended to spin back around and finish my beer, not willing to let myself become a gawking voyeur. But just as I'd made that decision, from across the bar, grey-blue eyes caught my own. I was sitting too far away to decipher a specific emotion if it passed across her visage – shock, confusion, embarrassment, or something else altogether. But I did observe her grab the attention of the girl dancing closest to her, and then she started to maneuver off the dance floor and walk directly toward me.

As I watched her weave through the crowded bar and steadily eliminate the distance between us, I felt a little like a deer in headlights. *This can't end well*, my brain warned me. *Shut up, brain*, I tossed back.

Her cheeks were flushed and a peculiar smile had found its way to her face. "Professor Graft?" Her voice was nervous, but not necessarily confused. It made me wonder if my sexuality was public knowledge among the small student body.

"How are you, Hunter?" I managed to stumble out. I self-consciously put my glass of beer on the bar top.

"I'm good," she said, routinely falling into polite small talk. This was safe territory. "And you?"

"Good, good," I returned. I bit down on my lower lip. I didn't know what to say. In the classroom, in my faculty office, or even in an off-campus coffee shop, I could muster up the courage for casual conversation. But not at a gay bar.

"Do you dance?" she asked.

I couldn't tell if she was asking me to dance with her or if she was just making conversation. I didn't want to read too much into it.

"Not when anyone's looking."

She glanced wistfully out at the dance floor. "Me either." Normally the space went unused, but on nights when they bothered to hire a DJ it always seemed to fill up. "But I'm here with some friends, and they dragged me out there."

I cleared my throat and shifted on my bar seat. "Well, don't let me keep you from them."

She shrugged, fine boney shoulders visible beneath her tank top. It was a far cry from the blue puffy winter jacket. "I'm not really in the dancing kind of mood anymore. It's so hard to just be 'on' all the time, you know?"

I nodded in understanding. After marking up so many papers that day, I'd felt emotionally and mentally exhausted. It was a wonder I had managed to drag myself here tonight, but I hadn't felt like being in an empty house all day.

She cast a furtive glance in my direction. "How about you? What brings you here tonight?"

"I was trying to drown my sorrows," I explained, looking down into the bottom of my glass, "but my sorrows learned to swim."

She leaned against the bar top, perceptively closer. "So not only do you teach English," she said, quirking an elegant eyebrow, "but you're also a poet?"

I shook my head. "I'm a writer." As if there was a world of difference. I'd paraphrased Frida Kahlo, but I didn't bother to explain that to her.

She smiled, truly beaming, and I knew I was in trouble.

I grabbed my drink and the paper napkin lifted with it. "What's the point?" I grumbled. I picked it off and threw the wilted napkin back down on the bar.

"I think it's for bar preservation," she smiled.

I stared hard at her face, hoping that the intensity of my gaze was masked by the dim bar lighting. She should smile all the time. I wish

I were funnier or wittier so I could produce that slow curl of generous lips spreading to reveal two rows of perfect, white teeth on demand. She smiled with her whole face, grey-blue eyes crinkling at the corners.

"I don't mean to pry," I said suddenly, "and you don't have to answer if you don't want to, but are you gay?"

The smile faltered. "I'm not sure," she said, looking away. "That's kind of why I'm here tonight." She looked back in my direction, her face looking full of remorse. "My friends mean well, but I'm just not a club kind of girl. I don't know what they thought I'd find here tonight." Her shoulders heaved as she sighed. "They're just excited for me, I guess. Like me exploring my sexuality is a shiny new car they want to take for a ride. But when do *I* get the keys to the car, you know?"

"I think that's the most I've ever heard you speak in one sitting."

She blushed prettily, eyes back on the bar top. "I'm sorry I wasn't a better student," she murmured.

"You were fine," I reassured her. I didn't really feel like talking shop. Not here. Not tonight. Not with her.

I took another drink of my beer. It was a good pale ale from one of my favorite local brewers. I might not know much about wine, but I was certainly a beer snob. As a university professor I should have been knowledgeable about floral bouquets instead and chatted nonstop about my most recent trip to Wine Country. But that wasn't me. Hell, I'd hardly ever left the Midwest. I'd always felt like a fraud – like a graduate student in professor clothing.

"I always had more to say," she noted wistfully, "I was just never brave enough to say it. I'd replay what I wanted to say over and over in my mind, but when I'd finally built up the courage to speak, we'd moved on to another question or another topic."

"I was like that in college too at first," I admitted with a slow nod. "You get over the fear with time though. You care less about making mistakes or looking bad in front of your peers."

"I'm sorry," she apologized. "This probably isn't how you imagined spending your night."

I shrugged. I had no plans. "How about you? How did you imagine the night turning out?"

"I don't know." She ran her thumbnail in a groove on the bar. "I'd meet some tall, dark stranger. She'd sweep me off my feet with her swagger, confidence, and whiskey mouth." She looked up, embarrassed. "I think I've been reading too many romance novels." She fiddled with an unoccupied drink coaster.

"Hunter," I said hesitantly. "I don't hide my sexuality at school – the other professors in my Department know – but I don't openly broadcast it." I gave her a wary glance. "So I'd appreciate if you didn't run home and post on Facebook about seeing me here."

"Oh! I wouldn't!" she insisted. Her grey-blue eyes were wide. "I mean, I don't even have a Facebook page, but even if I did I'd respect your privacy."

"You really don't have Facebook? I thought students these days weren't allowed to be in college without one." I was only partially kidding.

"I never really got into social networking," she shrugged. "I guess I don't see the point. I don't have a smart phone or an iPod either."

I sat up a little straighter on my stool. "Wow. It's like you're an alien."

She smiled pensively. "I guess I'm a little old-fashioned."

I stared at my hands, surrounding my half-filled beer glass. "Tell me about love on your planet," I murmured.

"Sorry?"

My eyes snapped back into focus. "It's from a movie. *Barbarella?*"

Her face scrunched up.

"Jane Fonda in a fur bikini?"

Hunter's pale eyebrows rose comically on her forehead.

I shook my head. "I'm really dating myself with these references, huh?"

She looked away suddenly. "You're barely older than me." Her voice sounded thin and far away, and I had to strain to hear her.

I brought my pint glass to my lips. "If *barely* means a decade, then sure," I winked. I wasn't sure where the sassiness had come from, but I was pretty sure the beer was to blame.

"Do you, um, want another beer?" Hunter stuttered out. It was as if she'd read my mind. "I could buy you one." She reached for her wallet and fumbled with the clasp.

Something about the offer endeared her to me even more. I put my hand over the top of my pint glass. "Thank you for the offer, but I should stop after this one." I offered her a small smile. "I've got papers to mark up tomorrow, and I can't be productive if I've got a hangover."

She nodded and put her wallet back out of sight.

"Speaking of age, are you even old enough to be here?" I asked. I tried to keep my tone light, like I wasn't policing her life.

Her expressive mouth tilted upside down. "Close enough. I'll be 21 in a few months."

I bit the tip of my tongue. The second beer was starting to get to my head and a teasing comment had wandered into my mouth. Even though she was no longer my student, I still felt the need to be somewhat professional in her presence.

"How did you know?"

"Know what?" I asked.

"That you were gay."

"Oh, uh." I fumbled momentarily. "Honestly, I was a late bloomer. I didn't know what gay was until college. And then I made up for lost time."

Her pale skin flushed, visible even in the darkened bar. I knew I was probably hedging on inappropriate, but this second beer was definitely starting to loosen my tongue.

"It was actually movies that made me realize I was gay," I continued. "I would find myself still thinking about the lead actress and not the male protagonist long after the movie had ended." I licked my lips. "What about you?""

Her grey-blue eyes momentarily widened as if she hadn't expected me to ask the same questions of her. "I, uh, I guess I'm still just trying to figure it all out still. Maybe I'm bisexual, maybe I'm lesbian."

"Are you attracted to men?"

Her features scrunched adorably like she was thinking really hard. "Objectively I can appreciate when men are attractive. But I can't really see myself ever having sex with one."

So many questions popped into my head. Was she a virgin? Had she ever had a boyfriend before? Had she ever kissed a girl? I tried to play it cool. She was a shiny gold star. I went for the question that seemed the safest. "So no boyfriends?"

She shrugged delicately. "Not really. A few short-lived relationships, but nothing ever serious. Most guys I knew in high school were jerks. I endured one too many sucking jokes."

"Sucking jokes?" I echoed, not getting the reference and dreading the response.

She smiled a little sadly. "My last name's Dyson."

"O-oh," I said, suddenly getting the reference. Her story made me want to scoop her up and protect her from the immature bullies in her past. But I stayed glued to the bar stool instead.

"So now you've got to tell me a story about yourself so I don't feel like I've been over-sharing." She laughed at herself and tucked a lock of hair behind her ear.

"Well..." An assortment of stories sprung to mind, and I mentally waded through the too-intimate-for-Peggy's tales in search of the perfect anecdote. But it never came. "So you liked *The Bell Jar*?" I asked instead.

"Is Esther gay for Doreen?"

I wasn't expecting that. "She, um, what do *you* think?"

Hunter looked momentarily thoughtful. "I think she's following what's comfortable and familiar with Buddy, but she doesn't love him. She sees something unconventional and wild about Janice. It's that lifestyle that she falls in love with."

I smiled. "Tell me again why you didn't talk more in class?"

She turned her face, and I heard her laugh. "I had my reasons."

I tried not to dwell on her vague response for too long. "I'd love to pick your brain more about Plath." I chewed on my lower lip. "But you should go back to your friends; I feel like I'm holding you back."

"I make it a rule never to be where I don't want to be." There was an unmistakable intensity that flickered behind her eyes. It faded when she shook her head. "Unless I'm sitting through one of Professor Witlan's lectures."

Doug Witlan was a biology professor who had the unfortunate luck of teaching the giant generalized biology lecture. "You have my sympathies. I haven't had to deal with him, but I've heard he's pretty monotone."

"Just imagine sitting through an 8am lecture with the man and everyone around you is either sleeping or texting."

"You know, when I was a student, we didn't have all that technology. We took notes on paper. And when professors lectured, they talked the entire time without visuals or PowerPoint or interactive classrooms."

"Do you have a hang-up about your age?"

I scrunched my eyebrows. "No," I said, a little taken aback by her forward tone. "Why?"

She shrugged. "It just seems like your mission tonight is to point out how much older you are than me."

I busied myself by drinking down the rest of my beer. I couldn't tell her that those comments were for my benefit – that my subconscious was reminding me to keep it professional. She was a student, and even though I wasn't her teacher anymore, I still needed to conduct myself appropriately. Even if we were sitting together at a gay bar. "Oh? I hadn't noticed I was doing that."

"Is this making you uncomfortable?"

Yes. "No. Why would it?" Lies. Lies. Lies. I hoped my poker face was in place.

"I'm sure you weren't expecting spending the evening with an ex-student."

I knew what she meant, but the way she had phrased it made me flush. My overly active imagination immediately went to an inappropriate place. "I didn't expect it," I answered honestly. "But that doesn't mean I'm not having fun."

She bit her lower lip and looked away; my stomach flip-flopped like I was free-falling.

"Another beer, Elle?" I looked away from Hunter to the bartender, Leah.

I looked back to Hunter. She stared back at me, unflinching. I'd already turned her down, not letting her buy me a drink with the excuse that I had grading.

"I suppose those papers can wait another day," I heard myself say.

Leah gave me a knowing smirk before turning away to retrieve my third beer.

I cleared my throat. "Can I get you anything?" I didn't look at Hunter, but there couldn't have been anyone else I was talking to. The bar area was still sparsely populated and we were practically alone. I knew she couldn't legally have alcohol, and I wasn't condoning under-aged drinking or about to put Peggy's liquor license in jeopardy, but she'd offered to buy me a drink earlier. It felt like the polite thing to do.

"No, no. I can handle getting a soda on my own. But thank you for the offer."

"Are you always so polite?" I asked.

"Would you rather I be rude?"

I didn't have a ready answer for her. Leah returned with my drink. "Something for you, sweetie?" Leah asked. It always annoyed me when bartenders used pet names to talk to girls. It annoyed me when men did it, and now it annoyed me when Leah did it to Hunter.

"Can I get a diet cola?" Hunter asked. "Whatever you've got is fine."

Leah pulled out the gun and filled a pint glass.

"How much?"

Leah pushed the glass across the bar. "It's on the house, hun," she said with a quick wink.

Hunter visibly reddened and looked down at her hands while mumbling her gratitude.

I felt myself getting unreasonably jealous. Leah never gave out free drinks, not even soda. She was notoriously stingy among the bar staff. I suddenly felt like I was in competition with Leah for Hunter's attention.

I didn't know what to talk about with her. I stared at the beer at the bottom of my pint as if the answer was swimming around in my glass. I hardly had game around beautiful women in the first place. I notoriously tripped all over myself, verbally and literally. I could always fall back on school talk and be the boring professor.

But the larger issue shouldn't have been what to talk about – it should have been why did I feel compelled to compete? It's not like I had any designs on seducing this girl. Sure, she'd played a starring role in most of my fantasies for the past year, but Hunter had been right about me – I was hung-up on the age difference.

And it wasn't as if Leah was a bad person from whom Hunter needed to be protected. And she wasn't that unattractive either. I took another look at the long-time bartender. She was a tall woman and tonight wore jeans, a studded belt, and a white tank top. Her bleached blonde hair was boyishly short and slightly spiked into a faux hawk. Her white tank top offset two impressive tattoo sleeves covering thinly muscled arms. She had a surprisingly feminine voice for such a hard exterior. If Leah wanted to make a play on Hunter, I knew it was best if I just stepped aside.

"Wow. It's getting late," I said, making a big show of checking the time on my cell phone.

I started to stand up until Hunter's hand came down to rest on top of mine. "You're leaving?" Those large grey-blue eyes bore into mine. "You've got a full beer. Isn't that breaking some kind of code?" I was highly aware that her hand had not moved away from mine. Her palm felt dry and warm.

"I know, but I probably should get going."

"If you leave, I'll have to go back to pretending to have fun with my friends."

"And you'd rather pretend to have fun with me?"

She smiled and nodded.

I might not have been an expert about these kinds of things, but I was pretty sure Hunter was flirting with me. And I was pretty sure I was flirting back.

We moved our conversation to one of the small tables that lined the perimeter of the bar. I reasoned it wasn't for the intimacy the private tables afforded; it just was more practical. Further away from the dance floor, we wouldn't have to shout to hear each other. But I still found myself leaning in closer as the night progressed.

My mouth had betrayed me enough that evening, so I nursed my third beer the rest of the night. We talked about a variety of things – school mostly, but I felt like I was talking with a friend, not an undergrad. I shared with her my anxieties about my upcoming tenure review and she talked about her own career uncertainties. Her internship was going well, but she wasn't sure yet what kind of nurse she wanted to be. We even discussed *The Bell Jar* again, and at some point in the conversation, I didn't know if we were still talking about the book anymore.

Before long, Leah was announcing Last Call and turning on the overhead lights. I hated Last Call; everyone scatters like cockroaches under the harsh, unflattering lights.

I took my time standing up and stretched out my limbs.

"I can't believe I'm still awake," Hunter laughed, shaking her head. "Normally I'd be in bed before 10pm on a Saturday."

"Now who's the grandma?" I teased.

"No talking about age, remember?" she admonished.

She'd caught me again. "Do you have a ride home?" I was worried for a moment that her friends had left her and then I'd feel obligated to give her another ride home. Okay, truthfully, I both worried and also secretly hoped that would happen.

She scanned the few people remaining in the bar, not looking worried. "No, I'm good. My friends are still here." She gave them a wave. I glanced in the direction of where she'd spotted them. Thankfully I still didn't recognize any of them as current or past students.

She turned to me and gave me a warm, brilliant smile. "Thanks for saving me tonight."

"Any time, Hunter."

I felt confident about going in for a hug. We'd spent all night talking to each other after all, and I was naturally hug-y. My immediate family had never showed that kind of open emotion, but Cady and her family were all about hugs, and it had worn off on me.

She must have misinterpreted my intentions, because as I leaned in for a hug, her arms weren't the only things touching me. I made a surprised noise when I realized her lips were pressed against mine. The kiss was short-lived, however, before she realized her mistake. When she pulled back, I'm sure the confusion was writ large on my face.

"Oh my God," she hastily mumbled. "I'm so sorry."

I was too startled to form complete sentences. "No. It's. No, don't worry about it."

She grabbed her bag from the table. I noticed how, for the first time since I'd met her, her eye contact faltered. She wouldn't lift her head to look at me. "Thank you for being so kind tonight."

I cleared my throat, self-conscious and aware of just how bright the overhead lights were now that the last patrons were milling out the front entrance. "No problem at all."

+++++

79

CHAPTER SEVEN

I stabbed at the top of the cellophane cover with a steak knife from the butcher block and threw the frozen dinner into the microwave. I knew how to cook, but nothing was more depressing than making a meal for one. As I pressed the pre-programmed buttons on the microwave, however, I began to rethink that statement.

I stared out the kitchen window into my backyard. Outside, the sky had turned a murky purple and the wind rattled my ancient windows. Rain fell, gentle at first, but progressively hit harder against the windows.

All day that day, I'd thrown myself into marking up student papers. I had to get the work done before tomorrow's Monday classes, but it also served as a decent distraction to what had happened at Peggy's the previous night. When I was busy circling grammatical mistakes and underlining awkward phrasing, I had little brain space left to dwell on the fact that Hunter Dyson had kissed me.

After eating my unsatisfying meal, I planned to continue distracting myself by rereading one of my favorite books. As an English professor, you'd think I would be sick of reading and tired of books in general, but I spent so much time either grading or writing myself that I had little time to actually read. No sooner had I curled up on the couch, thrown a blanket over my legs, and had started to immerse myself in 18th-century English society, when I heard a knock at the front door.

I unfolded my legs from beneath my body and rose. I heard

another knock, this time more tentative, and I hastened my step to the front door. I stood on my tiptoes to peer out through the small window at the top of the door. Outside, standing on the porch was a hooded figure. The slender, but angular shoulders and equally feminine legs indicated it was a woman, so my momentary panic faded. Although my neighborhood was relatively safe, as a woman who lived by herself, I was still wary of unannounced visitors.

"Yes?" I opened the door just a crack. "Can I help you?"

The woman took a small step forward, out of the rain, and pulled back the hood of her soggy sweatshirt.

"Hunter?"

My book would have to wait.

"Hi." She chewed on her lower lip, looking uncertain. Her normally meticulous hair was damp and flat against her forehead. Her clothes, a hooded sweatshirt and running shorts, were soaked through.

"Jesus...come in," I insisted, hurriedly. "Get out of this rain." I took a few steps back to make room for her.

She flashed me a quick, grateful smile and walked across the front threshold. I could hear the wet noises her socks and running shoes made on the hardwood floors. Once inside, she immediately peeled off her sweatshirt. It took some effort as it was soaked from the outside downpour. I felt tempted to help her when she looked stuck, but after a moment's struggle, she managed to pull the top off. Despite shedding the cumbersome sweatshirt, however, she was still wet. The t-shirt that had been hiding beneath her outer layer stuck to her skin.

"Did you jump in the lake with all your clothes on or something?"

She grimaced and pulled her hair out of its ponytail to shake out her dripping hair. "No," she noted drolly. She ran her fingers through the blonde locks like a wide-picked comb. "I was running and got caught in the rainstorm. Who knew it was monsoon season?"

I glanced past her and out the front picture window. The sky was dark and ominous and I could see the rain, slanted from the wind, wherever the streetlamps fought against the evening.

"Do you always run during an apocalypse?" I lightly teased. "And at night?" I hated that I sounded like an overly concerned mom.

She frowned. "No. But I needed to do some thinking, and I

always do my best thinking when I run."

"I do my best thinking in the shower," I said without thinking. Her eyes fixed on me, and I cleared my throat uncomfortably. "Um. Let me get you a towel," I offered. "You're dripping all over the floor like a melting snowman."

"Oh no," she gushed, noticing for the first time the puddle that had accumulated around her shoes. "I'm *so* sorry."

"Don't apologize," I waved off. I eyeballed her again. She looked a little bit like she'd just washed ashore. A mermaid who'd just been given legs. "Just...stay there."

I spun on my heel and took off for the linen closet in the hallway. I grabbed a clean towel, one from the top of the pile that still smelled like fabric softener. Realizing that a towel probably wasn't going to be enough, I took a detour to the guest bedroom. I had a walk-in closet upstairs in the master bedroom, but the guest bedroom's closet and wardrobe served as overflow. I mostly kept my workout clothes and pajamas in the second bedroom.

I pulled a clean, long-sleeved shirt from one of the dresser drawers and held it up. Hunter and I were about the same size, her bone structure a little finer, but it would fit. This particular shirt had shrunk from multiple washings and I rarely wore it myself. I hesitated before exiting the room. Should I bring her pants as well? All she was wearing was shorts. I mentally shook myself. No. That felt like crossing a line. It's not like I was inviting her over for a sleepover party. The shirt might have been inappropriate enough.

The longer I battled with myself in the guest bedroom, the more awkward I felt. Why was she even here in the first place? Maybe I should have found out before I'd bolted down the hallway and left her in the foyer. Maybe she wasn't planning on staying that long; maybe she was just returning my book. But why would she go for a run with a book, I reasoned. She probably just got caught in the rain and realized she was close to my house and was looking to wait it out. I nodded with some finality. Yes, that was probably it. And while I hesitated in the guest bedroom, she was probably politely freezing in the entranceway. I usually kept my house a few degrees chillier than necessary in the Fall to save on heating bills, and I'm sure in her damp clothes she was feeling it.

I left the room and found Hunter still standing in the front foyer looking strangely at ease in her soaked running outfit as she inspected the black and white photographs that hung in the entranceway. She looked up at the vaulted ceiling when the rain outside suddenly became louder.

"I think it's hailing." I announced, walking toward her. The tin roof that I'd thought was so charming when I'd originally purchased the house was romantic in the rain and horrible in the hail.

Hunter looked despondent. "I really chose an awesome day to go for a run, huh?"

"You're more than welcome to wait out the storm," I offered, shrugging. I didn't want to make a big deal out of it, but internally I was elated. The Weather Gods were certainly on my side tonight.

"I don't want to be a burden," she murmured. She shifted her weight from one squishy foot to the next.

"Don't be silly," I said. "It's not like you're keeping me from any plans. You apologize too much, by the way."

She nodded, but still looked uncertain about the genuineness of my hospitality.

"I got you a towel and a shirt," I said, awkwardly thrusting the objects in her direction. "Don't feel obligated to put on the shirt; I just thought you might be cold. There's pants and socks that go with that, too, if you want."

She took the offered towel and cotton shirt. "This is perfect. Thank you," she said quietly. The emotion I had originally identified as ease had slid off her features and was now replaced with something else, a little shiftless and uncomfortable. "I hate to ask, but could I get those pants, too?" She pulled at her nylon running shorts with a frown, and I noticed the goose bumps that covered her pale legs. "I'm kind of soaked through."

"Of course. I'll be right back." I hustled to the bedroom, faster than the original trip, and grabbed a pair of sweatpants from a bottom drawer that I hoped weren't too big for her.

When I returned, she looked a little more at ease than when I'd left her. "You can change in the bathroom," I said as I handed her the pants. "First door on the right."

I watched her squish down the corridor, her wet socks leaving foot-shaped puddles on the hardwood floor, until she reached the bathroom. When she closed the bathroom door, I immediately pulled my phone out of my hoodie front pocket and texted Troian.

Help. Winter Jacket is in my house. I stared at the sent message. Hunter was in my house. Hunter Dyson was in my bathroom, changing into my clothes. I desperately needed to do something to keep my mind from creating inappropriate mental images.

I left the front foyer in favor of the kitchen and filled the kettle with water for hot chocolate or tea. I didn't know if she drank either, but I was sure a quick warm-up would be appreciated, plus it gave me something to do instead of creepily lurking outside the bathroom door while she changed clothes.

I put the pot on the burner and turned from the stovetop when I heart the sound of bare feet padding against the wooden floor. Hunter had reappeared, looking far too comfortable in her borrowed clothes. We were about the same height, with myself being slightly taller and broader in the shoulders, but the clothes were a good fit. The top was thin from numerous washings and hugged at her waistline. Her small, round breasts swelled beneath the material. Jutting hipbones peeked out from the waistband of the sweatpants, and I found myself wondering what the rest of her body looked like.

"What should I do with these?" she asked. She awkwardly held out a small pile of damp clothes.

I cleared my throat, hoping my staring hadn't been too obvious. "Here," I offered, holding out a hand. "I'll hang those up for you by the fireplace."

She shook her head and pulled the damp pile against her chest like she was protecting it. "You've already done more than enough. I can certainly manage to hang them up myself."

I nodded, humming, and turned back to the stove. "I'm heating up some water if you'd like something hot to drink," I told her. "Tea? Hot Chocolate? Instant Coffee?"

"I'll take some tea if it's not too much of a bother."

"No trouble at all. You have a preference of flavor?"

She shrugged her bony shoulders. "Mint if you have it? It reminds me of my grandmother. She'd make it whenever I was sick."

"You planning on getting sick?" I asked, busying myself with the task of pulling out the tin container that held all my tea bags.

"Well, I'm sure running in this weather doesn't help," Hunter sighed. Her eyes flicked over to the window in my dining room. It still continued to storm outside.

I got her a mug, dropped the teabag in, and poured hot water to the cup's brim. "So what's on your mind?" I asked, pushing the cup across the kitchen island in her direction. I felt a little like a bartender. "What's this deep thinking you had to do so desperately that you went outside without a life preserver?"

Hunter hunched over the kitchen island. She shuffled her tea between her cupped hands. "There's this girl," she said after a moment's pause. "And I can't tell if it's just a silly crush on my part, or if it could actually be something."

My heart sank into my chest, which was a ridiculous reaction, I knew. Hunter was young and beautiful. It was just a matter of time before she found someone. I wondered if it was someone I knew. I wondered if they'd met at Peggy's. I wondered if it was Leah. I suddenly hated hedonistic Peggy's.

"Oh really?" I managed to get out. I knew I didn't sound like myself; my voice was wound tight and strained, and I wondered if she noticed.

She dipped the tip of her index finger into her mug and swirled the murky-colored beverage around. "I don't know what to do about it though. I've never had to pursue someone. I've always been the pursuee." She made a face. "That isn't even a word."

"I'll turn off my English professor button and let that one slide." I tried to make my tone light, but it still sounded stiff. I should have been flattered that she felt comfortable enough to bring this personal issue to me, but instead I felt miserable. I found myself becoming anxious for the storm to lighten up enough so she could leave, and I could start drinking.

My phone rattled, indicating I'd received a text message. *OMG. She wants you!!!* screamed Troian's over-exuberant text. I flicked the phone to silent and hastily shoved it into one of the kitchen drawers. It made an obvious noise as it banged against the other contents in the drawer, and Hunter gave me a perplexed look.

While my brain churned for something to say, she proceeded to pull her damp hair up in a bun. She didn't get very far, however, as a chunk of hair had gotten caught in the chain of the small, silver cross she always wore – apparently even while running. I heard her quietly curse as she tried to tug her hair free.

"Hold on," I called. "You're going to rip your hair out."

Her hands immediately stilled and she waited for me to come to her side of the kitchen island. I took the dainty chain in my hands and concentrated on releasing the fine strands from the links without breaking her hair or her necklace. I was acutely aware of how close we were; I hadn't been in such intimate proximity even at Peggy's last night when we'd had to lean into each other to be heard over the din of the bar.

"There," I said when I was satisfied I'd gotten the last of it. "All fixed with minimum carnage." The delicate chain lay attractively on her slightly flushed skin. She must have warmed up since coming in from the rain.

"Thank you," she breathed.

I should have taken a step back once I'd completed the task, but I was frozen to the spot. "Not a problem."

She turned around into my space. I still couldn't move. "Why won't you touch me?" If her voice had been any quieter, I would have thought I'd misheard her or that the voices in my head were at it again.

Before I could audibly express my confusion at her question, she had grabbed my hand and slid it over her chest. The cotton material felt slightly damp as though she hadn't completely toweled herself dry before putting it on, and her hardened nipple was taut against my palm. I yanked my hand away as if her body had scorched me.

"Oh my God. I'm sorry," she gasped; her angelic features twisted in horror. "I'm *so* sorry."

Tears immediately appeared in the corners of her eyes. "God, I'm such an idiot. I don't know why I thought you'd..." She shook her head hard. "You're amazing, and I'm such an idiot." She grabbed her still-damp clothes from where she'd hung them near the fireplace. "I-I'm just gonna change quick and then I'll go," she said shakily. "I'm sorry for taking advantage of your hospitality."

I stood there for a moment, just opening and closing my mouth like a goldfish feeding. I don't know how I managed to pull myself together.

I went after her, using my long legs to catch up before she could hide in the first floor bathroom and then catapult back into the stormy night. I grabbed her wrist and spun her around. "This is probably a giant mistake," I muttered more to myself than to her, before crushing my mouth against hers.

My hand moved to cup the nape of her neck, pulling her tighter into a languid kiss. She shuddered and grabbed onto my upper arms for stability. Her eyes fluttered, the light blue seemingly having a hard time focusing.

"Are you okay?" I asked. I searched her face, worried I had overstepped my boundaries or misread her intentions. I tucked a still-damp tendril that had worked its way free from her bun behind her ear. "I'm sorry," I panicked out loud. "Should I not have done that?"

My concern melted when her hand cupped the back of my neck. "I've wanted you to do that for so long."

I bent down and recaptured her lips with my own. I sucked her lower lip into my mouth and bit down lightly. I nipped at the delicate flesh, pulling a sharp intake of air from her.

"This isn't at all like how I imagined it," she breathed as she pulled away just slightly. Her soft lips brushed against mine, and I felt my knees buckle. "It wasn't supposed to be like this."

"How was it supposed to be?"

"I seduce you, but not looking like a wet mop."

I couldn't help the grin on my face. "You imagined this?"

She ducked her head sheepishly. "Maybe a few times."

I touched her chin, tilting her head back up to meet my gaze. "Well it's nice to know I wasn't alone in this."

"R-really?" she stuttered.

I mentally cringed, worried I'd revealed too much about my infatuation, but instead of scare her off, my words seemed to encourage and embolden her. She dropped to her knees, and before I could register what was happening, her fingers were tugging at the waistband of my yoga pants and pulling them down with her to the floor. She audibly groaned when she realized I wore no underwear beneath.

The question with the most obvious answer fell from my lips: "What are you doing?"

Apparently not one for teasing or foreplay, Hunter's mouth immediately found its way to my naked sex. Her tongue was eager, licking and sucking at me with the enthusiasm and inexperience of youth. She licked along my slit with the flat of her tongue, and her nose, deliberately or not, ground into my aching clit.

My knees buckled and I grabbed onto her slender shoulders for support. She licked against me hard, and I cursed quietly beneath my breath. She licked me again and my hips involuntarily jerked, lightly bumping my pelvic bone against her face. I was wet, so maddeningly wet; the heady scent of sex filled the air and she hadn't even really touched me yet. When her fingertips unexpectedly brushed along my outer lips, I instantly rethought my assessment of her as inexperienced.

"I can't," I grunted out in frustration. "Not like this."

She leaned back on her haunches and licked at her lower lip, tasting me on her mouth. "Why not?" she demanded. "I want this, and it's clear you do, too," she said boldly.

I pulled my pants back up as gracefully as one can. "That's...that's not what I meant," I said, biting back a chuckle. "I just mean I can't get off when I'm standing up. I was going to suggest we relocate."

Her eyes widened. "Oh. Well, now I'm embarrassed by that little outburst."

I took her hand in mine to pull her up from the floor. It nearly stole my breath how *natural* and *right* our hands felt together when I knew everything about this was wrong. I was no longer her teacher, and the university had no policy about professors and students fraternizing as long as there was no conflict of interest; but she was in *college* for Gods sake, and I was practically a decade her senior.

But as I watched her slowly lick along her lower lip and watched her tongue catch in the small cleft, my misgivings suddenly didn't seem so important anymore.

+++++

I felt my palms grow sweaty as I carefully maneuvered the stairs up to the master bedroom. It wasn't from the exertion of climbing stairs though; it had everything to do with the woman who held my hand and followed me upstairs. I blindly fumbled for light toggles in the dark that seemed to have relocated since I was last upstairs. I found the light switch for my bedroom as I guided her into the room.

"You have a lovely home," Hunter remarked. "I meant to tell you that when I was here for the English Department's party."

"Thank you," I reflexively replied.

My house was two-level bungalow style with the bedroom and bathroom upstairs dominating the entire floor. Instead of getting to comment on the Do-It-Yourself projects I'd recently completed, I was overwhelmed by the feeling of her pink mouth pressed once more against my lips and her tongue sliding along my bottom lip. My lips parted and she slipped her tongue into my mouth to slowly massage my tongue with her own. I gasped sharply as the intimacy heightened and metamorphosed from tender hesitation into the mashing of mouths and clashing of teeth. We clung to each other, full of need and desperation.

I ran my hands through her golden hair, tangling and twirling the damp strands around my fingers. Her hands wandered to the hem of my top and she toyed with the material. I couldn't help my own shiver when Hunter came in contact with my bare stomach, her hands sliding easily over the taunt skin.

Perhaps feeling her hands on my naked skin is what broke me from her spell. I pulled away. I had known when I first kissed her that it would be just a matter of time before I woke up from this dream or before my conscience realized what was happening and brought this all to a crashing halt. "At the bar last night you mentioned this was fairly new, um," I searched for an appropriate word, "*territory* for you."

She was a smart girl. Her kiss-swollen lips pursed. "And you want to know if this is my first time."

I nodded. I wasn't an entirely morality-free zone. I didn't want to take advantage of the situation or of her.

She tucked her lower lip into her mouth. "This *is* my first time," she haltingly admitted. "With a woman, I mean. I've had boyfriends."

"Who I really don't need to hear about," I interjected with a nervous laugh.

She looked away bashfully. "Sorry," she murmured.

"We don't have to do anything." I gently brushed a few errant strands of golden locks away from her face. She was so beautiful, it made my heart ache. "I can't stress that enough, Hunter. I don't want to pressure you if you're not ready or you're uncomfortable." I reluctantly let my hand fall from her features. "I can give you a ride home right now."

Her bashful smile stretched into a megawatt grin. "While I appreciate your concern – it's all very chivalrous of you," she added. "I *really* want this, Professor –."

"Okay, so as hot and incredibly taboo as that sounds," I hastily interrupted, hands flailing, "and I can't even *pretend* that doesn't play into practically every fantasy I've ever had," I unnecessarily added, "you *can't* call me Professor or Doctor Graft ever again. You have to call me Elle or I can't do this." I motioned between our bodies with my hand. "Whatever *this* might be."

Her eyelashes fluttered prettily. "I think I can manage that, *Elle*." I loved the way she said my name – the way it tripped and tickled across her tongue. I shivered slightly, anticipating just what that tongue might feel like on the rest of my body. I'd been privy to a sneak preview in the kitchen.

She made the next move, falling back onto my mattress, and in one fluid motion, she pulled me down on top of her. My knee instinctively went between her slightly parted thighs, and she was unable to stifle her moan. I kissed her open mouth again, not able to get enough of her. My tongue brushed against hers, and I smiled into the kiss when I felt her body melt into the embrace. With each touch, she became bolder and I became less anxious. I pressed my knee harder against the juncture between her thighs, and her body lifted from the mattress and molded against my curves.

I knew I would probably have a panic attack in the morning, but for now I tried to enjoy this moment that I had literally been dreaming about for a year. I pushed the naysayers and nagging voices from my thoughts. Hunter was in my bed. Hunter Dyson was hungrily pressing her mouth against mine; she was whimpering with need.

I pulled her up to a seated position and removed her long-sleeved shirt, mindful of her hair. Her hands went to the bottom hem of my own top, and she unceremoniously yanked it off. I cupped the back of her head and returned her to a reclined position. When our naked breasts touched for the first time, I kissed her fiercely; our tongues dueled and teeth gnashed unapologetically.

My right hand found its way between her thighs where my knee had been pressed. I cupped her there, hard, feeling her warmth burning through the thin material of her borrowed pants. I dug my heel in and rubbed in a wide circle, providing pressure – just enough to keep her clawing at me – but not enough for her to grow lazy from her own desire. It was a delicate balance, this give-and-take. Satisfy too soon and your own needs go unattended.

When she clung to my shoulders, erratically panting into my

mouth, I felt the desire crest within me, churning from the pit of my stomach and rushing down to my sex. I felt it defiantly flare, begging to be released, but I pushed it down. I shoved it down and censured it to never rise again. I knew it was just a matter of time, though; it would come back again, probably yet tonight. But I would blanket and snuff out that fire in my belly when it inevitably returned.

I summoned an unexpected willpower and tore myself away from her candy lips. *We had time,* I reassured myself. I didn't have to paw her like teenagers fumbling and groping in the back of a car in an abandoned parking lot. As eager as I was for my own orgasm, if this was her first time with a woman, I had an obligation to take my time.

Her breath was still uneven as she lay on her back, and I watched the ragged rise and fall of her chest. I ran my fingertips down the center of her body, down the fine column of her throat, between creamy, supple breasts, and down to her flat abdomen. Her grey-blue eyes fluttered shut, and she rounded her back into my touch.

She cried out when she felt the first contact – warm, wanting, wet kisses fluttering briefly over her naked breasts. I kissed the underside of her breast and slowly traced a line to her nipple with the tip of my tongue. She gasped at the sudden sensation as my tongue lashed against the sensitive bud before I took her nipple gently between my teeth. My tongue flicked the jumbled nerves back and forth from within the humid cavern of my open mouth. She arched her back even more, holding my mouth tight against her breast, crying out into the room.

With her arms holding my head tight against her, she relied on her legs. Her legs felt impossibly long as she wrapped me up in them. They were also deceptively strong. She pulled me tight against her, wrapping her legs around my torso and flexed. I may have been preoccupied with her hands and fingers and willowy arms when I first met her, but I should have never neglected those legs. I blame it on winter when she hid her toned thighs and calves beneath blue jeans.

I felt her lift her hips off the bed, straining for some form of contact. Rather than grind down against her, I undulated with her, denying her unspoken plea. Instead, I selfishly reveled at the sight of the frustrated woman pinned beneath me. It was as though along with her clothing, Hunter's innocence, her poise, had been stripped away as well. But she remained perfect, if not more so without her conservative clothing hiding the gentle dip at her waist, her jutting hipbones, and her modest, but more than adequate cleavage.

I shook my head, rattling me back to the moment. Hunter began to whimper from frustration. "Please, Elle," she pled.

My fingers curled beneath the waistband of the pants I'd let her borrow. I paused and wet my lips as I stared into those blue-grey eyes, silently begging permission. Her hips rose off the bed, and I held my breath as I pulled off her remaining clothes.

I took my time, running my palms over tender, flawless thighs. I dug my thumbs in and watched her come undone. I should have relented, should have given in to the overwhelming desire to lean in and run my tongue along the length of her folds. But I didn't want it to be over. I wanted to make it last in case this was just another dream or an experience limited to tonight.

I ran my hands up the length of her pale, inner thighs until my fingertips rested on her hipbones and my thumbs brushed against far more sensitive skin at the juncture between her legs. I kept my hands immobile, save for the rhythmic up and down motion of my thumbs. My short thumbnails stroked along her most vulnerable flesh.

I slid down to belly-button level and kissed and licked her bare skin, marveling at how my touch made her stomach tighten to form femininely defined muscles. I slid lower still and leaned in to breath warm air against her most sensitive parts. She moaned, and I felt her thighs tense beneath my hands. I wet my lips, preparing myself for what I was about to do.

I breathed in deeply, overcome from her scent. Tentatively, I inched my tongue closer to her shaved, satin skin. I slipped my tongue along her outside folds, tasting the early desire that had accumulated there. I heard her sigh above me as I gently parted her lips and blew onto the exposed skin before sinking my tongue deep inside.

"Oh my God." Hunter's hands immediately went to the back of my head, forcing my tongue deeper into her wet sex. I nuzzled my nose against her swollen clit, practically feeling her heart beat through the tiny bundle of flesh.

I moaned against her and tightened my grip on her upper thighs. She was delicious, tangy and clean; my eyes practically rolled back into my head at the taste. I licked deeper, allowing her arousal to coat my tongue and lips, and I hummed against her skin. I heard her sharp gasp as I continued my exploration.

"Elle!" she cried when my tongue finally came into contact with her sensitive clit. I flicked my tongue against the tiny nub, causing her hips to involuntarily cant toward the ceiling.

Her hips jerked and bucked. "Please, Elle. I need your fingers," she unabashedly begged.

Not wanting to waste anymore precious moonlight, I ran my hand down her stomach one final time before parting her lips with my fingers and sinking two digits deep inside. I glanced fleetingly up at her only to see her bite down hard on her lower lip to keep from crying out. I slowly withdrew my now-coated fingers, feeling her inner walls quickly adjust to the sudden intrusion. I lazily slid my fingers up and down her slit, rubbing her arousal over the smooth skin.

I pushed my fingers deep again and remained motionless while I captured her tiny bud between my lips. Hunter gasped. "Elle...Oh God. I'm so wet for you."

I withdrew my fingers and pushed them back in hard and began to attack her insides with even and steady strokes. I could feel her inner walls clamp tightly around my fingers, and the click of her wet sex filled the room.

I closed my eyes, freeing my mind of any misgivings. All that existed was the exquisite woman wrapped around my fingers and the burning ache between my own legs. I lapped and tongued her clit while I continued to thrust my fingers in and out, while her thighs quivered around my ears.

"I'm gonna..." Hunter gasped suddenly. "I...I'm so...so...close. I—Oh, God. Don't stop, please don't stop," she rambled.

I removed my mouth for a moment and stared deep into her pleading eyes. "That's it. Cum for me, Hunter. Let yourself go," I coaxed as I quickened my strokes.

"God, Elle," she moaned. "Fuck. Fuck. It's so good. I can't...I...oh God. Oh yes. Your fingers. Yes, just like that," she chanted. Her body shook uncontrollably and she bounced around the bed, practically fucking herself on my hand.

I took one last glance at the beautiful woman in my bed. "You're so gorgeous," I murmured, more to myself, and recaptured her clit between my parted lips.

"Oh shit!" Hunter cried, her body jolting upright in bed. She grabbed me and placed gentle, but desperate pressure on the back of my head, while entangling her fingers in my loose locks. "Elle," she panted. "I'm… Fuck!!"

I looked up when I heard a soft *thump* to see Hunter had fallen backwards onto the bed. Her eyes were closed tight, her mouth twisted into a small smile of satisfaction. She released the death-grip on my now-tangled hair and breathed out a soft sigh.

I slowly and gently eased my saturated fingers out of her and soothed her tender sex with small licks. I smiled serenely and wiped at my mouth with the aid of her inner thighs. "Good?" I asked with only a mild amount of trepidation.

She flexed and curled her toes. "God, Elle. *So* good."

I crawled up shakily, my arms sore and heart thumping heavily in my chest, my legs nearly asleep due to their prior stationary position. I snuggled into her naked and now sweaty form, pulling the tangled bed sheets up with me to cover us both.

I rested my head on her bare chest and listened to the rhythmic lub-dubbing as her heart struggled to return to its normal beat. Without exchanging words, we simultaneously breathed in deeply and slowly exhaled. She stroked my hair and I closed my eyes, relishing her gentle touch. I tried not to dwell on what had just happened. There would be time for that later. The sun would be awake soon.

+++++

CHAPTER EIGHT

The next morning I woke up to the sounds of the garbage truck outside. Sunshine crept through the wooden flats of the bedroom blinds. I stretched, arching my lower back and reaching my hands and flexing my fingers until they reached the headboard. My fingers wrapped around the sturdy, inlay wooden slats. I'd chosen this headboard specifically for its strength and the ease with which one could be tied to it. I hadn't gotten to really test its durability, however.

I glanced over at the bedside table and internally panicked when I saw the time illuminated on my alarm clock. With the previous night's events, I'd fallen asleep without setting my alarm. I hadn't missed class yet, but if I didn't hurry, I was going to be late. I'd showered the previous night, but I'd worked up quite a sweat spending the evening with Hunter. I unfortunately didn't have time to shower if I wanted to make it to my morning class.

My initial instinct was to bolt out of bed and rush around the house, but I had the presence of mind to remember the girl soundly sleeping beside me. I hazarded a glance in her direction. She lay on her side, facing me, with her hands curled near her face. Her eyes were loosely shut, the curve of her mouth planed flat.

As I watched her sleep, her lips parted and I could better hear the even intake and release of air. I knew I couldn't delay the inevitable. As much as I wanted to stay in bed and just keep looking at her, I needed to get to work. It was moments like this where I wished I had a more traditional job where I could just call in and take the entire day off. I could have canceled classes, I suppose, but I hated to do it.

I held my breath and slipped out of bed, careful not to wake up Hunter. My reasoning said I was just being thoughtful and letting her sleep. My conscience, however, knew I was being a coward and evading her waking up and telling me she'd made a horrible mistake by sleeping with me. I picked up the discarded clothes from the floor – my pajamas of yoga pants and t-shirt and the sweatpants and long-sleeved t-shirt I'd let Hunter borrow. I pulled up my clothes from the previous night and I dutifully folded Hunter's clothes and set them on top of my bureau.

Hunter remained sleeping through my minimum noises, and I padded out of the room, grimacing at how the wooden floorboards squeaked and groaned with each careful step. I made my way into the bathroom and had just enough time to brush my teeth, wash my face, toss my hair up in a loose ponytail, and put on mascara. I crept back into my bedroom to find an outfit.

My closet door was a single door that slid on rollers. I knew it would make an ugly sound, but I really needed to get some clothes and rush off to campus. I held my breath again and opened the door. The wheels shrieked terribly, metal on metal, and I looked once again in Hunter's direction. Her eyelashes fluttered, but she remained asleep. I pulled a skirt, cardigan, and blouse from my closet. The plastic hangers clattered against each other as I removed the clothes, but she continued to sleep through it all.

I changed clothes quickly and quietly. I went to finish the ensemble with some accessories from the jewelry box that sat on top of my bureau. I'd had the white container since I was very young. I'd gotten it as a present from my godparents for my First Communion in 1st grade. I lifted the lid, forgetting about the light tinkling song that played when open and the delicate ballerina who spun in tight concentric circles. My getting out of bed and creaking across the wood floor hadn't made her stir. The squeaky closet door had barely provoked any reaction. The plastic clatter of clothes hangers hadn't rendered on her radar. But apparently the quiet chime of a childhood jewelry box was enough to tug her out of sleep.

She stretched fully on the mattress and made an adorable little noise that best resembled a baby pterodactyl. I involuntarily stiffened, worried she might now be regretting staying the night. It had been a huge gamble sleeping with a former student. We needed to talk about what this was and what had happened. But for now I needed to get to campus and teach. And I was sure she had a busy day as well.

She sat up slightly in bed and leaned her weight on her elbows. As she straightened, the thin cotton sheet that had hid her nude form began to slip away. She wrapped the extra material around her torso and bound her breasts. Her pale skin contrasted attractively against the sage coloring of my sheets. Her grey eyes narrowed to slits as she squinted into the morning light. Her golden hair, long and loose, framed her face. The sun bounced off a few adorable strands wildly out of place on her normally impeccably styled hair.

"What time is it?" she mumbled. She rubbed at her eyes and the sheet slipped further south, revealing just the very top of dusky pink areolas.

"Just after 9."

She gave me a sleepy smile and raked her fingers through her hair. Sometime during the night it had fallen out of her ponytail. I swore under my breath. What I wouldn't give to play hooky today and go back to bed with her. I imagined the most deliciously languid day, drinking strong, rich coffee for breakfast, and only getting out of bed when necessary.

I knew I was going to be late if I didn't leave soon. But despite my time-phobia I sat down on the edge of the mattress. Hunter grabbed my hands and started playing with my fingers.

"Good morning," I greeted.

"Morning," she grumbled back.

I couldn't help the grin on my face. She was adorably disgruntled this morning. "Are you a morning person?"

She dropped one of my hands to rub at her eyes again. "Not really."

She wiggled a little closer, the thin covers the only thing hiding her beautiful body. "Last night you mentioned something about having a crush on someone."

"Mmhmm?" she said sleepily.

I dropped my eyes to my hands on my lap. "This might be silly to ask now, but is it me?"

Hunter's laugh was loud, but warm. "I thought you had a PhD?"

I scowled. "Stop it," I complained. "I just...I wanted to make sure there wasn't someone else I was competing with."

"Prof—." She caught herself, smiled, and started again. "I think that little black dress you wore at your house party made me gay."

"What? Really?"

"I couldn't keep my eyes off your legs." A small, shy smile crept onto her beautiful face. I couldn't mistake the way her gaze lingered on my legs now. "Why do you insist on teaching in skirts?" she murmured in a low burr. "It's all I could think about last semester. I'm surprised I managed a passing grade."

I cleared my throat, embarrassed. "I have to get to campus to teach, but don't feel like I'm kicking you out. Take your time, get something to eat. There's cereal and bagels and juice and coffee and all kinds of things in the kitchen. Just don't steal the family jewels." I grabbed a pair of heels from beneath the bed that I hadn't bothered to put away and slipped them on my bare feet.

"I know you have to go, but I wish you didn't." She shifted again in bed, and the sheets slipped down her body even more.

I sucked in a deep breath. "That makes two of us," I mumbled. I bent my head and pressed my lips against hers. Her mouth was so warm and her lips were so soft that it nearly made me forget my responsibilities that day. When her hand went to the side of my face and cupped my cheek, I nearly lost it. I deepened the kiss, running my tongue along the front of her even teeth. She made a muffled noise into my mouth.

Still mindful of the time, I pulled back before I was too long gone to care. Her eyes were still closed, lightly lidded, and her wide mouth curled at the edges. "Have a nice day," she murmured.

Mustering all my willpower, I stood up from the bedside. I smoothed my hands along the outside of my pencil skirt. "You too, Hunter."

++++++

The day moved by slowly, or at least it seemed to. It had been a long, late day filled with classes, committee meetings, and a senior seminar. Thinking about Hunter back at my house, wondering what she was currently doing, put me both on edge and at ease.

Because I'd abruptly stopped texting Troian after announcing Hunter's presence at my home the previous night, Troian had texted me repeatedly and left voicemails throughout the day, but I ignored them all.

When I returned home later that evening, the house was empty. I hunted for signs of life, but found only Sylvia. I searched for evidence that Hunter had in fact slept over, but my bed upstairs had been carefully remade and the clothes she'd borrowed were still folded on top of my bureau where I'd left them. The wet clothes she'd peeled out of, the catalyst for the shared evening, were gone, no longer hanging from hooks near the living room fireplace. I couldn't deny the feeling of disappointment that sat in the pit of my stomach to find her gone.

I didn't have her number. Since I was no longer her professor, I didn't have access to personal information like that minus her school email address, which was in the university directory. If she'd lived on campus the directory would at least have given me the extension to her dorm room's landline. But she lived off-campus. I could email her, but that felt cold and impersonal. I knew where she lived, having dropped her off at her apartment once, but that felt more stalker than sweet. Plus, if she had roommates, I didn't want to make things awkward or uncomfortable for her. Should I wait until she showed up again? Wait for her to contact me?

I grabbed my phone and flipped through my contacts until I came to the familiar number. I sent off a brief text: *Are you free right now? I need to see you.*

+++++

Half an hour later I found myself at Del Sol's, my favorite coffee shop. I'd ordered a mocha latte and was now seated at a small table by myself, waiting and idling trailing my fingertip along the top of my mug. Del Sol's was relatively empty; I was surprised there weren't more students flooding the place and cramming for midterms with the aid of copious caffeine.

I smiled pleasantly at a woman who walked by. She was wearing a t-shirt with the university's name printed across the front, but I didn't recognize her. I looked back down at my drink. My barista had manipulated the foam into the shape of a heart. Normally I got leaves. It seemed tragically foreboding.

"Still can't stop reading women's t-shirts, I see," a familiar voice called out. I looked back up and smiled when I saw my ex-girlfriend, Cady.

She always teased me about my compulsive reading. I couldn't help it; my eyes are naturally drawn to the printed word. It usually only becomes problematic when I'm driving or walking. Instead of paying attention to the road directly ahead, I'm reading billboards, road signs, mile markers, and license plates on the cars that pass me. When I walk, I inevitably end up reading the words on t-shirts. I considered wearing dark sunglasses, even at twilight, so no one could see the trajectory of my eyes and mistakenly believe I was checking out their breasts. I'm not a boob girl; I'm a *word* girl.

"If they didn't want me to look at their chest, they shouldn't have letters there," I countered.

Cady and I had been good together, but it had eventually become clear that we made better friends than girlfriends. Our busy schedules and the drive for respective successful careers had rendered us exhausted by the end of the workday. The dreaded Lesbian Death Bed had snuck into my life so quickly and without much protest that when I'd looked at the calendar and realized it had been several months since we'd last been intimate, I hardly protested its arrival.

Even though we could casually meet like this for coffee now without bloodshed, like most relationships, I suppose, the end of ours was messy. The end of relationships, no matter the length and intensity, had only ever been emotionally violent for me. I seemed to have a pattern of starting and ending romantic couplings in that way. I blamed it on being an Aries.

Time has the power to heal many things, and I was happy we'd come out the other side. She looked good. Happy. I knew she'd been seeing someone new and it was relatively serious, or so I'd gathered from our brief conversations.

"So what's new?" she asked as she slid into the chair across from me. "What's this urgent thing you need to talk to me about?"

I grunted noncommittally and looked down at my hands that cupped my coffee mug. Hunter's words from the previous night echoed in my head. "There's a girl."

Cady's face scrunched up. "There's always a girl."

I sighed and pushed my mug further away. I couldn't deny her wordless accusation. "I know. But this time it might get me in trouble."

An eyebrow arched. "Okay. I'll take the bait."

I looked down at my hands. I flexed and stretched my fingers, feeling the tendons pull. Just a few hours ago, these same hands were wandering Hunter's slight curves. "Her name is Hunter," I said warily. "And she's lovely."

"Sounds dangerous already," Cady quipped. She leaned back in her chair.

"She spent the night last night," I said. I dipped my finger into the foam of my drink, dashing out the heart shape.

"And the problem is?"

I looked up. "She used to be one of my students."

Cady's lips pursed. "'Used to be' as in years ago, or 'used to be' as in last week?"

I rested my forehead in the palm of my hand. "Last semester," I groaned.

Cady whistled lowly. "I don't know if I should high five you or call Child Services."

"She's 20," I snapped, irritated. "Practically 21. I'm not going to jail."

The cocky look on Cady's face turned to concern, and she leaned in slightly. "It's not going to get you fired is it?" she asked in a lower tone. "It's not, I don't know, *illegal* at your school or something?"

I shook my head. "I'm not her instructor anymore and don't have any control over her grades, so it's not a conflict of interest. There's no written rule that says I shouldn't be doing this."

"Doing *Hunter* you mean."

I set my jaw hard. "Right." I couldn't tell if this amused her or if this was a defense mechanism to hide her animosity. I didn't think she had a reason to be angry with me though. Not justifiably so, at least. We'd been broken up for nearly a year, and it wasn't like she'd been celibate since the break up either.

"So if there's no written rule against it," she asked, "what's your concern?"

"It's still, I don't know, frowned on? And there's the age thing to consider," I added.

"I know plenty of couples, straight and gay, who are more than a decade apart in age," Cady pointed out.

"But that's never been *me*," I said emphatically. "Two or three years, sure. But not *nine*."

"So was this just a one-time thing? Or do you genuinely see yourself in a relationship with this girl?"

"That's the thing I don't know," I admitted miserably. And it was the truth. I didn't know. I'd admittedly been a little obsessed with Hunter since she was originally my student. And now that we'd slept together, I kept waiting for that inevitable thrill to fade and my eye to get caught by the next cute thing in a short skirt. The thrill was still there though. But I didn't know if it would fade like it always did. I couldn't tell if this was worth the risk.

"Elle, you know I love you," Cady started cautiously, "so don't take this the wrong way, but I think you should stop sleeping with this girl until you figure out what it is you want from each other. If it's just physical, that's fine. But everyone involved should be on the same page. Talk to this girl," she urged. "Figure it out so no one gets hurt."

I nodded, agreeing. I knew all this, but it somehow helped to hear another person confirm it. Most of all I think I was just looking for permission to even entertain the thought that I could start a healthy relationship with someone so much younger than me. Cady hadn't exactly given me that, but it was better than nothing.

"Because speaking as someone whose heart you've recently trampled," she unnecessarily added, "it's a total bitch to not be on the same page as you."

+++++

I left Cady at Del Sol's and returned home in hopes of getting some work done. I had a stack of student outlines to struggle through while trying *not* to think about Hunter. At present, however, I was failing miserably. My entire being was on edge. I erratically checked and re-checked my campus email every few minutes, waiting for an email from her.

I hadn't yet told Troian or Nikole what had happened the previous night. They no doubt assumed that something noteworthy had happened though because my phone kept buzzing from text messages and missed voicemails, demanding to know where I was and what had happened last night. For the moment, I refrained myself from calling or texting them back. I still wasn't sure what had happened myself.

When I heard a sharp knock at my front door, I assumed that Troian and Nikole had given up on trying to call me and were coming to confront me face-to-face. I peered through the inset window and immediately recognized the figure standing on my front porch. It wasn't Troian and Nikole. My chest tightened, and I threw the door open.

"Hunter."

"Hi." She stepped close and gave me a brief, but lingering kiss, barely raising up on her toes to reach my lips. Her mouth was just as soft as I remembered, but the kiss itself was firm and assertive. It felt familiar and not forced as if this was a regular routine – her coming over at the end of the workday and kissing me hello.

When she pulled away, my fingers went to my lips. I hadn't expected a greeting like that. She tasted like strawberries.

"You left." I knew I sounded a little pouty.

She pulled off her oversized knit hat and fussed with her hair. Her hair was down, long and curled into loose spirals. She looked like perfection. "I had to go to the hospital to meet with someone about my internship. I couldn't lounge around your house all day."

"I didn't know how to get in touch with you."

"You know where I live," she reminded me. "And you have my e-mail."

"Yeah, but email felt too impersonal," I bristled, "and I didn't want to seem like a stalker just showing up at your place."

"Kind of like I'm doing right now?" she pointed out with a cheeky grin. "And like I did last night?"

She had a point. "Kind of."

She walked past me and into my house, her shoulder brushing against mine. My eyes shut of their own accord. "You're resourceful," she said. "You'd figure something out."

"You give me too much credit." Recovering, I tossed my phone at her. She caught it and gave me a perplexed look. "Put your number in there."

She arched an eyebrow. "Are you always so charming when you ask for girls' phone numbers?"

"Again, giving me too much credit," I said. "I may be older, but that doesn't mean I have more experience than you with these kinds of things."

When she gave me my phone back, she stroked her fingertips over my palm. "Oh, I don't know." Her voice dropped low, conspiratorially. "I thought you had plenty of experience last night."

I cleared my throat and took a few steps backwards, putting more space between us. Cady's advice played over and over in my head. I needed to figure out what exactly this was before I could entertain the possibility of Hunter and I being intimate again. And with her standing so close, I could think of little else but how good she smelled and how much I wanted her naked and in my bed again.

"Are you hungry?" I asked, turning away. I walked back in the direction of the kitchen and started rearranging stacks of unopened mail on the countertop. I didn't trust my idle hands.

"I could eat," she said, following me to the kitchen.

"Do you like Chinese? I could get delivery?" I offered. I realized I hadn't been to the grocery store in weeks. I wouldn't have been able to impress her with my minimal cooking skills even if I'd wanted to.

Hunter leaned her elbows on the kitchen island. The scooped neck of her shirt dipped low enough to provide a view of not only her chiseled collarbone, but also the slight swell of her breasts. I had to forcibly look away. Everything about her was tight, firm, and feminine.

"Or we could order something else," I said. I sifted through the stack of take-out menus I kept near the landline. A benefit of living in a college town was the number of restaurants that delivered. I liked cooking, especially when it wasn't just for me, but I liked convenience even more. "I like Chinese, but I'm always hungry a few hours later."

Even though I couldn't bring myself to look at her, I could still feel her eyes on me. "I'm sure we could find something else to eat if that happened." Her tone let me know she wasn't planning on rummaging through my pantry.

"So, Chinese?" I was proud of myself that my voice hadn't cracked like a prepubescent boy's.

Her bottom lip stuck out a little further than usual, but she made no further suggestive comments or complained about my deflections. I didn't want to reject her advances or entirely dismiss her attempts at flirting, especially because I didn't want her to think I was giving her the brush off. However, I needed to use some restraint with her.

"Chinese sounds great, thanks. Can I use your shower? I came straight from the hospital, and I'm feeling a little grungy."

"Of course you can." I was already on my way to the hallway linen closet to get her a clean towel. "Do you need something to change into?"

"Do I really need clothes?"

"I, uh." For having so many advanced degrees, it didn't take much for me to get tongue-tied around her.

For the second time since she'd arrived, she stepped close – too close – close enough for me to smell her skin. I knew that if I licked along the narrow column of her neck it would taste salty.

"You can use the shower down here or the one upstairs in the master bedroom." I held the folded towel between us like a protective shield. "Your choice."

Hunter took a step back and cocked her head, nonplussed. "Did I do something wrong?"

"Wrong? No. Why?"

"You just...I feel like I'm throwing myself at you and you're ignoring me."

"I'm sorry if I'm making you feel that way." My hands went to her hipbones and I squeezed. I pulled her a little closer – as close as I dared; she smelled like sunshine. "I'm horribly attracted to you, Hunter. It's taking all of my willpower to behave right now."

She frowned. "Why do you have to behave?"

"I just don't know if we should..."

She looked horrified. "Was it not good?" She tried to pull away, her ego no doubt scarred, but my arms around her waist drew her back in.

I nuzzled my nose in the crook of her neck. "Don't doubt yourself," I solemnly murmured against her skin. "Last night was amazing. *You're* amazing, Hunter."

I felt her rigid body relax beneath the soft caresses. "Then why do you keep putting on the breaks?"

I pulled back, just far enough so I could look her in the eyes. Steely blue eyes full of worry and inadequacies stared back at me. "I just want us to get to know each other better before we think about having sex again." I kissed the tip of her perfect nose. "I know it seems backwards, doing this *after* we've already had sex, but I want to do this right and not have a relationship that's based on the physical stuff." I scrutinized her beautiful features, searching for a reaction. "Is that okay with you?"

Hunter nodded, but her eyes looked watery. I latched onto her biceps and peered into her face. "Hunter." I loved the way her name felt falling off my tongue. I loved that I could hold her like this. I loved that I could say her name out loud without feeling guilty – well, not entirely. "What's wrong?"

"Nothing." She wiped at her eyes. "You're just not like anyone I've ever been with before."

I smiled mildly. "That's because I'm not a boy."

She shook her head. "I think there's something else."

"Can I take you on a date?" I inelegantly blurted out. The words felt immature in my mouth, but I couldn't take them back.

Her eyebrows rose. "Sure. What did you have in mind?"

"How do you feel about fish?"

+++++

CHAPTER NINE

When I drove up to the curb in front of her apartment the following Saturday, Hunter was already waiting outside on the front stoop. I wasn't late, so I was curious why she was waiting for me there. I parked my car and got out. I wondered if there was a reason she didn't want me to see the inside of her apartment. Maybe it was messy and she hadn't had time to pick up. Or maybe she had roommates and they were home, and she wasn't ready to introduce me. I didn't want to read into it too much though; I was already too cerebral with this girl.

I had finally caved and told Troian, who then promptly told Nikole, about my night with Winter Jacket. As expected, my friend was a mixture of jubilation and worry. She voiced every concern I had about pursuing a relationship with a former student, but she also didn't judge me for having gone through with it. Like the good friend she was, she was mindful of my career, but also said that if Hunter could make me happy, she was happy for the both of us. It was exactly the kind of pep talk I had needed.

When Hunter hopped down the concrete stairs and out into the sun, I promptly forgot any lingering anxieties. She was wearing a pleated a-line skirt that fell just above her knees, revealing long, lean calves and just a hint of the defined thighs I knew existed beneath the garment. It was a sunny Fall day, still early enough in the season that you didn't need a jacket, so she'd paired the skirt with a fitted scoop-neck top with three-quarter length sleeves that showed off the fine bones of her wrists.

Her smile grew as her ballet flats skipped along the sidewalk. I couldn't help my own smile and a warmth in my belly grew that I knew wasn't from the mild weather. She hastened her step as she got closer and practically crashed into me. I grabbed onto her hips to keep her from completely running me over.

"Hi," she breathed. Her cheeks flushed and those blue-grey eyes shifted in her skull as she searched my face.

"Hi," I returned, equally breathless.

She bit her lower lip. "Sorry I tackled you."

When my fingers perceptibly dug into her hips, she raised her eyebrows and wet the cleft in her lower lip. "Unless you don't mind." Her voice had taken on an audibly lower register and I had to suppress a shudder.

"You look great."

She ducked her head, looking bashful now instead of aggressive. "Thanks. I wasn't sure what to wear. I probably tried on half of my wardrobe before deciding on this. My roommate Sara thought it was hilarious."

I let my gaze linger a little longer on her long limbs and slight curves. "I'm sure you'd look good in a potato sack."

I could feel her smile on me like the sun's rays. I wanted to stand here a little longer and bask in the warmth of her grin, but we had a date to go on, and if I delayed any longer, we might never get to our destination.

+++++

"When you asked me about fish, this wasn't exactly what I had in mind."

The two of us stood, side-by-side, in front of a thousand-gallon tank at the local aquarium. Because it was a weekend, there was a decent-sized crowd, but there weren't so many people that you felt claustrophobic maneuvering through the dimly lit rooms.

"Do you not like it?" I worried out loud.

"I *love* aquariums. Except for ones that have giant animals in too-small tanks or ones that make the animals do tricks for entertainment."

"Duly noted," I said with a nod.

"So," she said, giving me a mega-watt smile, "have you done your homework so you can impress me on your knowledge of sea animals?"

"I became a professor so I'd never have to do homework ever again."

She stuck out her lower lip. "Not even to impress *me*?"

I bit the inside of my cheek. This gorgeous girl was pouting and flirting with me; she kept introducing me to new sides of her personality, each one more adorable than the previous. I shoved my hands into the back pockets of my jeans. If I didn't keep my hands busy I'd no doubt traumatize everyone at the aquarium.

"Well," she sighed dramatically, "I guess I should feel reassured by your lack of sea creature knowledge. At least I know that you don't bring *all* your women here in the hopes of wooing them by feeding penguins like you're starring in your own personal romantic comedy."

"You're not a rom-com fan?"

"I prefer horror films. The zombier, the better."

I shook my head. "I never would have guessed that about you."

"Hence why you need to take me on more dates," she winked.

I truly did love aquariums and zoos and aviaries – anything with animals, really. But I was having a hard time today enjoying my surroundings because of Hunter's proximity. I'd gotten so used to running from my instincts when it came to her that I was honestly unsure of how to act around her. Our hands kept brushing as we walked from one display to the next. I wanted to grab a hold of her hand and have our fingers intertwine, but I worried that she might not be comfortable with PDAs or that it might be too presumptuous of me.

I tapped my finger against the thick aquarium glass. "Why does that octopus have no legs?"

Hunter stood slightly on her tiptoes to get a better view of what I was pointing at. "Because it's not an octopus; it's a cuttlefish."

I quirked an eyebrow. "You just made that up."

"I did no such thing. I know my cuttlefish," she said, face serious. "It's one of my favorite sea animals."

I stared a little longer at the strange aquatic creature. I had never seen anything like it before. I had been to my share of aquariums, but not enough to be an encyclopedia of ocean animals. I could readily identify freshwater fish – my grandfather had loved fishing and took me often when I was little – but if its native habitat was the ocean, I was less knowledgeable.

The cuttlefish stared back at me with what I thought were two black, unblinking eyes. Where there should have been tentacles was a squiggly mass of tissue that rapidly fluttered, making the animal look like one of those ghosts from Pac-Man. "Is this where you take all *your* women?" I lightly teased.

Hunter pressed her palms flat against the aquarium glass and continued staring at the fish. "When I was little I wanted to be a marine biologist," she said. "My parents brought me to this aquarium all the time. I don't know if this is the same one, but they've always had a cuttlefish. I named him Sam."

"Why'd you stop wanting to be a marine biologist?"

"I grew up." Her eyes never left the tank, and I wondered if I'd broached a touchy subject. "Being a marine biologist is the kind of thing little kids want to be, like a dinosaur hunter or an astronaut or a princess. No one actually becomes what they wanted to be when they were five." She turned her head and looked at me. "Did you always want to be an English professor?"

I shook my head. "No. I wanted to be a documentarian."

"When you were five?"

I laughed. "No. I suppose back then I wanted to be a Muppeteer – you know, the people behind the movement and voices of the Muppets."

"That's adorable," she grinned, her deep-set dimples showing. All this talk about cuttlefish had me wanting to cut our date short and just cuddle *her*. "Will you put on a puppet show for me sometime?"

"Absolutely not," I snorted. "I've got a reputation to uphold."

"A reputation as what?"

"I don't know. An adult?"

Hunter waved a dismissive hand. "Being an adult is overrated." She released a heavy sigh and straightened her shoulders. "Let's go see Olivia."

"Who's Olivia?"

She took my hand and tugged me in a new direction. The smile had returned to her face, and for that I was thankful. "The sea turtle, obviously."

+++++

I wasn't disappointed. Olivia was a treat. We stood in front of the sea turtle's tank longer than the others, in a kind of quiet contemplation, watching the animal gracefully glide and slice through the water. The rest of the visit continued like that. We'd make our way to one tank after the next and Hunter would educate me all about the animals living inside. When I'd invited her on this date, I had no idea I'd be getting such an education. Did you know the temperature of the egg determines the gender of some species of turtles? I didn't. Hunter did.

Hunter stopped abruptly in front of a tank of seahorses. "Do you mind if we sit for a minute? My feet are killing me."

"Of course." I found us an empty bench that faced a tank filled with translucent jellyfish. I'd always been a little unnerved by jellyfish, but I could suffer through my aversion.

Hunter let out a quiet groan as she sat down. "I knew I should have worn more practical shoes," she sighed. "I haven't broken these in yet."

"They're cute shoes, if it's any consolation," I said as I sat beside her.

"Tell that to my blisters." She slipped off one of her shoes and rubbed at her arch.

"I could do that for you," I said, trying not to sound too eager.

Apparently she didn't need to be asked twice. Both shoes came off and her feet landed in my lap. Her feet, like the rest of her, were long and thin. I grabbed one of her feet and pressed my thumbs into her arch.

"If I start panting, I'm not to blame," she warned.

I smiled and continued applying pressure. I know some people are weird about feet, but not me. I certainly don't have a fetish, but I did feel envious towards women with perfect, proportionate feet. My own feet and toes better resembled a primate's. In fact, my mom's nickname for me was Monkey Toes. She teased me I could hang from trees – yet another reason I didn't get along with her.

My grandma, however, took the high road. She said I had special feet and, like a psychic reading tea leaves, told me the shape of my feet indicated I'd financially support my husband. She was a little off on the 'husband' part, but that prediction stuck with me. Someone thought I would be a financial success. That message meant a lot to a kid with working-class roots. Neither of my parents had gone to college, and now, here I was, not just a college graduate; I had a PhD.

"Why do you keep doing that?" she asked me. Her face was serious as she inspected me.

"Doing what?" I honestly didn't know what she was talking about.

"Every time someone walks by, you stop touching me."

"Really?" I had nothing against PDAs, but I suppose a part of me was still nervous about someone from school seeing us together. I didn't think it had been noticeable though.

"When that family stood next to us by the leafy sea dragon tank, you dropped my hand. When the custodian changed the garbage bag by the clownfish, you stopped touching my waist, and when that older couple smiled at us by the red-eared sliders, you removed your hand from the small of my back."

I blinked once. She'd apparently been keeping a journal.

Her face scrunched into a frown. "Are you usually so closeted?"

"Whoa," I said, dropping her feet. "I've been Out for a decade. I'm not in any kind of a closet."

"Then are you embarrassed to be seen with me?" She folded her arms across her chest.

"You're gorgeous, Hunter. Why would I want to hide you?"

She shrugged and her gaze slid to the floor. "Then why don't you want people to know we're here together?"

She only looked up when I gently lifted her chin with my fingers. "I'm sorry," I apologized, sure to make meaningful eye contact. "I guess I'm just nervous about someone from campus seeing us. And maybe on some level I wasn't sure how you felt about PDAs."

Her lips twisted. "Next time you're not sure how I feel about something, just ask." Her hand slid up my side and rested against my cheek. If I had been vigilant about it not looking like we were together before, that cautiousness left. She leaned in and pressed her lips against mine, soft and tender. When her tongue swabbed against my lower lip, I was lucky we were sitting down so my legs didn't give out. Instead, the sound of someone loudly clearing his or her throat snapped me out of the kiss.

"There's children here," a woman who looked to be in her mid-40s said crossly.

A self-conscious apology sprang to my lips, but Hunter had collected herself before I could.

"Are you the kissing police?" she challenged. "Because I hope you're going after that couple next." She pointed in the direction of a young, straight couple eagerly groping each other by the catfish.

The woman bristled and I saw her nostrils flare. She made a noise in the back of her throat, but thankfully didn't say anything else. Hunter watched the woman storm away, and I watched Hunter with curiosity.

"Are you sure you've never dated girls before? You're awfully good at this."

Hunter's gaze returned to me. I could see some of that heated anger still in her eyes. "Kissing?"

I couldn't help laughing. "That, too. But I meant facing off against the Purity Crusader over there," I clarified. "I've been with women who were too afraid to even hold my hand in public."

"I don't see it as a big deal," Hunter replied. "It shouldn't matter if a person is straight or gay or something in between. If I want to show I care about someone, I shouldn't have to hide it."

"Lots of people would disagree with you," I pointed out.

She set her jaw hard. "Those people are wrong."

I wasn't just learning about sea animals on this date, I was also learning about Hunter. Hunter Fact #1. She was amazing.

"You wanna get out of here?" she asked me. She stood up and brushed at the front of her skirt. "I've got a craving for pancakes."

+++++

Hunter Fact #2. She made amazing pancakes.

After being accosted by the woman at the aquarium, Hunter and I returned to my house. Hunter made herself at home, first scratching behind Sylvia's ears and murmuring a hello, and then setting up shop in my kitchen. I offered my help, but after I showed her where the cooking materials and utensils were, she sat me down on a stool at the kitchen island and assured me she could handle the rest on her own.

I was now getting to enjoy the fruits of her labor. I grinned around my fork and made a quiet moaning noise of approval. Hunter paused flipping pancakes on the griddle long enough to raise an eyebrow in my direction. "You okay over there?"

I swung my feet back and forth. Sitting on a stool at the kitchen island, eating warm pancakes covered in syrup made me feel like a kid again. "These may be the best pancakes I've ever had."

"Seriously?"

I nodded and enthusiastically tackled another bite. "Seriously," I said around my mouthful. "I never joke about food. Are you this talented with all cooking? Because I don't know if my waistline can handle it."

Hunter shook her head. "No. Just pancakes. I got really good making them for church-sponsored breakfasts."

I dropped my fork on the plate and it clattered noisily. I covered my face with my hands and groaned. "I'm corrupting a church girl. I'm going to Hell."

"Whatever," she scoffed, turning over a pancake on the cast-iron griddle, "I haven't been to Mass in a very long time – or at least not since I started crushing on my English professor."

I looked up from my hands and my eyebrows rose to my hairline. "Is that so?"

Hunter nodded and smiled coyly. "I couldn't go to church in good conscience when I kept thinking about how good her legs looked in skirts." Her voice had taken on an irresistible rasp.

"You are such trouble," I said, slowly shaking my head.

"Eat your pancakes."

I took another bite, and just to get back at her, I released another throaty moan.

She raised her spatula and waved it threateningly. "You know if you insist on holding out on me," she said sharply, "you're not allowed to make those kinds of noises."

I batted my eyelashes. "I have no idea what you're talking about." I took another bite and groaned loudly around the food. I rolled my eyes and dropped my fork so I could clench onto the countertop. "Oh, God," I panted.

I expected another scolding, but when I reopened my eyes, Hunter was no longer by the gas range. Distracted by my faux ecstasy, I hadn't noticed she'd relocated to a spot right next to where I currently sat. I was momentarily frozen, startled by her unexpected proximity.

Hunter smiled. "You should share," she said breathily. She took the fork from my rigid hand and stabbed a bite for herself. She slowly brought the fork to her lips, and I found myself entranced by the languid movement. Her lips parted and the tip of her pink tongue revealed itself. "Mm…that *is* good," she purred.

I swallowed hard. Apparently she had no intention of making this "getting to know you better," and "going slow" plan easy on me.

+++++

CHAPTER TEN

The weekend went by too quickly and soon enough it was Monday morning and I was back in my office. I didn't see Hunter on Sunday because we both had work to do – grading for me and studying for her – but I thought about her in her absence. I had spent a good portion of Sunday trying to figure out where I might take her on our next "getting to know you" date. I hadn't come up with anything definitive though, but I was anxious to see her again. I took that as a very good sign. We'd both agreed to the No Sex clause, and I was still excited to see her.

"So you haven't been sexed to death, I see." Troian breezed into my office, unannounced.

I set down my pen and grinned at my friend. "No, but what a way to go, right?"

"No arguing from me." She plopped down in the seat on the other side of my desk and crossed one leg over the other, getting comfortable. "So how's tricks?" she asked. "I haven't seen you in a while."

Troian and I hadn't really talked much since I'd told her about Hunter and me. I could tell she wanted to talk about it though; the purpose of her unexpected visit was hovering just beneath her calm exterior. Whenever she was this visibly stoical, there was usually something she wanted to talk about, but didn't know how to approach the topic.

"Things are good," I confirmed. "It's midterm week though so students are freaking out on schedule."

My phone buzzed with an incoming text message. I picked up my phone and read the screen: *Do I get to see you tonight?*

"That must be from Winter Jacket," Troian remarked casually.

"What makes you say that?" I asked as I typed a reply: *How much of me do you want to see?* Even though we'd agreed not to have sex again, that didn't mean I couldn't flirt.

"The smile on your face."

I put my phone down so I could pay attention to my friend. "Well it was."

Troian wrinkled her nose. "Gross. I don't want to know about your sexting."

"Whatever," I scoffed, putting my phone out of sight. I saw I had another message from Hunter, but I didn't want to be rude and ignore my friend for my phone. "We don't do that."

"Yet."

I shook my head. This is how Troian and I talked about anything serious. We'd joke, we'd tease each other, and then we'd get serious. "She has a name, you know."

Troian looked amused. She uncrossed her legs and leaned forward in her chair. "Oh really? You're going to let me use her real name now?"

I shrugged, trying to not make a big deal about it. "It just seems silly to keep calling her that."

"Why? Because you're dating her?"

"We went on *a* date," I corrected. It was premature to say we were "dating." I didn't want to get ahead of myself, but worried it was too late for that.

"And how was that?"

"Really great, actually." I smiled, remembering how much fun I'd had on Saturday. "We went to the aquarium and then she made me pancakes for dinner."

"Oh my God. You two sound perfect for each other. You're both cornballs."

"Whatever," I scoffed, "Miss-I-Get-My-Girlfriend-Elaborate-and-Thoughtful-Presents-For-Every-Anniversary." My friend's attitude irked me. It's not like she wasn't guilty of being over-the-top cheesy with Nikole all the time.

"Did you tell her about the nickname?"

Her question made me pause. "No. I don't want to scare her off."

117

"But you at least told her you obsessed over her for nearly a year, right?"

I wrinkled my nose. "Not in so many words, no."

"Keeping your cards close to the vest." Troian steepled her fingers and nodded her head sagely. "I approve."

"I'm not trying to keep secrets," I defended myself. "I just think those are unnecessary details. You're not supposed to spill that kind of stuff on the first date."

Troian quirked her eyebrow at me. I knew she wanted to say more, but if she disagreed with my decision, she kept it to herself. "So when do I get to meet this girl?" she asked. "You can't keep her chained to your bed forever."

"It's not like that."

"Uh huh," she deadpanned. "I'm surprised you two stopped fucking long enough for you to come to work today."

Troian's coarse language always made me cringe. "We decided to stop having sex after that first night." I cleared my throat. "We're taking things slow."

Troian rolled her eyes. "Jesus, Elle. You're the only person I know who slams on the breaks *after* you crash the car."

I didn't quite know what to make of the analogy. Did she think I was making a mistake? Did she think me sleeping with Hunter was a disaster? I tried not to overanalyze her word choice. I tried not to be me. "I know you think I rushed into it."

"No, I just know your *modus operandi*," she corrected. "You do this thing all the time with girls. Have sex with them the first night you meet them and then back peddle."

"It's not back peddling," I defended myself. "It's not like I think sleeping with her was a mistake; I just want to get to know her better before we think about doing that again."

"So what you're saying is, she was bad in bed."

"No. That's not it at all!" I was starting to get frustrated. I couldn't tell if Troian was teasing me or was just being obtuse. "The sex was good. Like really, really good. I mean, it was kind of one-sided, but I'm fine with that because she'd never been with a woman before."

Troian held up her hands. "I don't need a PowerPoint presentation."

I grit my back teeth and tried again. "I want to take things slow because I know how I am." I needed her to understand where I was coming from, but talking this over and actually saying the words out loud was also helping me. "I burn too hot in the beginning and my relationships all fizzle out. Nothing that intense can last forever. Besides," I added, "I don't want a relationship just based on sex."

Troian snorted. "You might be the only person on Earth."

I sighed deeply. This conversation wasn't going anywhere. I'd just have to be satisfied that my best friend didn't understand my worries.

"Enough about me," I deflected. "What are you up to today?"

"Writing," she sing-songed. "Staring at the Fall leaves and watching them change colors. The glamorous life of a writer. Do you have time to grab lunch with me?"

I shook my head. "Sorry. I've got class soon." I pointed to the wrapped sandwich on my desk. "I have like half an hour to shove food down my throat before I have to go teach again."

Troian nodded and stood up. "Okay, but let's hang out soon – with or without your Winter Jacket," she noted. "It's up to you when and if you ever want to introduce her to us."

"You guys will get to meet her," I promised, getting a little ahead of myself. "I just…it's a little too much too soon, you know?"

Troian nodded. "I get it. You wanna keep her all to yourself."

I laughed. "Right. It's not like you're a big sharer, either."

Troian shook her finger at me. "Stop drooling over my girlfriend, Bookworm," she scolded. "You've got one of your own now."

Troian didn't give me the opportunity to respond. She was out of my office and out of sight, leaving me to fret over her parting words. Did sex and a date constitute a relationship? Did I have a new girlfriend now?

Luckily, I didn't have much time to stress out over these questions. I had to eat my lunch and I had another class very soon. But before I could dive too deeply into my food, I had another unexpected visitor. Hunter.

"Hi, Professor Graft," she chirped pleasantly as she appeared in my doorway.

I dropped my sandwich on my desk. "Hunter, hi," I greeted, hastily wiping any crumbs from my face. I hated when people watched me eat. It made me feel vulnerable. "What are you doing here? I thought you were at the hospital all day." I stood from my desk and moved to close the office door. It occurred to me that Troian and Hunter had probably passed each other in the hallway or had just missed each other on the elevator.

"Well when you send me suggestive texts like that," she said, waving her cell phone, "how can you expect me to stay away?" She smirked and leaned dangerously close to me as I shut my office door. Her light perfume invaded my senses. "So how much of you *do* I get to see later?"

Ever since we'd slept together, Hunter's confidence seemed to have grown exponentially. She was no longer the reticent student sitting in the back corner of the classroom. I wondered if anyone else had noticed the change. "You're teasing me on purpose," I complained.

"You did it to yourself," Hunter grinned. "You're the masochist who wanted to take things slow." She spun on her heels and away from me before I lost it completely.

She sat down in the chair meant for students. Well, technically she was a student, just not one of mine anymore. "How are your classes this semester?" she asked conversationally. She crossed her long, long legs. Her hair was pulled back in a tight ponytail and her makeup was lightly applied. How anyone looked sexy in salmon-colored scrubs was beyond me.

I glanced at my closed office door. I wondered if I should re-open it to make sure I behaved. Instead, I steadied myself before going back to my chair. "They're good," I confirmed. "I'm teaching a creative writing course this semester which is a nice change of pace from the standard writing seminar."

Bob Birken, the Chair of my Department, had handed over the reins of the Creative Writing class to me. Normally Bob, with his poetry background, taught the course, but he was cutting back on classes as he'd just accepted the position as Assistant Dean of Faculty for the university. He would still be chairing the English Department, but with the extra administrative role as Assistant Dean, he'd had to drop one of his usual courses. With my interest in contemporary fiction and writing short stories I was the obvious choice to teach the course instead. Typically I was always stuck teaching multiple sections of the General Education writing seminar as low-woman on the tenure-totem pole, so it was exciting to have the opportunity to teach a class I'd never taught before.

"Sounds fun." Hunter licked her lips. "Any cute students?"

"I don't...I don't..." I stuttered. I wasn't expecting that question from her. From Troian, sure. She always asked me about each new crop of students; it's how I first told her about Hunter and her winter jacket.

Hunter's grin grew, but it didn't reach her eyes in that same playful manner. "I'm just curious, that's all. It's not like I have a claim on you."

Her statement made me frown. So much for the self-confidence. "Hunter, I don't do that. I can appreciate when someone is objectively attractive, but as soon as I grade their first papers and read all of those sentence fragments..." I shook my head. "Ruined."

"But I wasn't a perfect student," she pointed out, frowning. "I had run-on sentences and a weak thesis statement."

"Because you're different!" I jumped to my feet, no longer comfortable with the distance my office desk put between us. She was still sitting though, so I didn't know what to do with myself. I could keep standing and feel like I was towering over her, I could dramatically fall to my knees beside her, I could sit on the floor awkwardly in my pencil skirt. Instead, I perched on the corner of my desk closest to her.

"Hunter." So many endearments came to my mouth – sweetie, darling, baby – but it felt forced and too soon. Just calling her Hunter seemed intimate. "You don't have to worry about me crushing on some other student," I stressed. "I'm not going anywhere."

"Really?" Her voice lilted hopefully.

I nodded. "Really."

Her shoulders sagged as if she'd been holding herself erect for an exhaustive amount of time. "I'm sorry I'm such a worrier. This is just still really new for me, and I'm afraid you're going to get tired of me."

"I'm a boring English professor." I slowly shook my head at her anxieties. It was strangely reassuring to know that she had worries as well. "Don't you think I worry that exact thing? That you'd rather be out with your friends, having fun, and being young?"

"You're not boring."

"Tell that to the freshmen who fall asleep in my classes," I snorted.

She looked properly offended on my behalf. "Give me their

names and I'll knock some sense into them. They should never insult the hottest professor on campus like that."

"Speaking of which," I mused out loud, eager for the opportunity to turn the tables on her, "any cute professors I should feel threatened by?"

Unlike me, Hunter didn't stutter. "My teachers are all men this semester. You know I'm in it for the skirts." The way her eyes trailed down my bare legs wasn't lost on me.

I cleared my throat. "How do you feel about dirt?"

"Is this like your fish question?" She quirked an elegant eyebrow. Everything about her was elegant. "You'll have to be a little more specific. I don't want to end up at a Monster Truck Rally."

"I want to plant a flower garden in my backyard," I explained, "but I'm kind of hopeless when it comes to those kinds of things."

"You're in luck," Hunter beamed, her previous apprehension quieted for the moment. "I happen to be an expert."

"Oh really?"

"Well, maybe not an *expert*," she qualified, "but I've got some experience with gardening."

"You're hired. Can you come over this evening?"

Her generous mouth twisted into a wry smile. "Don't you want to see my resume first? I've got references."

"I trust you," I said, grinning back. "You've got an honest face."

"That's funny; my parole officer says the same thing."

I shook my head and laughed. Hunter Fact #3. She had a way with dirt. I bent down and kissed her.

+++++

Later that afternoon, I waited on my front porch for Hunter to finish at the hospital. For once I didn't have grading to do, so I used the free time to finish up the final story in my anthology. Soon I would start shopping it around to trade presses for publication. I had decided to go ahead with my idea and write a story about Hunter, but I was going to keep it a secret until the book was published. I suppose that's one of the dangers of dating a writer; you often show up on the printed page.

Around 6pm, she appeared in my front yard, walking from the direction of her apartment. As she strolled up the sidewalk to the front of my house, I took a moment to admire how good she looked. She'd changed out of her scrubs and looked amazing in torn jeans and a t-shirt that fit snugly around her thin biceps. She strode up the front walkway with long, lean legs that never ended and a small, perfect ass I was now openly ogling.

When she reached the front stoop, she held up a canvas bag with the local grocery chain's logo screen printed on it. "I didn't know if you had eaten dinner or not already," she announced, "but I stopped by the grocery store and picked us up some sandwiches from the deli."

I stood up and gave her a quick peck on the cheek. "That was awfully thoughtful." The kiss felt like a very couple-y thing to do, and once I'd done it, I worried maybe I was moving too fast. We'd slept together, but that didn't mean we were ready to merge like amoebas. She didn't look like she minded it though, so I pushed the worry from my mind.

"You feed me all the time," she said shrugging. "I thought it was time I repaid the favor."

"You made pancakes," I pointed out. "And they were amazing."

"With *your* kitchen supplies," she countered. "And you paid for admission to the aquarium." Her grin widened. "You should let me treat you once in a while."

I wrinkled my nose at her logic. "But I've got a job and you're still in school. I don't mind paying for things."

"I'm not looking for a Sugar Mama, Elle," she said, shaking her head. "I'm looking for a partner."

This woman was a marvel. I tried to not drool too visibly. "Duly noted."

"So what kinds of flowers did you get?" she asked.

"Oh, some pink ones and some purple ones, and I think some orange and yellow ones."

Her eyes widened. "Oh Lord, you're not serious are you?"

I laughed. "I'm joking. I know a little about these things. I got some bulbs from the garden center. Tulips and things like that. I figure I'd get a head start on them now so I could have a little color come Spring and then plant another round of perennials in the Summer."

"Sounds like you've got it all figured out."

"But I still need your help."

Hunter rubbed her hands together and grinned eagerly. "Okay. Let's get started on this garden."

+++++

Hunter handled the bulbs I'd purchased with such dedication and such care, you'd think they were fragile eggs rather than tightly bundled roots. As I sat on the grass beside her and watched her dig a small hole with a trowel, I felt a warmth spread over me. It wasn't purely arousal, although watching her hands work the earth certainly brought back memories of what else she could do with those hands.

"You're awfully good with your hands." Whoops. I hadn't meant to say that out loud.

Hunter paused mid-hole. "Is this an elaborate set-up? Did you buy all of these bulbs and supplies just so you could throw sexual innuendos at me?"

I ducked my head. I really had meant to keep that thought to myself. "No, I've actually been planning a flower garden since I bought the place," I defended. I plucked a blade of grass from the earth and rolled it between my thumb and pointer finger. "I just haven't had the time to do anything about it until now."

"Or the cheap labor," she teased.

"How did you get so good at this?" I asked. When I'd shown her the space along my garage in the backyard where I intended to have my flower garden, she hadn't waited for any further instruction. She'd taken the lead, immediately digging into the dirt and opening up the bags of bulbs I'd purchased. She'd asked me for feedback on the design of the garden, but beyond that, I hadn't had to do much.

Hunter looked up after placing a cluster of small bulbs into another hole in the ground. She wiped at her forehead with the back of her hand, mindful not to get dirt on her face. "My grandparents always had a big garden at their house. My grandma used to babysit my brother and me in the summers when my parents were at work – we were cheap labor." She picked up another bag of bulbs and inspected the label. "After my grandpa died and my grandma's arthritis got bad, I used to go over and help her keep the garden going."

"You're determined to make me fall for you, aren't you?"

She looked away from the bag of bulbs and raised a pale, blonde eyebrow at me.

"A girl who helps out her arthritic grandmother?" I clarified. "You're making me melt, Hunter."

She bit her lower lip and cast her gaze low. "It's not a big deal," she murmured modestly. "Plus she always paid me with rhubarb pie."

"How do you propose *I* pay you back for your help?" I asked. I really hadn't done much since we'd gone to the backyard except hand her a few bulbs whenever she asked me for them.

Her lips twisted into a wry grin, and she shook her head. "You're making it very hard for me," she mumbled in warning.

"I have no idea what you're talking about."

She shook her head again and stabbed the trowel deeper into the soft earth. The movement was a little aggressive. "This going slow stuff sucks." She breathed out a frustrated puff of air that ruffled at her bangs.

I reached out and wiped at a smudge of dirt on her cheek. I only made it worse, but I wasn't about to lick my thumb like a mom and wipe it off.

Her eyes shifted and trained on my hand. The blue orbs looked bluer than usual with the low afternoon sun reflecting against them. "Can I make you breakfast in the morning?"

I pulled my hand away from her face. "Is that your way of asking to spend the night?"

Hunter's gaze slipped demurely to the side. "Well, your bed *is* ridiculously comfortable. From what I remember, I mean."

"And you're a ridiculously talented cuddler." I licked my lips. "From what I remember," I added. "It's like you studied at a school for cats. No wonder Sylvia adores you."

She looked up from her work and leveled me with that intense blue-grey gaze. I hadn't felt the intensity of her stare in a while, but it affected me just as much as it had before we started dating. "*Just* Sylvia?"

I bit my lower lip. *Damn it.* I was in so much trouble with this girl.

+++++

125

CHAPTER ELEVEN

Midterm Week is just as stressful on professors as it is for the students who take them, and by the end of the week I was exhausted. On Friday, when I didn't have to teach, I did something I hadn't done in a very long time – I took a nap. Usually my brain never lets me sleep during the day because of my inability to turn it off, but I had finished enough work that morning to warrant taking the rest of the afternoon off. Hunter had said she would come over after her classes finished for the day, but that wouldn't be for a few more hours.

I hadn't seen Hunter since our Monday evening and subsequent morning together. After we'd finished planting the bulbs in the backyard, we had the sandwiches she'd brought and I'd rounded up some fresh fruit and other snacks for us to graze on throughout the night. We'd cuddled up on the couch and watched TV like it was the most natural thing in the world. Even though I wasn't sure about letting her spend the night again, worried that I wouldn't be able to restrain myself if she continued to tease me, we'd both behaved. Sylvia, for the first time since I'd adopted her, slept at the end of the bed. I'm sure it had something to do with the woman sleeping soundly beside me.

Waking up next to Hunter the following morning had felt equally comfortable and as natural as the night before. It was something I could get used to very quickly. It was an uneasy thought that I'd gotten so emotionally invested in this woman so soon. She'd made good on her promise of making me breakfast Tuesday morning and I discovered that not only did she make a killer pancake, but she also made some of the best French toast I'd ever had.

When I finally woke up from my nap Friday afternoon and went downstairs, I heard voices, or at least *a* voice. I walked closer in the direction of the noise, until the voice became clearer and finally identifiable. "Hunter?" I called out.

Her response was immediate. "Yes?"

I found her in my home office sitting on the little red couch. "Were you talking to yourself?" I leaned against the door jam, almost afraid to enter my own space as if I was interrupting. Bright sunlight streamed through the office windows, wiggling past the slanted blinds. The way the sunrays reflected off her already light blonde hair gave her an ethereal glow. I felt like I needed to whisper in her presence.

"No. I was talking to Sylvia."

From where I stood I couldn't see the cat, but I didn't doubt she was crouched somewhere, maybe hiding behind a stack of books or a potted plant. My office had the best natural light in the house, and she was attracted to the sunny spots cast on the floor and furniture. I wondered if Hunter was, too. Maybe she was part cat, which helped explain why she and my disgruntled pet got along so well. They spoke the same language.

"I never realized she was such a conversationalist."

Hunter tilted her head to the side. "You must not be listening close enough."

I crossed the room and sat beside her. I could now see the cat, Sylvia, perched like a rabbit on my wheeled office chair. Her tail flicked back and forth erratically. She must have been irritated with me for interrupting what was certainly a complex conversation.

"Have you been down here long?"

Hunter checked the time on the grandfather clock in the office. "About an hour. I went upstairs looking for you, but you were so adorable passed out on the bed, I decided to let you sleep."

"I'm kind of a heavy sleeper," I admitted. "I guess it's a good thing I didn't bother locking the front door or I never would have heard you ring the bell." My hand found hers. "What would you like to do today?" I loved how our fingers seemed to be puzzle pieces that were meant to find each other to be complete.

"I've got some homework to do," she said, "but it shouldn't take long."

"Homework on a Friday night?"

She smirked. "If I get it done tonight I have all weekend to play."

"Can you do it here?" I didn't want to sound clingy or controlling, but I didn't want her to go.

She smiled and tilted toward me to rest her head on my shoulder. I kissed the crown of her head, taking a moment to inhale her sweet scent. "If I stay," she murmured, "will I actually get anything done? Or are you going to distract me?"

"I would never get between you and school." I held up three fingers, lined up in a row. "Scouts honor."

She yawned and stretched, that adorable prehistoric noise falling past her lips. "It's so cozy in here. I don't know how you get anything done. I'd want to nap all day long." My suspicions were confirmed; she was part cat.

"Is all your homework stuff here, or do you have to go home first?"

She buried her face back into my shoulder. "It's all in my bag in the kitchen."

If she kept being so cute and cuddly, we'd spend all day in this room. I was totally fine with that plan, but that shred of responsible adult was nagging at me to let her get her work done.

I regretfully pulled away. She tilted her chin up; her face was crumpled and disgruntled. "I'm going to grab your bag and some coffee for you," I explained. "You can set up right here and use my desk if you want."

"Mmmm. That sounds nice," she purred. "Why are you so perfect?"

"You give me too much credit," I waved off. All my life, praise had made me uncomfortable, especially when it came to significant others. Hunter wasn't my significant other, but it very much felt like we were moving to that point. "I'm bound to screw up sooner or later."

While I had napped, Troian had been blowing up my phone. I had multiple missed messages from her:

Where are you?
Is Winter Jacket holding you hostage?
I miss my friend!

I didn't want to become one of those people who, as soon as they coupled up, forgot about the rest of the world. It was oh-so-tempting with Hunter to just hide away in my house and forget about everyone else, but Troian was my best friend. I missed her, too.

I'm still alive, I replied.

My screen lit up with an instant response: *Put on clothes. I'm coming over.*

Her message sent me into a panic. Was I ready to introduce Hunter to the people in my life? I wasn't worried about Troian and Nikole. They had no connection to my university, and I trusted them both with my deepest secrets. It wasn't that Hunter was a secret, but I certainly wasn't advertising that I was spending an unreasonable amount of time with a former student. I knew Troian would give me more grief about it, but after the initial mockery and judging had subsided, we could all enjoy a nice evening together.

I was more worried about Hunter. Letting her meet my friends definitely meant this was more than a one-night-stand. I didn't just let every girl I'd ever slept with meet the people in my inner circle.

I looked over at the girl in question. She was still sitting on the red couch, her long legs tucked beneath her body. On her lap was a thick, cumbersome textbook that I assumed was for one of her nursing classes – science stuff I hadn't thought about since high school. She looked deep in thought – brow furrowed, eyes narrowed and focused. Every once in a while she'd bite on her lower lip.

I wanted this.

I wanted her.

My thumb tapped out a message for Troian. *Let's do dinner tonight. You guys free?*

Her return text hid nothing. *You mean we actually get to meet this girl??? I'll clear our schedule. See you at 6.*

I exhaled deeply and tucked my phone away. Now I just had to make sure Hunter was even interested in meeting my friends.

"Hey, Hunter?"

She didn't look up. "Mmhmm?" she hummed, turning a page.

"Do you want to go out to dinner tonight?" I asked.

"That sounds nice." She sounded distracted.

"Would it be okay if Troian and Nikole came along?"

That caught her attention. She looked up from her textbook with wide eyes. "Your friends?" Her voice pitched.

I tried to not make a big deal about it. "Yeah. I just got a text from Troian seeing if we wanted to hang out with them tonight."

"Like a double date?" I couldn't interpret the emotion in her voice. Was she excited? Scared? Hesitant?

Because I couldn't decipher her reaction, I didn't quite know how to respond. "Maybe? I guess so."

The smile on her face started out small, just the ends of her mouth curling up. It soon broadened across her face.

"So I take it that's a yes?"

"Of course it's a yes!" she exclaimed. The excitement on her face was quickly replaced with a look of horror. "Oh no. I don't have anything to wear."

"It's not a black-tie affair," I teased.

She hopped up from the couch. "I have to start getting ready," she said in a panicked tone.

"What about your homework?"

She dug through her bag, pulling out one article of clothing after the next. Her backpack was apparently a clown car. When I'd brought her bag from the kitchen to my office, I'd had no idea her wardrobe was stored inside. "That can wait until tomorrow," she dismissed. "I have to take a shower."

+++++

I looked up when I heard the sound of high heels on the wooden stairs. Hunter descended the staircase, ghosting one hand down the banister. I let my eyes linger a little longer than necessary on her slight curves. She was tall and thin, but with just enough meat in all the right areas. Her skirt and fitted top accentuated the narrowness of her waist and the gentle swell at her hips. I licked my lips and allowed myself this indulgence. I didn't smoke, I drank in moderation, and I was mindful of what I ate. Beautiful women, however, were my vice.

Hunter sensed the eyes on her form, and she looked down at herself self-consciously. "Do I not look okay?" she worried.

"You look fantastic." I wrapped an arm around her waist and

pulled her close to place a soft kiss near her ear.

She fidgeted with her hair; she'd been wearing it back in a ponytail lately, but for tonight she had taken the time to straighten and style it.

I noticed her uneasiness, and I took the fidgeting hand in my own and brought her knuckles to my lips. "Are you nervous?"

Her upper lip curled. "A little," she admitted. "I just want to make a good first impression. I want your friends to like me."

"You're absolutely adorable," I placated. "Of course they'll like you."

"And you're sure this is an okay outfit?" She tugged at the bottom hem of her top. "I don't want to be over or underdressed."

"Oh, you're definitely overdressed."

She looked perplexed until she saw the predatory look on my face.

"I love it when you wear skirts," I openly admired. "Although this one is a little long for my tastes."

She shook her head. "It's too cold tonight for a skirt, let alone a shorter one. I just didn't have any nice jeans in my bag."

I made a big production of pouting. "But that makes it harder for me to slip my hand up your dress during dinner."

Her grey eyes widened. "Don't you dare. I get tongue-tied enough around strangers without your wandering hands making me forget my own name."

"You don't have to remember your own name though." I licked along the outer shell of her ear. I didn't know what had come over me. "Just mine."

She closed her eyes and released a shuttering breath. "What time do we have to meet up with your friends?" Her willpower was admirable.

"We have plenty of time," I reassured her.

"Because I hate being late; it's bad manners." She wobbled unsteadily when I slipped my hand beneath her top and stroked her stomach.

"We won't be late," I assured in a low, melodic tone. "I can be very quick when I want to."

"Does this mean...does this mean..." Her voice wavered when I raked my nails across her abdomen, "that we're done going slow?"

"That's up to you," I said hotly into her ear.

Her response was immediate. "I want you."

Her flexibility shouldn't have come as a surprise, but I made a startled noise into her open mouth when I felt her knee nudging my hip. I hadn't figured the material of her skirt would allow for the movement. I quickly recovered though and grabbed her leg, my fingers holding her tight behind the back of her knee.

"Up," I commanded.

She didn't need to be told twice. Her other leg appeared at my side, and soon her long legs were wrapped around my waist. I was thankful for upper body strength that allowed me to maneuver us closer to the kitchen countertop. I stabilized her with one arm tight around her waist and the other in the small of her back until I had her against the kitchen island. I let go briefly, just long enough to sweep my hand across the granite surface and knock everything to the floor. Her thighs squeezed my ribs tighter to compensate.

We were both wearing too many clothes. She seemed to have the same idea as her hands went to the bottom hem of her top and she haphazardly yanked it off, elbows flying. As soon as her top came off, my mouth was on her breast. The sheer fabric of her bra left little to the imagination, and I sucked her hard through the material. Her nipple hardened and pebbled, and I roughly licked against it with the length of my tongue. Her hand went to the v-cut of my t-shirt and she yanked down hard until I heard a faint ripping sound. I could have cared less though. She could have gone Hulk Hogan on me and shred my shirt in half, and I wouldn't have been fazed.

When I reached beneath her skirt and maneuvered past flimsy undergarments, I found her wet and ready for me. My single digit slid into her easily.

"More," she groaned.

I withdrew my finger and placed both my index and middle finger at her entrance. I gently pushed against her. "Like this?" I asked, meeting her eyes.

Her top row of straight, white teeth bit into her bottom lip and she nodded.

I pushed just to the first knuckle. "This okay?"

She nodded and whimpered so I pushed deeper yet.

I curled my two fingers inside her, pulling a sharp gasp from her. She clutched onto my shoulders and leaned in close until I could feel her breath, hot and coming in ragged bursts against the outer shell of my ear. "I need you deeper, Elle."

I was only too happy to oblige.

I grabbed on to her bucking hipbone with my free hand while the other began to piston in and out of her. She was so tight and so wet that whenever she clenched around me, I was sure my fingers were going to snap off.

Her hand clamped onto my right shoulder. For a moment I thought she was going to stop me, but then her hand traveled to rest on my right bicep. Before long I felt her jerking back and forth on my arm, controlling the pace and depth of my thrusts. She pushed and pulled my two fingers in and out of her warm center in long, deep strokes. She made me bottom out on each thrust, and my knuckles rammed hard against her tender flesh. I groaned with want but continued letting her manipulate my movements to get herself off.

I felt her rapidly tightening around me and knew it was just a matter of time before she crashed over the edge. I swiped the pad of my thumb across her swollen clit and she howled. When her orgasm crested, she threw her head back and moaned. I continued my steady assault on her insides until the telltale tightening of her sex halted and her vice-grip on my bicep relaxed.

I felt exhausted and disoriented when it was over. I gently eased my fingers out of her sex.

"What just happened?" she asked, sounding breathless. I hoped that would never change. I hoped I would always have that effect on her.

I looked around at my kitchen and at the objects strewn on the floor. It had seemed like a good idea at the time. Quick. Efficient. "We either just had sex or a tornado swirled through this room."

She pushed her bangs off her forehead and looked a little dazed. "Or a sex tornado."

"Someone call the Weather Channel," I smirked.

Her blue eyes widened. "Oh, no. We're going to be late now."

"I'll text Troi. They'll be fine delaying coming over. Nikole always takes forever to primp, anyway."

"Wait." Her features looked more panicked than before. "They're meeting us *here*?"

"Yeah, the restaurant's within walking distance from my house, so they're going to stop here first, we'll have a drink, and then we'll go to the restaurant."

As if on cue, there was a knock at the front door.

Hunter hopped off the countertop and snatched her discarded top from the kitchen floor. "Oh my God. I'm not ready to meet your friends." She scampered away, as fast as her long legs could take her and disappeared up the stairs.

I still felt lightheaded and disoriented, but I couldn't let Troian and Nikole hang outside on my porch all night. I left the kitchen and its disarray for the front door.

"Hey guys. Come on in," I greeted when I opened the door and discovered that it was my friends who had, for probably the first time in the entirety of our friendship, shown up on time. "Hunter's just finishing getting ready upstairs."

Troian eyeballed me suspiciously as she stepped inside. "You have sex hair."

I touched my hand to my head. "I do not," I protested self-consciously. My normally tame, spiraled curls felt a little more unruly than usual, but nothing out of the ordinary.

"Whatever," Troian said, making a face. "I hope you washed your hands."

When I welcomed both of my friends inside, I heard a surprised noise from the top of the staircase. "Nikole?"

"Hunter," Nikole grinned, seemingly unperturbed. I don't think I'd ever seen that woman look confused or unsettled. "Huh. Small world. I kind of wondered if Elle's Hunter was you. It's not a very common name."

"You two know each other?" I felt a rumbling of petty jealousy in the pit of my stomach. Nikole was not an ugly girl by any stretch of the imagination.

Hunter descended the second floor stairs and stopped next to me. I quickly appraised her; I don't know how she'd managed to put herself back together so quickly, but she looked as perfect as usual, if not a little flushed in her normally alabaster cheeks.

"Nikole was my boss last summer." She smiled at me. "It's how I got to be so good with my hands."

"What?!" Troian squawked.

Hunter's already pale features blanched even more. "Oh my God. I didn't mean it like *that*. It's an inside joke between Elle and me. We were planting bulbs in her backyard last week and there was dirt and digging, and she made a comment about my fingers and…" She snapped her mouth shut and blushed to the tips of her ears.

"It's okay," Nikole reassured. "Troi's just the insanely jealous type."

"Can you blame me?" Troian pulled herself to her full height – all 5 feet of her. "You're insanely hot. I've gotta protect my interests."

"Oh God." I ran my hand over my face. "This can't end well."

"So now I'm your property?" Nikole scoffed. "And do you really think I'd cheat on you with one of my student employees?"

"Well, Elle sleeps with her students," Troian countered. "Maybe she's a bad influence on you."

"*Student.* Singular," I corrected, raising my voice and jumping into the fray. "It's not like I do this kind of thing all the time. Just Hunter." I could feel the heat of Hunter's pointed stare. I had never even given a student a second-glance until her. Troian was going to ruin everything if she didn't get her mouth under control. "And she's not even my student anymore, so that really shouldn't count."

"I need a drink," Nikole muttered.

I wanted to second that motion, but I kept my mouth shut for fear of getting myself into more trouble.

"Oh my god," Troian blurted out. "You *both* have sex hair."

Hunter blushed furiously while I scowled at my friend.

"So now that we got *that* out of the way, when are we going to dinner?" Troian asked, stomping her foot a little. "I'm hungry."

+++++

After a rocky start, dinner with my friends had gone much better than I had expected. Conversation had been effortless among the four of us as if we'd been going on double dates together forever. After dinner, we'd all returned to my house. Nikole and I each had one more beer while Troian and Hunter bonded over their mutual lack of drinking. Hunter still had about a month to go before she was 21 while Troian's allergies kept her the permanent Designated Driver.

I grabbed Nikole and Troian's jackets from the front coat closet as they prepared to go home. "So what do you think of her?" I asked in a hushed tone.

"I've always liked Hunter; she was very mature and hardworking when she worked for me last summer," Nikole pragmatically stated. It wasn't exactly the review I'd hoped for. "Plus, she clearly adores you."

I lifted an eyebrow. I'd noticed no such thing. "How can you tell?"

Nikole shrugged into her jacket. "I have eyes," she smirked. "The way she looked at you during dinner – every time you talked, she looked at you like there were hearts in her eyes."

"It was honestly gross," Troian said in her usual dour tone. She hated anything cute that didn't involve her.

"Serves you right," I deflected. "Now you know what the rest of us suffer through seeing the two of you dote on each other." I paused and worried my bottom lip. "You think she really likes me?"

They both laughed at what they perceived as naivety. Nikole clapped me on the shoulder. "Trust us on this one, Bookie."

I walked my friends to the front door. "Hang out again soon?"

Troian rolled her eyes. "Sure. If we can drag you two out of bed long enough for brunch. Because from the way you looked when we first showed up," she snorted, "I'd guess you guys gave up on taking things slow."

I cleared my throat, but didn't confirm nor deny her assumption.

"Leave Elle alone, hun," Nikole chastised. "She looks happy."

"I do?"

Nikole chuckled as they walked out onto the front porch. "Hunter wasn't the only one at dinner tonight with hearts in her eyes."

I watched Troian and Nikole walk down the concrete path to the curb in front of my house and waited at the front door until they had made it safely into Nikole's Jeep. I waved once more before shutting the door and returned my attention to the last woman left in my house.

I grabbed myself another beer from the kitchen and found Hunter sitting in the living room on the couch. She had poured herself a glass of water and now fiddled with the cup in her hands. She looked up when I walked into the room. "Did I do alright tonight?" she worried. "Do your friends approve?"

"It was touch and go for a while," I teased, taking a quick pull from my bottle, "but we officially have their stamp of approval." I actually hadn't been worried at all. I knew they'd think she was charming and thoughtful and beautiful, inside and out. "They want to go out again soon, if you'd be into that."

The tension seemed to leave her face, and her body language became less rigid. I knew she'd been worried about meeting my best friends, but she'd been so natural at dinner with them, I hadn't realized it had weighed so heavily on her.

I sat down on the couch beside her and set my beer down on the coffee table. "Did you like *them*? This wasn't just about them liking you, you know."

She nodded. "They're nice," she confirmed. "Knowing Nikole from before made things easier. And Troian seems fun, but she scares me a little."

Hunter was at least 5 foot, 7 inches tall, and Troian barely broke 5 feet. I knew what she meant though; Troian could be pretty intense. "Her bark is worse than her bite," I assured her. "She's just protective of the people in her life."

"They're a good couple," Hunter said with a thoughtful look. "How long have they been together?"

"Forever. At least eight years."

She made a noise. "Wow. I think my longest relationship was 8 months. What about you?"

Uh oh. I really didn't want to talk about my exes. If there was a prize for worst girlfriend ever, I'd win it year after year. My relationships seemed to have a limited shelf life before they inevitably imploded.

"Um, not that much longer," I confessed. "Maybe a year and a half?"

She drank the rest of her water and set the empty glass on the coffee table next to my beer. I smiled fondly when she was purposeful about putting the glass on a coaster. I didn't care about things like that, but the fact that she did was endearing. I wondered what her life had been like growing up to have produced such a careful, meticulous person. One moment she could be rigid and careful, but I knew how quickly she could shrug off that cautious persona and say something so explicit and teasing she'd have me blushing from the tips of my ears down to my toes. It was like she was at war with herself, trying to break free from whomever she'd been earlier in life. We had that in common.

She twisted to face me. "How long have you been dating girls?"

"Exclusively, since I was 21," I said. "But I went back and forth between guys and girls for about a year before then." I thought back to my first official girlfriend. Growing up in a tiny, isolated Midwestern town, I hadn't even realized being gay was an option.

"Have you ever been in love?"

I sucked in a breath. I wondered if she'd had these questions on her mind for a while now or if this was spontaneous. Maybe she was just now feeling comfortable enough to ask since I'd introduced her to my friends, and in doing so, had opened up my world a little more to her.

"At the time, I know I thought it was love," I started slowly. "Looking back at it now, though...I'm not sure."

She silently nodded. I thought she'd continue asking questions, but when no more came, I posed one of my own: "I have to ask – why did you never take off your jacket in class?"

Her pale eyebrows rose. "You noticed that?"

I nodded. I was tempted to reveal my fixation on her because of that jacket, but for now I kept that to myself.

"It was a cramped classroom," she explained simply, "and I didn't want to take up too much space. It was just as easy to keep on my jacket instead of hitting someone with my elbows when I took it off."

Her reasoning baffled me. "But the room was like a total sauna."

Hunter looked unperturbed. "It was just a little heat. Better that than embarrassing myself."

The grandfather clock in my study chimed loudly, echoing through the rest of the house, indicating how late it was. We'd been at dinner for several hours between appetizers at the beginning and coffee at the end of the meal. I didn't have a reason to wake up early the next day, but I didn't want to assume Hunter didn't have any plans.

"Do you need to be getting home?" I asked. "I can give you a ride."

A frown twisted her face. "Am I wearing out my welcome?"

"No, no, no. I didn't mean it like that," I appeased. For being a writing teacher, I was a klutz when it came to words. "It's just that it's getting late; I don't want to monopolize your time if you have to get up early tomorrow."

"I'm fine." Her head lolled to one side and rested against my shoulder. She reached for my hand and settled it on her lap. It felt so familiar, like she'd done it a million times before. "I just have some

138

homework tomorrow, but it won't take too long."

I don't know why I felt compelled to ask, but I did. Perhaps it was because we'd started opening up to each other. Perhaps it was because most of the women I'd dated had a habit of hiding me. "Does your roommate know about me?"

"No," she revealed, not lifting her head from my shoulder. "But we don't really share things like that."

"Why not? You live together."

"It's complicated." She sat up straight and I instantly missed the weight of her body gently pressed against mine. "Sara..." She paused and scrunched up her nose. "We were close friends in high school. Now though, we don't have much in common. We don't have classes together, we hang out with different people, and we have different schedules."

I could understand that. I had few friends from high school with whom I was still close. I had lost touch with most of them during college when I'd gone to school out-of-state and most of them had attended the local state university. Plus, after word spread that I was gay, few reached out to me. I was okay with that though. Mostly.

"Where does she think you are when you're with me or when you spend the night?"

"I don't know. She's my roommate, not my keeper. I just text her when I won't be coming home so she knows I'm okay."

I looked down to our enjoined hands. Her fingers were a marvel, long and sturdy-looking, yet still feminine. "Are you going to text her tonight?"

"I could." Her grey-blue eyes narrowed, lids looking heavy. "Remember that sex tornado from earlier today?"

"How could I forget?" I felt flushed just from the memory. At her prompt I easily recalled how wet she'd been for me. I wanted to be with her again, but properly naked this time.

"The tornado was one-sided."

"I don't mind." I didn't think of myself as a stone butch at all, but getting to touch her had been enough. "Besides, we didn't exactly have enough time to do anything about that."

She gave me a small smile, bashful as she dropped her gaze. "How about now? Do we have enough time?"

I cleared my throat. "All the time in the world."

She slowly licked her lips; I watched the trajectory of her pink tongue and suppressed a shudder thinking of all the things I wanted her to do with that tongue. "Why don't you take off your granny panties and finish that drink so I can return the favor?"

I quirked an eyebrow and brought the beer bottle to my lips. "You know very well I don't wear granny panties."

A smile started at the corners of her mouth and slowly took over her entire face. "What do you have on right now?"

"Why should I tell you?" I felt like playing hard to get after all the taunting I'd endured when we were taking things slow.

Her lips pursed. "I suppose I could just check for myself." Her voice had taken on a low burr that told me she had no intention of asking for permission.

She stood up and took my beer bottle and set it out of the way on the coffee table. She repositioned herself so she was straddling my lap. I gazed up at the nimble form practically floating above me. She brought her hands to her own firm, upturned breasts, cupping the small globes in her hands. I gaped in awe and released a low groan at this overtly sexual creature now tweaking and pinching her own nipples through her sheer top as she began to grind against my pelvic bone. Hunter Dyson was giving me a lap dance. This certainly wasn't what I had expected from my understated former student. I clutched her upper thighs and attempted to sit up. But refusing my attempt to reclaim dominance, Hunter placed her hands on my shoulders and pinned me flat on my back.

"Patience," she admonished. She grabbed onto my wrists and pinned them against my sides. "I've been imagining this moment for far too long."

I was never very good at following orders, but for her I stayed still. This was a new side to Hunter that I'd never experienced before, and I was pretty sure I was totally into it. Even though I self-identified as a Top and a bit of a Dom, there was something truly delicious about surrendering and giving up control to someone else. I couldn't ever be a full-time bottom— it wasn't in my personality— but I could relinquish this to her for the night.

She breathed heavily, directly into my ear, and I squirmed and began heavy breathing of my own. I groaned when she slid the tip of her tongue up my neck to my right earlobe, which received prompt attention from her chewing and nipping mouth.

She dipped her head and covered my mouth with her own. I

moaned into her mouth and attempted to grind against her pelvic bone, greedily craving more stimulation. I wasn't going to last long. Her hands went to the bottom hem of my v-neck top and she broke the kiss long enough to pull my shirt off. Tenderly, gently, she placed small, butterfly-soft kisses on my collarbone. She licked and nipped at the bare skin, eliciting small sighs and moans from me.

She slid lower down my body, eventually releasing her grip on my wrists. She kissed and licked a trail down my torso, stopping briefly to stimulate my sensitive nipples through my bra, which grew hard under her touch, her tongue, and her teeth.

She slid off the couch entirely and onto her knees. I sucked in a sharp breath when her hands went to the waistband of my jeans. She deftly popped open the top button and slowly, very slowly, unzipped them. She placed deliberate kisses on my stomach, down to my hips, licking hard at the bone that peeked out just above the waistband of my pants.

She ran her fingertips up the outsides of my thighs and curled them underneath the waistband, ready to remove my jeans. I was only too happy to lift my backside off the couch and allow her better access. She dragged the jeans down my thighs, past my knees, down the length of my calves, until she reached my ankles. I expected her to completely remove my pants, but she left them pooled at my feet.

She raked her short fingernails down my abdomen. I bit down on my lower lip, hard, without really realizing. When I let up, I ran the tip of my tongue over my lip and felt the deep indentations I'd given myself.

I heard her quietly groan as she rocked on her knees and leaned forward until her nose practically bumped against my panty-covered clit. I squirmed against the couch and bit down on my bottom lip again. She rested her hands on my upper thighs. She ran them along the naked flesh of my inner thighs, and I bit back a needy moan.

She seemed content to hover there, just over the place where I needed her the most. She groaned again, this time a little louder and more desperate. I clenched my hands around the pliable couch material and dug in my barely-there nails. Hearing how much she was enjoying this role-reversal was nearly enough to shove me over the edge, and she'd barely even touched me.

"Please, Hunter," came the pained whisper choked out of my mouth. Her head snapped up to meet my gaze. Her steely blue-grey irises met my own darker blue. Cornflower, I thought to myself. That's what they were.

"What is it, Ellio?" she asked sweetly. Her wide, pink mouth curved into a coy smile. She leaned closer and breathed against me, warm and wet.

I made a frustrated noise and slammed my head back against the couch cushions. I wasn't used to being in this position – not in control and allowing someone else to give or deny my pleasure. But as much as I hated getting teased, I also loved it. Anyone who gave me what I wanted right away usually didn't last too long. The delayed gratification, regardless of the situation leading up to it, was worth the delay. I could beg her to touch me, which is what she wanted to hear from me, no doubt, or I could wait it out and enjoy my torture.

I wanted to feel her hands ghost over my inner thighs. I wanted her breath, labored and hot, tickling my skin. But more than anything, I wanted her mouth intimately pressed against me, roughly tonguing my clit through my underwear. I wanted her fingertips harshly digging into my hipbones as she pulled my underwear tight against my throbbing sex. I wanted her mouth sucking me through the narrow column of material between my splayed thighs until I no longer knew where my arousal ended and her saliva began. I wanted her fingers urgently pressing against me, dipping as far inside me as the material would allow. I wanted to hear the material tear and groan and stretch as she tried to pierce me deeper. I wanted to beg for it, to be desperate to feel her shove that damp swatch of material to the side, and to finally feel her with no barriers separating us.

I breathed in sharply when I felt the sudden heat and moisture of Hunter breathing hotly over my covered skin. Her nose bumped along the length of my slit over the thin material of my underwear. She placed her mouth over my cotton-clad sex and gently tongued my clit through the soft material. I groaned at the sensation of the wet material brushing and rubbing against my most sensitive skin. She continued to flick my clit back and forth, rolling the nub around and breathing warm, wet air onto the covered skin. I squirmed beneath her wet touch. I'm sure she could sense my frustration and impatience.

She stared hard at my body, her eyes glazed over with desire. "So beautiful…" she whispered. With one smooth motion, she pulled my remaining clothing past my hips and down my legs.

When I looked down and saw the graceful sweep of long lashes, the flush bright on her normally porcelain skin, it took all I had not to grab her by the back of her neck and press her against where I needed her mouth the most. I didn't want to scare her or make her feel inadequate – like I needed to be in the driver's seat to thoroughly enjoy her.

Her touch was tentative, thoughtful, and delicate. This was not the desperation of youth eager to please for fear of rejection. It was as if she sensed that we had all the time we wanted or needed, as if she too wanted to languish over the act in case it wasn't real. I rested my head against the couch pillow and let myself enjoy the dedicated attention.

When her fingers parted my lips and sank deep inside, I knew I wouldn't last long. It had felt like a solid year of foreplay. Two long fingers slid in and out with a dedicated rhythm. I felt the sudden wave of heat and pleasure rake over me starting deep in my core, expanding to my fingertips, and down to my painted toenails as the orgasm took over.

She raised her fingers to her mouth and carefully licked them clean. I unabashedly moaned at the sight of this gorgeous creature feasting on my arousal.

"Are you *sure* you've never done that before?" I rasped.

The corner of her mouth twitched. "So it was okay?" she asked, her tone meek. She wiped at her mouth with the back of her hand and stood up from the floor so she could return to her previous position, straddling my lap. My hands fell easily to her hips.

I let my head fall back against the couch pillow, and I laughed at the space above my face. "It was *amazing*. I've never gotten off so hard or so quickly in my life. I kind of feel like a teenage boy now."

Before more self-doubt or feelings of inadequacy could trouble her, I grabbed her waist and spun us, so I flipped positions with her. She let out an adorable squeak of surprise when her back hit the couch cushions.

I let my gaze linger over her figure. She looked flushed and altogether delectable. "My turn," I grinned.

++++

CHAPTER TWELVE

I woke up early the next morning and watched while Hunter continued to sleep. I don't think I'd ever seen someone sleep so hard or be so trusting in bed next to me. I didn't need much sleep myself and usually stayed up late working or writing and got up a few hours later to work out. But dating someone meant spending more time in bed. I didn't mind, but it took some getting used to. When you're constantly busy, constantly at motion, it can feel strange to just be still for too long. I'd have to get over the guilt of thinking I should be grading or working on my next book or doing something else productive. I had a hard time shutting myself off.

I knew it was just a matter of time before she woke up and caught me staring, so I drank her in while I could. Hunter's breath fell in long, even breaths. She made the cutest little noises when she slept – not quite talking in her sleep, but definite noises. I'd also discovered that she had a habit of reaching for me in her sleep. Her fingers would curl around my bicep or her hand would innocently slip beneath the waistband of my pajama pants and rest against my hipbone, or she'd bunch the material of my cotton t-shirt in her fist. With anyone else it would have felt suffocating. I liked my space when I slept. I wasn't anti-cuddling, but it was rare for me to actually fall asleep like that. I could handle a few minutes of spooning before I needed space.

Hunter gently stirred beside me, her blonde eyelashes fluttering open. When she saw me watching her, instead of getting weirded out, her smile grew. "Morning." Her voice was deeper, raspier than usual from sleep.

I propped myself on my elbow. "Morning," I returned.

She shifted in bed besides me with slow, careful movements. I watched her with interest. "What are you doing?" I asked.

"I think Sylvia slept on me last night. My leg is asleep." I felt her move again beside me. "I'm just trying to get my legs back without waking her up."

"She's just a cat," I quietly chuckled. "It's okay. If you disturb her, she'll fall right back asleep anyway."

"Do you think I'm too polite?" Her gaze was on me, disturbingly intense and serious for the early hour.

"Because you put my cat's comfort above your own?"

"People say I'm too polite."

I stared at her, perplexed. "There's nothing wrong with having good manners."

"I think it makes people uncomfortable. Like they don't know how to talk to me," she frowned. "Like they can't be their real selves around me for fear of offending my 'delicate sensibilities.'"

"For what it's worth, I don't feel like that." I rolled onto my side so I could take one of her hands in mind. I ran my thumbs along her palm. "You're one of the most complex women I've ever met."

"I don't know if that's a good thing or not."

She looked so serious, I kept my laugh to myself. "I just mean that there's so much more to you than this polite exterior." I tightened my hold on her hand. Her skin was incredibly soft. "Your personality keeps me guessing."

She made a face. "Now I sound like Sybil Dorsett."

"I can't believe you know that reference," I gushed.

"I spent a lot of time in my high school library over lunch periods. I found *Sybil* when I was getting lost in the stacks. I was painfully shy," she told me. "And the combination of that with my tendency to be too polite made people think I was stuck up."

The idea of this amazing woman being taunted or feeling awkward and ostracized angered me. So many things about her made more sense. Why she hadn't voluntarily spoken up in my class more. Why she hadn't wanted to draw attention to herself by taking off her jacket. The scars from her past remained at the surface.

"I suppose we can't stay in bed all day," she sighed, looking up at the ceiling.

"I suppose not," I said, still thinking about Hunter Dyson – the woman she had been and the woman she was becoming.

"I'm going to hop in the shower," she said, her voice no longer melancholy and serious. "Join me? We could whittle away at that carbon footprint together."

Butterflies organized a mass assault on my stomach and I forgot my mental musings. I wanted to take a shower with her in the worst way, but I also needed to show a little willpower. We'd decided to stop "going slow" just yesterday and we'd already had sex twice. Normally that would be cause for a parade down Main Street, but I didn't want our relationship to revolve around physicality. I'd fallen into that trap too many times. I needed to pace myself with this girl so we didn't burn too hot, too intense, too soon.

"I don't want you to get tired of me."

"Fat chance of that happening." She wiggled her eyebrows at me. When I still didn't take the bait, she threw the covers off her body. "Fine, fine," she huffed. She made a disgruntled noise as she got out of bed. "I suppose I can handle showering on my own."

"Well if you need help soaping up your back, just give me a holler." I didn't want her to think I was rejecting her. I was rejecting the very real fear that we wouldn't last if I didn't show some self-restraint.

She made a humming noise of approval. "I'll totally take you up on that."

"Think about what you might want to do today. I know you've got some work to do, so we could stay in or go out – whatever you want."

"My choice?" she asked, leaning down and playfully batting her eyelashes. "Who knew you were so good at letting go of control, Ellio?"

I found the nickname entirely endearing. She'd used it once the previous night, teasing me. I'd never had a nickname before besides Troian's nickname of Bookworm and its multiple shortened forms – Book, Bookie, Booklet. She'd tried Worm once, but I'd quickly put an end to that. I could get used to Ellio. I could get used to this playful, sexual side of Hunter as well.

I felt myself blushing furiously. If our latest intimacy was any indication of the rewards I received when I relinquished control, I'd let her Top me any day of the week.

+++++

While Hunter showered, I started to piece together something for breakfast. I didn't have the same pancake skill-set that she did, but I could manage toasting bagels and brewing coffee. Maybe I would even make some blueberry muffins – from a box though. I wasn't *that* talented.

I tried not to think about Hunter being naked in my shower as I cleaned and cut up fresh fruit. I tried not imagining her body, stripped bare with water droplets cascading down her smooth flesh, running down her neck, past her collarbone, between the valley of her breasts, down her flat abdomen, and disappearing at the juncture between her thighs. While I dug through the cabinets to produce a box of muffin mix I tried not to think about where my lucky loofa was currently touching as she soaped up her limber body. It was nearly enough to make me abandon my breakfast scavenger hunt.

A knock at my front door pulled me from my X-rated thoughts. I went to the front entrance, the box of muffin mix still in hand, and opened the door. The woman standing on my front stoop was probably the last person I'd ever anticipated seeing again.

"Ruby? What the fuck?" Normally I didn't drop f-bombs. It was kind of my thing.

My unexpected visitor didn't wait for an invite. She welcomed herself inside. "Good morning to you, too," she greeted as she walked past me and into the house. She inhaled deeply. "Mmmm. That smells good. Care to spare a cup of coffee for an old friend?"

"Not really." I folded my arms across my chest. "What brings you to town?" I tried to keep my voice emotionless.

Ruby pulled off her jacket, revealing the small, trim figure it hid. She dangled the coat at the edge of her fingers; I knew she expected me to take the jacket from her and hang it up, but this was one person from whom I didn't mind withholding a few pleasantries. She wasn't completely obtuse. She hung her jacket over her right arm. "A conference. I thought I'd pop in and see how my old friend was doing these days." She gave me a steely look. "You haven't returned any of my emails."

"I haven't *read* any of your emails," I corrected her. I glanced nervously in the direction of the staircase. I sincerely hoped Hunter

147

would be taking a long shower. I closed the front door even though I had no intention of letting this woman stay.

Ruby and I had attended graduate school for our doctorates together, years ago. We'd entered the program at the same time, and I'd instantly disliked her. She had made it clear early on that the feeling was mutual. I usually found a way to get along with everyone I met, but there was something about this woman that made it impossible for the two of us to ever be friendly. She was fiercely competitive and neither modest nor gracious about her accomplishments, about which she'd be the first to remind you there were many. Being in the same program and studying the same topics, we often found ourselves in direct competition with each other for grants and fellowships and other awards.

Our mutual animosity had continued until the final year. By that time we had both finished course work and comprehensive exams. The only thing left was to write the dissertation and I'd be Dr. Elle Graft. Because I no longer had need to be on campus everyday while I worked on my manuscript, several months had passed without the bad luck of running into Ruby, my personal nemesis.

I'd been on campus that day to support another grad school friend who had just successfully defended his dissertation proposal. A group of us had gotten together afterwards to celebrate at a local bar. Somewhere between the third and fourth pint, I'd realized that Ruby was also at that same bar, just not with our group. She was sitting by herself at the bar, drinking and watching whatever sports game was on. With my tongue and usual reservations loosened by alcohol, I'd launched into a rant about my displeasure at seeing her there. I hadn't cared that my voice probably carried and that she might have heard every hateful word.

Later, when I had excused myself to use the bathroom, I had practically stumbled over a woman on my way out of the partitioned bathroom stall. I'd apologized for my clumsiness until I recognized who it was — Ruby. I was still harboring massive resentment and she looked equally displeased to see me as well. One moment we were arguing about something whose topic currently evaded me, and the next, my backside was pinned against the row of bathroom sinks and her hand was shoved down the front of my pants.

I hadn't even known she was gay. But then again, my gaydar had never been fine-tuned. That moment signaled the beginning of a very intense affair. We hadn't exactly had a relationship; we'd never gone out on a proper date, and we didn't celebrate anniversaries of any kind. I didn't talk about her to any of my friends, and she never introduced me to any of hers. We had come to an understanding. We used each other as a release for all the stress we were under between finishing the dissertation and job interviews for university teaching jobs.

Ruby was fearless in bed and she'd challenged me to try things I hadn't ever thought I'd be into. We discovered early on that we were both on the dominant side, which in hindsight probably explained why we'd never gotten along outside of the bedroom. Even then, however, I still didn't really like her and was only so happy to take that aggression out on her body.

It had been a particularly intense few months, but after we had graduated and had procured teaching jobs in different parts of the country, it had ended. There had been no exchange of belongings; neither of us had kept things at the other person's apartment because we never had sleepovers. It ended as quickly as it had started, and I only had my memories and one faint scar on my hip (we had very briefly explored knife-play) as evidence that it had ever really happened.

But none of this helped explain the minimally veiled animosity I currently felt as she stood in my foyer. But I wasn't really angry with her; I was angry with myself.

About a year into teaching at my current school, I had met Cady, my most recent ex-girlfriend. We'd met at a book club that Troian insisted I join. She worried I wasn't getting out and meeting anyone outside of the campus bubble. It was one of those feminist book groups that pretends to be about the literature, but generally turns into too much wine and hooking up.

I was never any good at delayed gratification, unless it was a bedroom game, and so I fell into bed with Cady, a lovely, bright woman, after only the second group meeting. And that would have been fine if it hadn't developed into something more. Instead, it turned into the one-night-stand that lasted a year and a half. One minute we were mapping each other's bodies with fingers and mouths, and the next we were picking out new linens for my master bedroom.

Nearly a year into the relationship, and I had grown restless with the status quo. And that was when the emails from Ruby had started. It began innocuously enough, two colleagues from grad school comparing notes about their first academic jobs. I'm not sure now who had started flirting with whom first, but once that door had been reopened it was just a matter of time before I was texting suggestive messages and she was reciprocating.

I thought it was okay if I limited myself to an online affair, fooled myself into believing it wasn't really cheating if we didn't meet face to face, but the more explicit I became with Ruby, the less attentive I became to Cady. I was living a double life and egotistical enough to think I could get away with it.

When summer break had arrived, I'd recommitted myself to my relationship with Cady. We had even taken our first vacation together. But when the academic year rolled around again and my inbox started filling up with Ruby's emails, I was at a crossroads – end things with Cady or cut off communication from Ruby. I had decided to do both.

"How did you find me?" I tried to keep my anger in check. "I never gave you my home address."

Ruby inspected the parts of my home that were in view. "I sent an email to your Departmental Secretary explaining how I was an old friend from grad school looking to reconnect. She was more than helpful."

Damn it. I made a mental note to remind Tricia first thing on Monday morning not to give out personal information.

"I like your house, Elle," she commented. "It's a far cry from that shithole studio you had in school." She turned her face toward me. "Where's the bedroom?"

"Hey, Elle?" I heard Hunter's voice call from upstairs and I froze. "Are you interested in Mexican tonight? I've got a craving."

Ruby leaned forward and one hand slid along the banister. I flinched, thinking she was about to bound up the stairs, two at a time. "Is that Cady up there?" she asked with a far too eager look on her face. "I can't believe you two are still together after all this time."

I should have let her believe whatever she had in her head about my life. I don't know why I felt compelled to correct her. "No. Cady and I broke up."

Her smile broadened. "Who's your company?"

"My, uh, my girlfriend," I stammered out. Hunter and I hadn't exactly had a conversation about labels or being mutually exclusive, but Ruby didn't need to know that.

How do I get rid of this woman? I wondered in a panic. Why wouldn't she take a hint? It wasn't like I'd invited her to sit down and had made her a sandwich.

"Elle?" Hunter's steps were light on the wood stairs. I heard her stop short, however, when she realized I wasn't alone. "Sorry. I, uh, didn't know, anyone else was here," she sputtered about halfway down the staircase. She self-consciously tugged the white towel wrapped around her body just a little tighter even though it covered her well.

"Good thing you thought to put on a towel," Ruby purred.

I snapped a warning glance in Ruby's direction.

Hunter looked justifiably uncomfortable and her blue-grey eyes moved from my face to Ruby and back to me again. "I'll just…get a little less comfortable," she mumbled. She silently crept back up the stairs and out of sight.

As soon as Hunter was out of earshot, I glared at Ruby. "You need to leave."

Her lips pursed and she stood up on her tiptoes, gazing in the direction from which Hunter had just come. "Call me crazy, but isn't she a little *young* for your tastes?"

"Her age isn't your concern," I barked. "There's nothing illegal about any of this."

Ruby made a humming noise, but didn't comment.

Sooner than I had expected, Hunter was back. Her courageousness amazed me sometimes. Put in her situation, I would have just hid out in the bedroom until I was sure the stranger on the first floor was gone.

"Hi. I'm Ruby," my unwanted visitor greeted, sticking out her hand. "I'm an old friend of Elle's."

Hunter accepted Ruby's hand and shook it cordially. "Hunter," she returned. "It's nice to meet you," she said in a mildly pleasant tone. I could tell she still felt a little uncomfortable since she'd just recently been in nothing but a towel; her trained politeness curled at the edges.

"I was just in town and thought I'd drop by and invite your girl to dinner." Ruby flashed a winning, but calculating grin in Hunter's direction. "You're more than welcome to come along."

"And I was just about to decline the offer," I spoke up. My voice sounded too loud in my head. "We have other plans tonight."

"Elle, we could always reschedule," Hunter said, her critical eyes not leaving Ruby. "You should make time for your friends."

I wanted to snap that Ruby and I weren't friends, but then I'd be forced to rehash how exactly Ruby and I knew each other. It would dig up too many skeletons that I wasn't ready to tell Hunter about just yet. She was already self-conscious enough without hearing about my past infidelities. Instead, I pushed a pained smile to my lips. "Fine."

Ruby clapped gleefully. "Then it's settled. We'll all go out for dinner tonight, my treat."

I knew nothing good would come from this, but I didn't know what else I could do.

+++++

Soon after Ruby thankfully left, Hunter disappeared back upstairs. I didn't know if she was upset by Ruby's visit and was trying to get away from me, but I wanted to give her any space she might need. Because of Ruby's visit, we hadn't had that breakfast I'd been planning, so I returned to the bagels and coffee. I stopped when I heard a strange sound coming from upstairs. I paused, eyeballs shifting in my head as I tried to figure out what I was hearing upstairs.

"Hunter?" I called out. I stood still, but heard no reply. I left the kitchen and walked to the foot of the stairs. "Hunter?" I tried again.

When she still didn't respond, but the unidentifiable noise continued, I cautiously crept up the stairs. The noise got louder as I got closer. When I reached the door to my bedroom, I recognized the noise – Hunter was blow-drying her hair.

I silently padded to the master bathroom and found her standing in front of the large vanity mirror that hung over the double sinks. Her face was impassive, her expressive mouth forming a hard, straight line. I'd never seen someone look so serious while doing such a mundane task.

When she finally turned off the hairdryer, I saw my window of opportunity. "You know you don't have to primp for me."

She visibly jumped at the sound of my voice, unaware that I'd been watching her, but she quickly recovered her composure. "I like looking good for you."

"You always look good," I countered.

She picked up her flatiron and began attacking her hair, one chunk of hair at a time. "You've only ever seen me done up."

I narrowed my eyes a little, examining her. "Do you wake up before me and get ready while I sleep so I don't see you with bed-head?"

"No. But I may have thought about it," she revealed.

I folded my arms across my chest. I might have been projecting my own uneasiness, but whatever was going on right now didn't feel right. "I'm not just dating you because you're beautiful, you know."

"Why *are* you dating me?"

I felt a frown curling at the edges of my mouth. "Is that a real question?"

She set her flatiron down on the vanity top. "Maybe I'm a little curious."

"I'm sure this is a conversation to be had when you're not busy curling your hair."

"I'm flat-ironing it," she corrected me. "There's a difference."

I bit my bottom lip. "You really don't have to come to dinner tonight."

She looked at me via her reflection in the mirror. "Why not?"

"It's just that, Ruby and I…" I trailed off. I didn't know how to voice my misgivings without giving myself away.

Hunter tilted her head. "How *do* you know her? Is she a professor, too?"

"We went to graduate school together," I said. "She teaches in California though."

"Did you date her?" she asked me pointedly.

"Not exactly."

Hunter was a very smart woman. "But you had sex."

"Yeah."

She made a little noise of displeasure and returned to the mirror. "Do I have anything to be worried about?"

"Absolutely not." I wanted to wrap her up in a tight hug, but I worried she might brand me with her flatiron, so I continued to keep my distance instead.

Her eyes gazed on her own reflection. She pursed her lips. "Are you sure you don't want me to come tonight because you're embarrassed of me?"

"If I stop my hang-ups about my age," I frowned, "you've got to promise to give up this self-doubting thing."

"We just haven't gone out a lot, that's all," she shrugged. "There was the aquarium and then dinner with Nikole and Troian, but really nothing else. I thought maybe you were embarrassed to be seen with me in public."

"You're absolutely wrong," I said, shaking my head. I tightened my arms across my chest. "I *want* to show you off. You've seen yourself, right?"

Hunter turned once again to face me. "I'd still really like to come out to dinner tonight," she said in a quiet, even voice. "Meet other people in your life."

"She's not really in my life," I argued.

"But she's from your past," she pointed out.

I pushed out a deep breath. "Yeah. And I wish she would have stayed there."

+++++

Hunter and I met up with Ruby at an Italian restaurant out in the suburbs later that evening. I had never been to this specific place before as I rarely ventured out into exurbia. Everything I needed was near campus, and it was generally better than anything the suburbs had to offer. But Ruby had read about this place and their stuffed gnocchi, and Hunter, herself born and raised in the suburbs, was able to vouch for the positive reviews. Normally I'd be excited to try a new restaurant, but tonight I felt more apprehension than anything.

"Why don't you choose the wine, Elle," Ruby suggested as she folded her menu closed. "You've always had good taste."

I knew for a fact that Ruby and I had never split a bottle of wine before. I didn't know what her game was, but that feeling of foreboding deepened the longer the three of us sat together at the table.

She trained her calculating gaze on Hunter next. "Do you like Reds, Hunter?"

Hunter's brow furrowed and she didn't look up from her menu. "I don't drink." She wasn't 21 yet. I'd started planning a party for her with Nikole's help.

"Oh, is that like a religious thing?" Ruby asked.

Hunter turned the menu page. Her face was impassive. "No. I just don't drink." I tried catching her eye to give her a reassuring smile, but she looked too focused on her menu to notice me.

"Wow. That's unexpected what with Elle loving microbrews so much." Ruby laughed. "But I suppose opposites attract." How Ruby knew anything about me beyond the strawberry birthmark on my left shoulder blade was a mystery.

"We manage somehow," I said sardonically. I stared down at my menu, itching for this dinner to be over. I hoped no one wanted an appetizer or dessert.

The awkwardness was momentarily broken up when our waiter came by to take our drink and food order. Ruby looked amused when I, like Hunter, stuck with water.

"So, Hunter," Ruby asked, folding her hands on her lap when the waiter had taken our orders and collected the menus, "are you an athlete? A body like that, you must work out."

I glared at Ruby. If her goal tonight was to make Hunter feel uncomfortable, she was well on her way.

"I, uh, I run."

"Marathons?"

"No. Nothing serious like that."

"She's just being modest," I jumped in. "She runs half marathons. That's over 13 miles, which is 12 miles longer than I've ever run."

"Oh, if memory serves me right, Elle," Ruby smirked, "you never had a hard time keeping up." She ran her fingertips along the top of her water glass.

"Not appropriate dinner conversation," I grit out between clenched teeth.

"Oh, we're all adults here," Ruby breezed. "Or at least most of us are." The wink she threw at Hunter was over the top.

Hunter's hand found my knee beneath the table. She steadied me before my anger got the best of me and I made a scene. Thankfully the waiter returned with our food and the uncomfortable conversation was tabled while we ate. Despite Ruby's presence, my stuffed gnocchi in basil cream sauce was worth the trip. I'd have to bring Hunter back here, just the two of us, so we could have a do-over.

"I hope you're saving room for dessert," Ruby announced near the end of the meal. "I read some great reviews about their raspberry mousse." Just when I thought Ruby was finally acting like a human being and I was starting to relax, she opened her mouth again. "Or we could get a To Go box and bring it back to my hotel room." She laughed at something, but I didn't see the humor. "Remember that time I brought chocolate sauce to your apartment, Elle, and you got so upset with me for staining your sheets?"

Hunter wiped at her mouth with her napkin and set it on her half-finished dinner plate. "Excuse me," she said, the words mumbled under her breath. She stood from her chair and I rose as well.

I reached for her before she could run off. I caught her wrist and I kissed near her temple. "I'm sorry about her," I said for only her to hear.

"It's okay, Ellio. You warned me." Her hand went to the side of my face and my heart fluttered at the endearment. "I'll be right back. Just going to the bathroom."

"Don't be long," I murmured, unabashedly leaning into the touch. "I'll miss you." I let my hand linger in the small of her back. I couldn't help myself. My hands wanted to be touching her all the time and dinner had been long enough.

I sat down when she left the table to go to the restroom. "You two are so cute, it makes me want to puke," Ruby snorted. I didn't appreciate the way her gaze followed the slight sway of my girlfriend's backside. While I flushed with anger at her lack of decorum, I couldn't deny how much I loved referring to Hunter as *my girlfriend*. I hoped she would be okay with it.

"You lack subtlety."

Her eyes didn't stray. "I don't know what you're talking about."

"Stop hitting on my girlfriend," I snapped. "And stop rubbing her nose in our past. It's not cute."

"I was just thinking about how much fun the three of us could have together."

"Never going to happen," I growled.

She turned her eyes toward me. "How about just you and me

then?"

"What part of I-have-a-girlfriend don't you understand?" I hissed.

"Never stopped you before," she shrugged.

"That's not who I am anymore."

Ruby leaned in and lowered her voice.

"Give me one night, Elle. One fuck. That's all I'm looking for; then I'll be out of your life forever." A vicious smile crept onto her face. "I won't say anything to your little plaything, either."

I slammed my fist down on the table, upsetting the water glasses. "That's it," I growled. "I knew this was a bad idea. I only agreed to dinner because I wanted to prove to Hunter that I'm not embarrassed by our relationship. But I see now that that was a mistake."

Ruby didn't appear disturbed that water had saturated the tablecloth and was now dripping onto the floor. "Do this one thing, Elle, and I won't let your secret slip to the wrong people."

I hesitated, only momentarily. "What *secret* do you think you have over me? I've already told Cady about what happened between you and me. It's one of the reasons why we broke up."

Ruby's lips curled at the edges. "But have you told your Dean that you're dating a student?"

+++++

I was quiet on the drive back to the city, and I was pretty sure Hunter could tell there was something wrong, but she didn't press me about it. She just simply held my free hand in her lap as I drove and played with my fingers while looking out the passenger-side window. Her touch was light and warm. It felt familiar, comforting, and I hated it.

I hated it because I didn't deserve it – because I was actually considering Ruby's ultimatum.

+++++

157

CHAPTER THIRTEEN

The next evening when Ruby answered the knock at her hotel room door and saw me standing in the hallway, her face morphed from surprise to a knowing leer. I'd just caught her out of the shower. She wore an oversized towel wrapped tightly around her torso and her hair was wet and twisted in dark tendrils down her back.

"I knew you couldn't stay away."

My own face was emotionless. Without waiting for an invite, much as she'd done yesterday morning, I strode past her and welcomed myself inside. Her hotel room had two queen-sized mattresses, but only one looked slept in. The television was on, but the volume was low. On screen was one of those Housewives shows. That she might like Reality Television was a surprise, but I realized that even after all this time I knew little about Ruby's interests.

"Can I get you a drink?" her voice tugged me back into reality.

Just being in this room made me feel sick. It felt a whole lot like cheating, even if I had no intention of giving in to Ruby's threats. But I had to be here. I had to at least try and plead my case. I'd worked too hard to get where I was at professionally to let a ghost from my past – Ruby – ruin it all for me.

After dinner the previous night, I'd dropped Hunter off at her apartment and once back home, with a glass of wine in hand, I'd thought about my options. The easy solution would be to break it off with Hunter. If I wasn't in a relationship with her anymore, there was nothing worthy over which to blackmail me. But there was something there with Hunter – something I couldn't divorce myself from so thoughtlessly to save my own hide.

Ruby had no concrete proof that I was dating a former student, so even if she called my Dean, there would be a brief investigation; Hunter and I would temporarily keep our distance, and the matter would be dropped. But that also meant we would have to continue seeing each other in secret until she graduated. I couldn't ask her to do that for me. I didn't want her first relationship with another woman to be shrouded in secrecy and deceit.

I also knew better than to give in to Ruby's demands. She might have promised to be discreet if I slept with her, but what was stopping her from coming back again and again? If I slept with her even once, she could use that against me to sour my relationship with Hunter. As usual, sex was not the answer.

"I'm not here for that."

She ignored me and poured me a drink – an airplane-sized travel bottle of vodka in a glass-filled tumbler. "What did you tell your little blonde about tonight?" she asked coolly. Her cocky grin was maddening, and I wanted to knock it from her face.

"Don't talk about her like that," I bit off.

My anger was only mildly contained. I knew I was being blackmailed, and I wasn't taking her manipulation lightly. She was riling me up on purpose, too. She wanted me angry and she wanted me to take out that anger on her body. In a previous life, a different version of myself would have been only too happy to give her what she wanted. I'd had one-night-stands before, but even those I'd felt at least *something* for my partner, even if only through an alcohol-drenched haze. I couldn't be with Ruby. Maybe we could have worked out before, but with what she was trying to do to me, I felt nothing except disgust and contempt.

She held up her hands in the universal sign of surrender before passing me the drink. I tossed back the entirety of the liquid like it was a shot of courage and set the empty glass on the bedside table. I wanted this to be over with as soon as possible so I could go home and take a scalding, punishing hot shower.

While I was distracted by my glass, her hand grabbed the tight knot that corded between her cleavage. She tugged at the twist of the towel and it fell to the floor, leaving her entirely naked.

"Oh, God." My hands flew up to cover my eyes. "Put some

clothes on, Ruby. I beg you."

"If memory serves me right," she snickered, "I was usually the one begging *you.*"

I kept my hand shielding my eyes. "I'm serious, Ruby. I'm not here for that. I'm just here to talk."

I heard her sigh deeply, followed by the sound of cotton material rustling. "Ok. It's safe," she announced. "You can look now."

I hazarded a peek to make sure she wasn't lying. She'd gone beneath the sheets on her bed. It wasn't exactly putting clothes on, but at least she wasn't parading around naked anymore.

She slid her hands behind her head and grinned at me. "So why is this girl off-limits?" she asked. "You didn't care when I used to talk about Cady."

"And look how well that turned out," I pointed out sourly. I felt awkward standing in the middle of the room while she reclined naked in bed, but there was no way in hell I was sitting down on the mattress. I shoved my hands in the back of my jean pockets.

"When did you and Cady break up?" I expected to see that maddeningly cocky grin on her face, but instead she genuinely looked remorseful.

I did the math in my head. "Little more than a year ago."

She seemed to be doing the same math. "Was it because of me?" She didn't sound cocky anymore. In fact, she almost sounded *sorry.*

"The relationship had run its course," I said honestly. "You were a..." I searched for the right word. "...symptom of my unhappiness in the relationship, but you weren't the reason we broke up."

"So what's so special about this new girl that you're willing to jeopardize your career for her? It feels very un-Elle-like," Ruby noted. "I thought you were more cutthroat than that."

I bristled at her comment. It hurt my ego to have someone like Ruby think I'd gone soft or that my career still wasn't my main concern. "Securing tenure is still a priority," I forcefully declared, "but realistically I know it's not the end of the world if things don't go as planned."

Ruby stared at me and slowly shook her head. "Who are you and what have you done with Elle Graft?"

I'd been forfeiting my happiness for too long all in the name of career and money and success. I had always told myself during school that there would be time for love once I'd achieved my goals.

But even after graduation and getting my tenure-track job I found that there was always something else – papers to grade, books to write, committee meetings to lead – that made me postpone really living my life.

The latest hoop to jump through was my upcoming tenure review, the leap from being an Assistant Professor to an Associate Professor. It also meant job security. I had been telling myself this was the final obstacle, but I was beginning to recognize as my review crept closer, that there would always be something new to overcome.

"How did you know she was one of my students? I could have met her anywhere," I pointed out. That question had been nagging me since Ruby had originally propositioned me at the restaurant.

"I had a hunch when you reacted the way you did at your house when I mentioned her age. It just took another call to your ever-helpful departmental secretary asking to confirm something about a student transcript. You small schools are *so* trusting," she said with a peculiar smile. "I only had to say I was from a graduate program considering Hunter for our program. Your secretary provided the rest. I didn't know Hunter's last name, but luckily for me, it's a pretty unique name."

I cursed under my breath. Tricia had never been the best administrative assistant, but now she was breaking federal laws.

Ruby sat up in bed and pulled the covers back. I quickly looked away again, uncomfortable with her nakedness. I remained silent while I heard her rummaging around. I started to get angry with myself. I should have called her to meet me at a neutral location to talk. I didn't have to come to her hotel room where she could make me uncomfortable like this.

"Applesauce."

I looked back to see she had put on clothes – a tank top and shorts. "What?" I recognized her safe word from our time together. Hers had always struck me as an odd choice, but I'd never questioned its origins.

"I can't do this." Ruby looked disgruntled. She sat on the edge of the bed and ran her fingers through her still-damp hair. "I'm sorry, Elle. I shouldn't have done this to you. I just got a little jealous, a little crazy, I guess. I thought I wanted to do this, whether you wanted it or not. But this isn't fun for either of us. I'd be emotionally raping you by forcing you to cheat on your little

161

wallflower."

The tension, the anger that had been building up since I entered her hotel room, started to leave my body. I felt exhausted by the drama of the past two days. "Are you still going to tell my Dean?"

She shook her head. "Who am I to begrudge you this little kink?"

I finally joined Ruby at the edge of the mattress. "I really care for her, Ruby," I said. "This isn't just a student-teacher fling to me."

She grimaced. "I know," she nodded. "And that's why I can't do this to you." Without further fanfare, she stood up. "You should go before I change my mind."

As she walked me to her hotel room door, I considered maybe we'd actually come out of this thing as friends. I said my goodbyes, but refrained from giving her a hug or shaking hands. Any kind of physical contact would have felt unnecessary at this point.

I left her room and stopped in the hallway when I heard her call after me. "Hey, Elle?" I turned back. Her hands curled around the edge of the door. "Call me when you come to your senses about this girl and want to hook up."

Maybe not.

+++++

The next day I was distracted by an uneasy, heavy feeling that left my stomach in knots. Despite our meeting, I still didn't entirely trust Ruby to not go back on her promise. Every time the phone rang or I received a new email, I tensed, anticipating it was someone from the university telling me that I was fired.

When I got home from work that day, I decided to call Ruby just to double-check that we were okay. My sanity wouldn't survive this not knowing for much longer. She answered her hotel room phone after the third ring.

"Hello?"

"It's 5 o'clock in the afternoon," I remarked. "Why do you sound like I just woke you up from a dead sleep?"

"Because you did." She coughed, clearing the sleep from her voice. "I didn't expect to hear from you before I left town. Don't tell me you changed your mind."

"No. Of course not," I said hastily. I didn't want to linger too long on the phone. Ruby had a talent for weaving an uncomfortable web. "I just want to make sure you're still planning on upholding your side of the bargain."

"I didn't realize there was a bargain in place." I could hear the amusement in her voice. "After all, you didn't complete your part of the agreement. Which, I have to say I'm still surprised. I thought you *liked* my breasts. But maybe I shouldn't have covered up so soon. You might have had a change of heart."

"Stop it," I scolded. I hated how she twisted conversations. I used to find her explicit language exciting. Now it was just annoying. "Can I trust you with this?"

She chuckled, but it sounded humorless. "Your dirty little secret is safe with me, Elle. I won't tell your Dean. *And* I won't tell your little blonde cherub about your late night visit to my hotel room, either."

I heard a quiet gasp on the phone line, but it wasn't from me and it wasn't from Ruby.

Shit.

I didn't bother hanging up the phone. I was out of my desk chair in a flash and racing down the hallway toward the front door. Hunter was there, yanking on her winter jacket – the same jacket that had endeared me to her nearly a year ago. The tears were already streaming down her face.

"I knocked," she explained wetly. "The door was unlocked, so I just came in. I wanted to surprise you with dinner."

I spotted a paper bag full of groceries by the door. It was tipped over, its contents spilling onto the floor.

"I wasn't eavesdropping," she choked through a particularly vicious sob. The wounded look on her face was unmistakable. "The battery on my cell phone died and I was going to leave a message for Sara. I didn't know you were already on the line."

"Hunter." I was breathless. It was like someone was sitting on top of my chest. "It's not...it isn't what it sounds like." I wanted to cut off my own tongue for the tragic cliché.

Her lips tightened to form a straight line. I knew she was putting on a brave face. "I have to go."

Without waiting for me to explain myself, she left me, tongue-tied and stunned in the front entrance. She didn't even bother closing the door behind her. I felt clammy with sweat and frozen by indecision. Did I let her run away and have this dramatic storm-off moment or should I immediately go after her? This was normally the moment in my relationships when I emotionally closed up. I'd always fought hard for the things I'd wanted in life, but for some reason, that had never extended into my love life. I was prone to fighting and arguments – I was an Aries, after all – but I'd always fought to save face or to be right. But I'd never worked hard enough to save a relationship.

After a moment, too long of a moment I thought, of indecision, I raced out the front door. I looked both ways down the sidewalk, but didn't see her. I took off running in the direction of her apartment. I wasn't much of a runner – that was Hunter's territory. It wasn't long before sweat trickled down my hairline, making my scalp itch. I tried not to think of what I looked like, a maniac bolting down the sidewalk in clothes that were not meant to be run in.

My calves started to loosen up finally, so I lengthened my stride, pushing myself to run just a little faster. She still wasn't anywhere in sight. My heart pounded along with the rhythmic crunching of loose gravel beneath my shoes, which should have lulled me into a serene blanket of safety. Instead, my feet, echoing against the sidewalk, punctuated the urgency that I felt. I could feel my upper abdominal muscles pull and flex slightly with every step. It wasn't even hot out, yet the sweat beaded on my forehead and slowly trickled down to my nose before I wiped it away with the back of my hand.

I was breathless and panting by the time I reached the front entrance of Hunter's apartment building. I sprinted up the short concrete stairs to the entrance and pressed the button for apartment number 3 – Dyson and Sharon. Hunter's apartment. I knew she wouldn't buzz me upstairs if she was furious with me, but I had to still try. After getting no response, I pressed the button again.

"Hello?" A feminine voice I didn't recognize, slightly muffled and crackling, came through the tiny speaker.

I pressed the button to speak. "Is Hunter there?"

"No," came the reply. "Do you want to leave a message?"

Hunter very well could be inside the apartment, but was having Sara lie for her. I had no choice but to take this woman's word as truth. It's not like I could bust into the apartment. I wasn't about to toss tiny stones at her bedroom window, either. I didn't even know which window was her bedroom window in the first place. I could have always waited for one of the other residents to come home and put on my best innocent face to be let inside the building, but that felt too desperate. I'd have to get in contact with Hunter some other way.

"Can you tell her Elle stopped by?"

I had no idea if Hunter had told her roommate about me yet. I had no idea if the woman on the intercom was even her roommate in the first place.

"Sure."

The sky darkened overhead, becoming overcast and gloomy, mirroring my own emotions. I felt drained after my short sprint and the resulting adrenaline. I started the walk back to my apartment, alone.

When I got back home, I popped a microwavable dinner into the microwave. Ever since Hunter and I had started dating I had no need to buy any more of the depressing one-person meals, but after some digging in the freezer I found a neglected meal that didn't look too freezer-burned. I wasn't really hungry anymore, but I needed to make myself eat.

While I waited for my dinner to heat up, I tried calling Hunter's phone. As expected, she didn't pick up. After about the fourth time I called her in a row, her phone went straight to mailbox. Sighing heavily, I tossed my phone onto the kitchen counter and slumped over until my forehead pressed against the cool granite top. My house was silent besides the eternal ticking of the grandfather clock and the gentle humming of the microwave.

My cell phone rang and I instantly righted myself. I grabbed my phone from the counter, but frowned when the number flashing on the screen was not Hunter's. I answered it anyway even though I wasn't in the mood to talk.

A familiar voice, angrier than I had ever heard it, barked at me: "What the hell did you do, Elle Graft?"

Whatever stoical wall I'd built up since returning home quickly fell apart. "I fucked up, Troi," I cried, swallowing back a sob. "I really fucked it up."

"I know. Hunter told me all about it," my best friend's voice chastised me over the phone. "And of all the people in the world, why did it have to be *Ruby*?" Troian's voice rose in anger. "Why is she like your fucking monogamy kryptonite? You and I aren't dating and even *I* feel betrayed by this."

"I know it's no excuse, but I was scared," I explained. "She was going to tell Dean Krauss about Hunter. How I-I'm dating a student," I stammered out. I think that might have been the first time I'd actually said the words out loud. "I didn't know what to do. She said if I just did this one thing…" I couldn't say the rest. It was too horrible.

"So you fucked her," Troian said flatly. Her tone was almost worse than when she yelled at me. It was like my best friend had officially given up caring. "You wanted to save your professional ass, so you did Ruby's ass."

"I didn't!" I protested. "I swear to you that I didn't, Troi. I just went to her hotel room to plead my case. But Hunter overheard us on the phone today, and I'm pretty sure she thinks we had sex."

"Okay, this story just gets crazier and crazier."

A snot-filled laugh filled my lungs. "I know," I sighed, wiping at my eyes. "She's not answering her phone, and she wasn't at her apartment. I need to explain myself, Troi. I'm going crazy over here."

"Good," she responded in a clipped tone. I could almost picture her face in my mind. Eyes narrowed, mouth angry and scowling. "You deserve to go a little crazy after what you did to her."

I tugged at my hair in frustration. I knew I deserved this. I'd been an idiot about everything since the heater broke in my classroom two semesters ago. It's like my brain broke as well. I should have just told Hunter what was going on so there would be no need for hurt feelings or miscommunication. "I just need to know that she's alright."

"She's as alright as can be expected," Troian told me stonily. I heard her sigh heavily, her resolve to be angry with me softening at the edges. "She's here with Nik and me, okay? Nikole ran into her on the way home from work, and you know how much she likes to coax life back into withering seedlings." She sighed again. "We'll keep an eye on her."

I closed my eyes and clutched my phone a little tighter. "Thank you," I murmured.

"Now stop calling her," Troi chastised, her tone infinitely lighter. "You look like a crazy woman and that's bad for your rep."

I tried to laugh, but it sounded hollow to my ears. If I hadn't been so concerned about my "rep" at my university, none of this would be happening.

"Are you coming at all tonight?" Even though Troian had insisted she didn't want to do a party to celebrate she and Nikole buying their condo, the lure of having a party at all had been too great. Nikole loved planning get-togethers.

"No. I probably shouldn't," I sighed. "Not until I get the chance to work this out with Hunter. And you guys have been planning this party forever. My being there would just be awkward for everyone involved." It was terrible timing, and the reminder of my friend's event made me hate myself even more. I had been looking forward to taking Hunter there as my official girlfriend.

"You're probably right about that," she conceded. Troian hated confrontations and hated witnessing them even more. I wanted to go to her party, but this would be easier on everyone. It was cowardly, but hopefully the right thing to do.

"Just, um, can you do one thing for me?" I asked hesitantly. "Can you kind of keep an eye on her tonight? I mean, I want her to have fun and I don't want you to be her babysitter, but just, I don't know, keep her out of trouble? And I'm not asking you to spy on her either for me, but I know it's just going to be a bunch of lesbians there tonight, and if she," I sucked in a deep breath, "wants to forget about me, and there's someone at your party…" I trailed off.

God, I was an idiot. I should be at Troian's condo right now, apologizing with my heart in my hands, not begging my best friend to be Hunter's keeper.

Troian sighed. I wondered if we were sharing the same thought. "Yeah. I can do that."

"Thanks, Troi. You're the best friend a girl could ask for."

"Yeah, yeah," she said, grumbling. "Just fix this, okay? I don't need all this drama."

I ended up throwing away my uninspired dinner without touching it. That night, while Nikole and Troian's party raged on, I tried reading a book, but my mind kept wandering. I was going crazy, continually looking at the clock while the party was going on, wondering what Hunter was doing at that exact moment. I wanted to text Troian and demand status updates. How was Hunter? What was Hunter doing? Was she making new friends? Was she off in a room someplace getting felt up by a stranger? On two occasions I even went so far as to grab my jacket from the front hall. One of those times I made it as far as my detached garage. Both times, however, I realized I was being obsessive and needed to take my punishment.

To make matters worse, Sylvia was in a bad mood. I tried picking her up and putting her on my lap to cuddle, but she'd bit me and scampered away down the hallway. I wondered if she knew what I'd done and was punishing me, too.

I spent the remainder of my night making gin and tonics, light on the tonic and heavy on the gin. By the time I was ready to pass out, I reeked of a Christmas tree.

I stumbled to bed and grabbed onto the pillow Hunter usually slept on. I don't know if it was just in my head, but I could still smell her light scent on the pillowcase. I hugged it against my body and tried to get some sleep.

+++++

The next morning I woke up abruptly when a noise exploded in my bedroom. I slapped at my clock radio, mistakenly believing it was my alarm that was making that horrible noise. When the sound continued, I sat up in bed, unable to pinpoint what had snapped me out of a dreamless sleep. I sat up too quickly though and the room began to spin. I swallowed down a wave of nausea and kicked my right leg out from under my covers. I let gravity do its thing and stomped my foot down on the floor and the room stabilized. It was a trick an ex-boyfriend had taught me in college to get rid of the room spins. I have no idea why it worked, but it always did. I hadn't had to use it in years though. Damn that hard liquor.

The mystery noise cut off as abruptly as it had started and I flopped back down in bed, my head hitting the pillow hard. My mouth felt like ass. My head was pounding. I'd fallen asleep with my contacts in and my eyes ached. I wanted to die.

The same noise from before started up again. I got out of bed and played a solitary game of Hotter/Colder until I found the source of the obnoxious noise – my cell phone. I had specific ring tones assigned to the people who called me the most frequently and I didn't recognize the phone number and there was no way in hell I would have purposely chosen that noise.

I thought about letting the call go to voicemail because I wasn't done feeling sorry for myself yet, but something made me answer.

"Hello?"

"Hey." It was Troian.

"What the hell is this number?" I barked into the phone.

"Good morning to you, too, asshole. It's the phone my work gave me. My cell died and I'm too lazy to plug it in."

"Stop it," I chastised. I sat down on the edge of my mattress and cradled my head in my free hand. "You're scaring me. A house warming party *and* a phone just for work? It's like I don't know you at all."

"Listen, Elle." Troian's serious tone indicated there was an actual purpose to her call. It was our pattern again – tease, be mean, get real. "If you have any intention of making things right with your girl, then you'll do it now before she moves on to the next warm bed."

"She's not like that," I defended her.

"She certainly looked like she was last night."

I gripped my phone tighter. "What?" My voice came out little more than a choked whisper.

"It's not my place to be telling you any of this," Troian said, dropping her tone, "but I think Hunter fooled around with someone at the party last night."

"I think I'm going to be sick." My stomach soured and the previous night's gin and tonics had nothing to do with it. "Where is she right now?" My worst nightmare was that Hunter had gone home with someone else after the party.

"She's in the shower. We wouldn't let her leave the party after she'd had so much to drink. But if she pukes in there and clogs the drain, I'm billing you for the plumber."

That Troian let Hunter drink kind of surprised me. It wasn't just the under-aged thing, but usually Troian was Captain Sobriety. Nikole was the only reason they kept alcohol in the house and even then it had been an epic fight over what kind and how much she'd be allowed to store in their liquor cabinet.

"Now before you jump to conclusions and go all self-destructive, I don't know exactly what went down," Troian revealed. "Hunter was pretty drunk and I saw her wander off with this girl Nik knows. There were a lot more people at the party than I'd expected and I kind of lost track of her."

"No, that's okay. I don't need to hear the details," I said, cutting her off from divulging anymore. "Thank you for telling me, and thank you for taking care of her this morning."

"Sure. The girl deserved to be a little irresponsible," Troian unhelpfully reasoned. "She's put up with dating you, after all. I'm surprised you hadn't led the poor girl to drink earlier."

Troian had a particular talent for calling my bullshit and putting me in my place when I acted out. "Thanks."

"So what are you going to do?"

I sighed and rubbed at her face. "The only thing I know how to do."

"I don't know if I like the sound of that."

"Thanks for the heads up, Troi," I told my friend. "I'll talk to you later."

+++++

CHAPTER FOURTEEN

The hallway leading to Hunter's apartment smelled like Indian food. The lighting wasn't the best either, kind of an unattractive halogen glow, but it wasn't like there was anything I really wanted to see better in the hallway. It was one of those places where you have to buzz at the front door to gain entrance to the complex. But I guess I had an honest face because one of the neighbors had let me in on their way out.

I hadn't been to her apartment before. I'd dropped her off that once before we started dating and I'd picked her up before the aquarium, but I'd never been inside. And for as long as we'd been together, I always preferred my own house and wanted to sleep in my own bed instead of coming back here. Hunter had never complained, but the thought made me realize just how horribly selfish I'd been.

I straightened my shoulders as I stood outside her apartment. I was going to fix this. I knocked and waited for the door to open.

"Elle." Hunter stood, dumbstruck.

I lowered my gaze. "Hi. Can I come in?"

She hesitated, perhaps unnerved by my unannounced appearance, or simply just debating if I should be admitted entrance. After a painful moment where I had begun to rethink this whole 'showing up uninvited' strategy, she finally took a few steps backward and lifted her hand, ushering me inside.

I followed her into the apartment, not yet knowing what to say or do. I had rehearsed a lengthy apology, but the moment she had opened the door, the practiced, articulate words had abandoned me. I turned to close the door behind me, careful and deliberate with my movements. The heavy door shut and the lock latched with a solemn click.

When I turned back around to face her, my breath caught in my throat. Hunter was invading my personal bubble. She stood so close, I could tell she wasn't wearing makeup because her eyelashes were blonde. Her breathing sounded strained as if she was holding back emotions bubbling just beneath the surface.

I opened my mouth to speak – to say what, I don't know. But before I could launch into some semblance of a cobbled apology, my words were cut off by her mouth crashing into mine. She kissed me with such force that I stumbled backwards and my back hit against her front door.

She pressed the full length of her body against mine, pinning me to the door. Her tongue sought entrance to my mouth, which I could not deny her. Her hands went to either side of my face, practically holding me by the ears. It took me a moment to figure out why my face was wet. Her streaming tears were warm against my skin and showed no sign of stopping. Her mouth tasted different to me. I could taste the salty mixture of her tears and the lingering taste of tequila.

Her lips moved against mine, in a rapid, desperate motion. I realized she was talking to me through the kiss. "I couldn't do it," she kept mumbling into my mouth. "I'm so sorry."

"Shhh," I hushed, stroking the side of her face. "You don't have anything to be sorry about, Hunter. I'm the one who messed up. And you –."

She cut me off. "I fucked up, too."

She violently let go of my head and her hands went to the front button of my jeans. She fumbled with the fasten just long enough for me to grab onto her wrists and gently pull her shaking hands away.

Her face took on a hard, ugly edge. "Isn't this what you wanted?"

I didn't know what she was talking about, but I was too afraid to ask. I was too afraid to say anything.

"Just sex," she spit out. "Isn't that why you went running to Ruby?"

I opened and closed my mouth a few times like a feeding fish. "I messed up," I willfully admitted. "But I didn't have sex with her, Hunter. I didn't cheat on you."

"Why should I believe you?" Her voice had taken on a bitterness to which I wasn't accustomed. She always had a smile in her tone. Warm. Laughing. Joyful. As if life hadn't yet broken her. I suppose this is what I had done to her. "I know you cheated on your last girlfriend with her. Why should I think I'm any different?"

She spun away from me. I watched her shoulders shake, but I couldn't tell if she was crying or simply vibrating in anger. Maybe it was both. I wanted to reach out to her, to hold her and console her. But I had to get these words out.

"She tried to blackmail me," I said meekly. The words felt strange in my mouth. It was like I was living out a *Lifetime* movie. I watched Hunter's body intently, desperate to read her emotions. "She threatened to tell my Dean about you and me, so I went to her hotel to ask her not to. But nothing happened, Hunter. I promise."

At my admission, she slowly turned in my direction. Her eyes looked angry and red at the edges and her cheeks were blotched with tear tracks. Her arms still hugged her own form, something I wanted to do for her. "I thought dating me wasn't a big deal now that you aren't my teacher anymore."

I sighed and rubbed at my face. "Technically, it's fine. But this, I don't know, *concept* of a teacher being intimate with a student? They make bad porno about this kind of stuff."

"So you didn't cheat on me."

"No," I said slowly, letting the word and syllable weigh on my tongue. I took a tentative step closer to her. "I didn't cheat on you. But I know I should have just told you about Ruby. I should have been honest and upfront about everything that was happening instead of trying to cover my ass and deal with it on my own."

"You're right." My heart ached in my chest; she looked so defeated and so drained. I had done this to her. I felt like she had her fingers curled around the bloody, beating, mass of muscle and was slowly squeezing.

"I know I messed up, Hunter. I kept secrets from you, and I betrayed your trust." I could feel my own emotions start to well up. Tears pricked at the corners of my eyes. "I'm no good at any of this." *Keep it together.* "Relationships. Monogamy." I shook my head. "Being a grown-up."

I didn't like where this conversation was headed, but she deserved to know my ugly truth. "Ruby and I have history, which you know," I started vaguely. "It's nothing I'm particularly proud of. She came into town this week thinking we had some unfinished business. She just didn't know I was already dating someone." I made a soured face. "Not that that has ever stopped me before." I took a deep, shuddering breath. "I cheated on my last girlfriend with her because I was bored."

"And you're tired of me already?"

"No! Not even close!"

"At Troian and Nikole's party last night...I was so...so *angry* with you."

I swallowed hard. I'd told her my truth and now she was telling me hers. I felt like running away so it wouldn't hurt so much.

"I don't want us to have any secrets," she prefaced.

"Me either."

Hunter shook her head. "Nothing happened. I mean, I kissed this girl, but I stopped before anything really happened. I wanted to forget. I wanted to get back at you. But we mostly just talked about you," she admitted.

"I'm so sorry I put you through this, Hunter. This is all my fault," I choked through my bruised ego. "If I had just told you..." I shook my head.

"I'm sorry I kissed someone else," she said quietly.

"I don't want anyone else touching you," I said impulsively. "The thought of it – it seriously makes me sick to my stomach." I looked down at my hands, afraid I'd said too much or that my territorial nature might freak her out.

She reached for me and gently brushed a few stray strands of hair out of my face, carefully tucking them behind my ear. I wanted to sob over how delicate her touch was. "And I only want to be with you," she whispered back. "I only want to be touched by you."

I stroked my thumbs across her cheekbones, picking up any stray tears. I stared hard at her bright blue eyes, brighter than usual from crying.

"Will you stay with me tonight?" she asked me.

"Anything you want."

She offered me her hand and I gladly intertwined our fingers. She led me down a narrow hallway, past the living room, past a bathroom, and into a bedroom. The first thing I noticed when I walked into her bedroom was the scent. When I had entered the apartment I'd noticed the slight musty odor of an old building. Hunter's bedroom, however, smelled 100% feminine.

The dresser and bedside table were littered with framed photographs of people I didn't recognize. That thought alone made me feel horrible. Not only had I never been in her bedroom or her apartment before, I'd invited Hunter to live in my world without taking the time to get to know hers. If I had been the girlfriend she deserved, I'd know everyone pictured in those photographs. I'd know how they'd met, and how often they got together, and about that embarrassing story I wasn't supposed to bring up in conversation.

Not letting go of her hand, I sat down on the corner of her mattress. She sat beside me, looking wistful.

"What are you thinking about?" I hated when people asked me the same thing, but she looked so thoughtful and I was so paranoid about where we stood, I had to know.

"We just had our first fight as a couple," she remarked. "Aren't we supposed to have make-up sex now?"

My stomach lurched. "Where's your roommate?"

"Not here, but she'll probably be home soon. I could put a sock on the door though," Hunter smirked. "She'll find some other place to go."

I cleared my throat. "Are you serious?"

"She's done it to me enough."

As much as I never wanted to turn down sex, especially with this woman, I hesitated. "I still feel like I have apologizing to do."

"But I'm the one who kissed another girl," she said. "I never should have kissed her, no matter how angry and confused I felt."

Her words twisted my stomach uncomfortably. "But if I had just been open with you instead of keeping secrets, it wouldn't have happened. I'm at fault."

"Are you always such a martyr?" She stroked the tips of her fingers up and down my arm. It was the most soothing, reassuring thing I'd felt in a long time.

"I'm usually never wrong, actually," I said with a crooked smile. "Cady hated that about me."

She stared at me with that intense, unwavering gaze. "Well

175

regardless of who's in the wrong, I'm still sorry."

"And I'm sorry too, baby."

We were quiet for a while, the two of us perched on the edge of her bed.

"Elle, can I ask you something?" She chewed on her lower lip.

"Of course."

"Do you *like* our sex?"

I was sure I'd misheard her. "What are you...um...huh?"

She looked away bashfully. "When I was drowning my sorrows last night, I asked Troi about you and Ruby. I was trying to figure out why you'd chosen her over me. What she had that I didn't." She dropped her gaze. "And Troi might have mentioned something about you liking, um, *certain things* in bed."

I was going to *kill* that tiny Asian. I grabbed Hunter's hands and trapped them between our torsos as if the movement would make her stop this topic. "I like you just the way you are," I insisted. And it was the truth. I didn't need all the bells and whistles and bondage and spanking. It was fun, sure. But I wasn't going to die without it.

"Are you sure? I don't want you to get bored," she said. "I don't want you to lose interest in me once the newness has worn off."

I frowned guiltily. I couldn't promise her that would never happen. Part of the fun was the chase, and any woman who had given in too easily usually had no chance of a serious, long-term relationship with me.

"I would only do that with you if it was something you're genuinely interested in," I said carefully. "I don't want you to do it because you think it's something I need."

"I want to try it with you."

I could hear my heart thudding in my ears. "Only if you want me to."

"I trust you, Elle. And I want to try it all with you."

I didn't want to hurt her. I didn't want her humiliated. Part of the reason I was able to go there with Ruby is because I didn't respect her. She was a nemesis and her submission was my pleasure. I let Hunter's words weigh on me before I asked a question, not sure how she'd react. "How do you feel about restraints?"

Hunter visibly swallowed. "Uh, what did you have in mind?"

"Normally I wouldn't ask for permission or for preference from a Sub, but if you had your choice, would you want your wrists bound or your ankles?"

She blushed prettily and her long eyelashes fluttered. "I don't know anything about this kind of thing."

I stroked my hand down her cheek and gently coaxed her to meet my eyes. "And I'm not expecting you to. But if you have a preference, I'd like to try that with you."

"O-oh. Uhm. I guess I...uh...do *you* have a favorite?"

"I actually prefer the wrists over the ankles," I noted. "Spreaders are amazing to work with – I've used those before." I realized I was rambling and probably shouldn't be talking about past conquests, but I couldn't seem to stop. "But I think the helplessness of being bound at the wrists is more appealing." I paused to scrutinize her reaction. "How does that sound?"

She nodded and licked her lips. "Do I call you Mistress or something?"

I arched an eyebrow. "Do you want to?"

"Not really. Could I call you 'Professor,' instead?"

I swallowed hard. "Uh, yeah. That works, too." I felt lightheaded. I remembered asking her during our first night together not to call me that because it had felt too taboo. She apparently remembered that conversation, too.

"I'll be right back," she announced, standing up. "I need to wash my face. My skin feels salty after all that crying."

While she disappeared down the hallway, I flopped down on my back on her bed and released a deep breath. Her mattress was firm, but not too hard. Out of curiosity, I reached up and tested the strength of her headboard by giving it a few firm tugs. The bed looked like it had come from IKEA, and I had no intention of destroying her bed frame even if it sounded like a fun idea.

Thinking about exploring that kind of physicality with Hunter reminded me of Troian's indiscretion. I pulled my phone from my back pocket and texted my best friend: *You are in such trouble.*

A few seconds later, Troian responded. *Hello to you, too.*

Forgive my lack of propriety, I returned, *but I'm mad at you.*

Two messages lit up my screen in rapid succession.

Why? What did I do?

Did you make up with your girl?

I grumbled and sent my reply: *What possessed you to tell Hunter about the things Ruby and I used to do together?*

It's not like I drew her pictures, she returned.

She wanted me to Top her! I typed back.

1. Ew. You know I hate hearing about your sex life and 2. You're welcome.

Hunter watched from the doorway. "On your phone already?" she clucked. "Maybe I should be the one tying *you* up so you can't multitask when we're spending time together."

"Next time," I promised with a cheeky grin.

"Is everything going to be okay?"

I turned my phone to silent and set it on her bedside table, out of sight. "What do you mean?"

"Is Ruby going to get you in trouble?"

I sighed. In my bliss of reconciliation, I'd nearly forgotten about that. I patted the space beside me and Hunter crawled onto the mattress to curl beside me. "She said she wasn't going to tell the Dean," I said slowly, unsure myself.

"And you trust her?"

I shook my head. "Not really."

"Are you sure you want to be with me? I-I'd understand if I'm not worth the risk."

I twisted to look at her and rested my weight on my elbow. "Hunter, I'll tell you this every day if it'll make you feel more confident, but I want to be with you. It'll take more than one bitch from my past to keep me away. I'm not giving up on this."

My answer appeared to be satisfactory because she was smiling again. "Then I've got a request."

I brought her knuckles up to my lips. "Anything."

"Will you meet my parents?"

+++++

CHAPTER FIFTEEN

"Are you nervous?"

I made a scoffing sound. "I don't get nervous."

"Not even to meet your girlfriend's parents?" Hunter grinned.

The calm exterior I had been stoically clinging to seemed to crack before Hunter's eyes. "I thought I was done with this kind of thing, honestly," I sighed.

Hunter leaned into the sink, closer to the vanity mirror to apply her mascara. "Done with what?"

"Breaking in parents to the idea that their little girl is gay."

Hunter laughed pleasantly, but said nothing.

"Wait. You told them I'm a girl, right?" I panicked out loud. "I may like classic movies, but I have no desire to act out a scene from *Look Who's Coming to Dinner*."

Hunter rolled her eyes. "Well I certainly *hope* they realize that my girlfriend *Elle* is an actual girl."

"And they're fine with it?"

She shrugged. "As fine as you can expect parents to be. I mean, they're the ones who wanted to have this dinner. If they wanted nothing to do with us, I don't think they would have gone to all the trouble."

"What about the age thing?"

"What about it?" she shot back.

"Did you tell them that I'm, uh, a little older than you?"

Hunter arched an eyebrow. "Do you think that's going to matter?"

"Hunter!"

"Ellio," she said, pulling away from the mirror and giving me an exasperated look, "you need to calm down. "It's not like you're *their* age," she pointed out. "Sure you may not be in your 20s anymore, but really, we're not that far apart in age. You really need to stop making a big deal about this."

"I still feel like a dinosaur sometimes," I grumbled.

Hunter tugged at the bottom hem of my shirt so she could place her hands on my abdomen. "You're damn sexy for an old lady," she teased. She trapped my bottom lip between her top and lower teeth and tugged.

I pulled at her waist and pressed my lips harder against hers. She smelled sweet. "And you're lucky you're so gorgeous that I put up with this," I murmured into her mouth.

Hunter laughed again and pushed me away. "Stop distracting me. I have to finish getting ready."

"Why?" I leaned against the inside of the doorframe. She looked amazing all the time; she didn't need to primp. "You're not the one who has to impress anyone. They already know what you look like."

"You don't want my parents to think that since dating you I've let myself go, do you?" she said as she went back to her makeup. "I've still got appearances to keep up."

She had a point. "Fair enough; just don't take too long, okay? I don't want to be late."

She smiled knowingly into the mirror. "Not nervous, huh?"

I shook my head emphatically. "Being punctual is just good manners."

I don't know why the question came into my head at that moment, but I felt inclined to ask: "Hey, Hunter, when you went to the Department's end-of-the-year party at my house..." I trailed off because the implications seemed far-fetched.

She twisted so she could look me in the eyes. "Did I go just so I could see you one more time?"

"I wasn't going to put it like that. That makes me sound like I have a huge ego."

She smiled broadly. "One of the girls in my program mentioned you were hosting the party. She'd suggested we crash because the English department is the only end-of-year party that provides free booze. We'd all had to take the writing seminar at some point, so we figured we were *de facto* English majors."

"Is it pathetic that hearing you use the phrase *de facto* is a huge turn on?"

She smiled warmly, but didn't say anything in return. She went back to getting herself ready, picking up her mascara.

+++++

I stared at the small rack of wine I kept in the dining room, pondering if I should bring a bottle to dinner with us. I sighed – another incident of meeting the parents. I could still vividly remember the first time I had met the parents of a girl I had been dating. I was 21 at the time, like Hunter, and we were each other's first girlfriends. Her parents had been divorced for a while and her mom had been the one to raise her along with her two younger siblings. She'd basically raised herself though. I remember meeting her mom for the first time – it had been dinner, just the three of us, pizza and Mountain Dew. It wasn't her mom's fault; she was doing the best she could with the hand Life had dealt her. She knew how to protect her daughters from teenaged boys. She knew how to warn 21-year-old boys to keep their distance. She just didn't know what to do about me. I remember thinking at the time that I never wanted to feel that way ever again. And for the most part, I'd never been anyone's first girlfriend again.

I looked away from the wine rack when I heard Hunter clearing her throat to garner my attention. She stood at the foot of the staircase with her jacket in her hands. Her hair was down, straightened and falling past her thin shoulders.

"Ready?" Her voice sounded small, not its usually roundness. It was as if the syllables had gotten stuck on the way out.

I smiled through my own nerves. "Why do you sound like we're about to face a firing squad? You're not allowed to be nervous."

She arched a manicured eyebrow. I had the strangest urge to kiss the space just above it. "I'm not allowed?" she playfully mused. She switched her jacket from one hand to the other. "I'm only bringing my very first girlfriend to meet my parents," she scoffed.

I stepped close and inhaled her sweet scent. It still made me a little light-headed. "We could always cancel." It was a cowardly thing to say, but I wasn't above self-preservation.

She shook her head. "No. I have to do this," she said with some finality. "I feel like I'm keeping secrets."

I sighed and nodded. I knew too well that feeling. Hunter was still very much my own secret. The people closest to me knew, but it wasn't as though I was advertising the information. I wasn't particularly close with my own immediate family, so I felt no immediacy to reach out to them.

My parents had separated when I was young and despite the time and distance, they still couldn't stand each other. When I'd gotten old enough, I'd divorced myself from them both. I hadn't seen them since I graduated from graduate school. I had a younger sister, but we rarely talked. We liked each other just fine, but had little in common as adults.

"Should I bring a bottle of wine?" I asked.

Hunter pulled on her jacket. "Probably shouldn't. Neither of my parents drinks."

I don't know why, but that single admission made my stomach drop. I don't think I knew anyone who didn't drink besides Troian, but she was allergic. It felt like a huge foreboding microcosm for the difference between my world and Hunter's.

"Do I look alright?" As soon as I blurted out the question, I felt foolish.

The tense look on her face softened. "Oh, sweetie." She touched the side of my face and I couldn't help but flutter my eyes and lean into her warmth. "You look great."

I opened my eyes and looked down at my camisole, cardigan, and skinny jeans ensemble. "Are you sure?"

She smiled that warm-honey grin that made me want to curl up on the couch with her, buried beneath layers of afghans. "You're perfect," she breathed.

I nodded, letting her know it was enough. What was happening to me? I wasn't this nervous, tongue-tied person. I was strong, independent, and self-assured. I was adept at public speaking, being the most captivating person in a room to keep the attention of a room full of co-eds. I wasn't this fidgeting, self-doubting, anxious stomach. Maybe I'd bring the bottle of wine after all and drink it on the drive there.

+++++

I followed Hunter's directions out of the city and into the suburbs. The buildings flattened and became more sprawled out the further away from the city center I drove. She pointed me into a subdivision that was the poster child for all subdivisions – violently green lawns, adolescent trees, and rows and rows of houses that all looked the same.

Hunter must have sensed my silent judgment. "We didn't always live out here. I grew up in a bungalow in the city, kind of like your house. But my dad got a new, better paying job, and they built out here when I started high school."

I pulled into a cul-de-sac with a basketball hoop at one end. "So you had to change schools?"

She stared out the passenger window at her parents' home. It was a big two-story pre-fabrication house like the others in the neighborhood. "Hence the no friend thing. I probably only became friends with Sara because her parents lived next door."

The more I learned about Hunter's past, the more my heart ached for her, and the more I wanted to protect her. But I knew she didn't want or need that from me. She'd made it clear many times she didn't need to be coddled. She needed to be treated like an equal.

I parked the car and unfastened my seatbelt. Her story had momentarily distracted me from my own nerves, but now that we were here, my anxieties had returned. I let out a shaky breath.

I heard her soft laugh. "It's cute you're so nervous about this."

I wiped my clammy palms against my thighs. "How is this cute? My stomach is in knots."

She leaned across the center consol and brushed the hair away from my forehead. "You're always so calm and collected. It's refreshing to see you frazzled."

I let out a sardonic laugh. "Well I'm glad my nervous breakdown is productive."

She leaned over a little more and brushed her lips against mine. "We should stop delaying the inevitable."

"Or we could stay here and make-out in front of your parents' house," I mumbled against her lips.

"Mmm...tempting," she hummed. Her eyes fluttered and I wanted to drive away from this cul-de-sac as fast as my car could go and take her back to my house.

Instead, showing an unreasonable amount of willpower, I pulled away. "Come on," I breathed, trying not to stare at her wide mouth. "Let's do this."

I climbed out of my car and started up the sidewalk that led to the front door. Hunter's hand slid into mine and we walked the rest of the way, hand-in-hand. I glanced at her as we ascended the concrete stairs to the front stoop, trying to read the emotions on her face. If she was still nervous, it didn't show. It settled my stomach a little more.

The front door swung open before we could even ring the doorbell. A boy, who I guessed to be Hunter's younger brother, Brian, stood in the threshold. My gut reaction was to drop Hunter's hand, but she squeezed my hand harder, refusing to let me pull away.

"It's about time," the boy grinned. He and Hunter had the same wide-set mouth. Brian's blond hair was shortly cropped; not one of those shaggy cuts popular with high school and college boys. He looked just as crisply put-together as his older sister in a polo button up and fitted flat-front khakis. "Mom was going crazy that you'd be late and she'd have to re-heat dinner."

Hunter put her free hand on her hip. "How long have you been spying on us, creep?" she said affectionately.

If possible, her brother's grin grew even broader. "Long enough." He wiggled his eyebrows suggestively.

"Elle, this is my perverted little brother, Brian."

He turned his attention to me and, like his sister, switched on his politeness. "It's nice to meet you, Elle. We've heard nothing about you." I felt his eyes on me. "I can see why you went gay, Grunt. I mean, I get it. I can't blame you. I like girls, too. "

I stood there, a little dumbstruck. So maybe Brian didn't quite have the same polite charm of his sister. I shouldn't have been surprised by his response, however. Brian, a typical teenage boy, wouldn't know how to react to seeing the two of us together. I'm sure his hormones were racing with typical straight boy girl-on-girl fantasies, but were complicated because one of those girls was his sister.

Hunter didn't appear to be affected by his behavior. She rolled her eyes. "Cute. Real cute."

Brian took a step backwards, and Hunter and I stepped inside. I took a moment to appraise the house, or at least what I could see of it. The front foyer was generous and was tastefully and simply decorated. The vaulted ceilings were impressive and the open-floor layout was refreshing.

I didn't know much about her family besides the fact that her parents were still together. I knew Brian was younger, still in high school, but I didn't know his age. Her dad worked somewhere in the city, doing something financial, but I didn't know what his actual job was. And what I knew about her mother mirrored the rest of her family. She had been an interior decorator before Hunter was born, but since then had been a fulltime homemaker. I had tried to get as much information to prepare for dinner, but Hunter hadn't been forthcoming.

"Where's Mom and Dad?" Hunter asked, slipping out of her jacket. I instinctively took it from her even though I didn't know where to hang it up.

"Mom's in the kitchen fretting like she's making dinner for the President. And Dad's still at work."

Hunter frowned. "But he's planning on coming home for dinner, right?"

"Who knows. Mom's pissed though."

Hunter's mouth went tight. "Great."

I cleared my throat, breaking up the sibling reunion. "Where should I hang this up?" I asked, pointing to Hunter's jacket.

Hunter's face lit up with recognition. "Oh! Sorry! The closet's over there."

I nodded, thankful for the task. When I met families for the first time I liked to launch myself into chores and being helpful in the kitchen. It was the right thing to do, but also lessened the likeliness of me being awkward if I had something busying my hands and my brain.

When I opened the closet, I was attacked by falling board game boxes. "Holy board games," I mumbled. "Does your family own stock in Milton Bradley or something?"

"No. We just love board games. We're pretty competitive." She shrugged it off. "Ready to meet my mom?"

I took a deep breath. "Ready as I'll ever be."

+++++

Ellen Dyson was a striking woman – tall and blonde with the same intense grey-blue eyes as her children. I wasn't sure if she liked me though. I had received a warm welcome from Brian, but the same courtesy hadn't been extended from his mother. I tried not to be too off-put by the chilly reception. She was clearly upset her husband hadn't made it back in time for dinner, and everyone who sat around the dining room table knew that. Brian had barely looked up from his plate since we'd sat down, and Hunter looked equally uncomfortable. I felt decades younger and the meal brought me back to my youth and similarly tense family sit-downs.

"Hey, Elle," Brian interrupted my thoughts. "Did you know that Hunter was supposed to be a boy?"

I glanced in the direction of my girlfriend, who was currently rolling her eyes. "I wasn't supposed to be a boy, dummy. Mom and Dad just wanted to be surprised by the gender when they had me and didn't request to find out beforehand."

"Then why do you have a *boy* name?" Brian grinned around a mouthful of mashed potatoes.

Their mother cleared her throat. "That's enough, Brian," she gently corrected. "So, how did you two meet?" It was the first time Hunter's mother had really spoken beyond a few polite requests for someone to pass the butter and rolls.

I turned my eyes toward Hunter. We'd been anticipating this question for some time now; I'd expected the question to have come up much earlier than this, however. In a perfect world, we wouldn't be testing the reception of the answer on her parents first. But, in a perfect world, we would have met some other way. Although I suppose there are worst ways to have met. Prison comes to mind.

Hunter wiped her mouth with her napkin and carefully set it on the table next to her utensils. If the reception went poorly we'd already discussed making a hasty exit rather than linger and hash it out.

"We met at school, actually," Hunter said without pretense. I could see her make eye contact with her mom. I couldn't tell if it was an unspoken challenge or just her way of showing she wasn't ashamed.

Mrs. Dyson trained her attention to her plate as she carefully cut up her chicken breast into uniform bites. "What's your major, Elle?"

I'm sure my eyes grew about two sizes. I looked to Hunter for direction, but she only frowned and shook her head. "I'm actually not a student." I gripped onto the table's edge, knuckles turning white. "I'm a professor."

"A professor?" her mother echoed, eyes still trained on her protein. "You look...young to have a PhD."

"Good genes, I guess," I said with a nervous laugh. "I moved through graduate school pretty quickly," I admitted before pausing, "but I'm 30."

Her shoulders went tense. "Brian," she said in a quiet voice, "you may be excused."

Hunter's brother looked annoyed. "But I haven't finished—."

"I *said*, you may be excused," his mother interrupted sharply.

The teen boy grumbled something unintelligible before grabbing a roll, shoving himself away from the table, and storming out of the dining room. Mrs. Dyson watched as he left the room. When he'd gone, her grey-blue eyes returned to me. Even though Hunter and her mom had the same eyes, I'd never seen Hunter look at me like this, though. "And what do you teach?" she asked.

I cleared my throat. "English," I managed to croak out. "I specialize in Composition and Creative Writing."

Her mouth pinched and she glanced at her daughter. "Sweetie, didn't you tell me you were taking an English class?"

Hunter looked paler than usual. "A writing seminar last semester," she confirmed with a nod. "It was Elle's class."

The somewhat jovial atmosphere immediately turned tense – tenser than it had been when her mom had discovered I was older than her daughter. Hunter's mom dropped her silverware onto her plate, creating a wincing ceramic clatter.

Hunter raised her hand, palm out, anticipating an explosion. "Mom," she said in a shaky voice, "before you go off the deep end, just hear me out. We didn't start dating until after the semester ended. Nothing inappropriate happened, I promise."

Mrs. Dyson seemed to be taking a few calming breaths. "I think I've been relatively accepting of this situation, all things considered."

"Mom."

"No," her mother, calmly interrupted. "Let me say my peace. I won't lie and say that your decision to date girls didn't come as a surprise."

Hunter made a motion to interject, but her mom effectively

silenced her again. "You never really had any serious boyfriends in high school, but no parent ever expects that one of their children is gay." I had to give this woman credit. She said the g-word without stuttering or blushing. "But then you expect me to be, what, *okay*, with you dating your professor? It's a little much to take."

Hunter's gaze, which had started out locked on her mother's disappointed expression, had now drifted to the little flower pattern on her plate. "She's not my professor anymore," she grumbled.

I sat on the edge of my chair, watching the exchange like a particularly tense tennis match. I knew I should say something, but what magic words could I possibly offer when I myself still felt uneasy about the circumstances under which we'd met and the age difference? But I had to say *something*. I couldn't sit back and let Hunter take this punishment. I was just as much, if not more, culpable.

"Mrs. Dyson." Her head spun as if on a swivel. I wondered if she'd forgotten my presence.

"Ellen," she corrected.

I nodded. "Ellen," I repeated. This was the part where I was supposed to be eloquent, gracious, and reassuring – three things I currently wasn't feeling. "I know this isn't an ideal situation," I started, fumbling for the right words, "but I want you to know that I care very much for Hunter, and I truly just want to make her happy."

I felt Hunter's hand search under the table to find my knee. She squeezed just above my kneecap.

Mrs. Dyson removed the cloth napkin from her lap and set it on top of her plate. Apparently dinner was over. "And I appreciate hearing that," she countered, "but you'll forgive me if I have a hard time understanding what a 30-year-old woman could possibly gain from a relationship with a 21-year-old."

Hunter's chair made a horrible scratching noise as she abruptly stood up and the legs of her seat scraped against the wood floor. "Thank you for dinner, Mom," she said in a clipped tone, "but we have to go."

"Hunter." I knew we'd talked about leaving like this if things got too tense, but now that it was actually happening, I didn't want to run away, leaving things so broken.

Hunter, ignoring my plea, threw open the big, colonial-style door and nearly ran into a man as she blustered outside.

"There's my little girl!" the man greeted. "What's your hurry? Where's the fire?"

"Hi, Dad," she said flatly. "We're leaving."

Hunter's father was a handsome man, probably in his mid-50s. He had a full head of hair, brown with a little grey peppering his temples. He was wearing a grey suit, with a white dress shirt, and his dark tie was loose around his neck. "Leaving?" His heavy eyebrows furrowed. "But I didn't get to meet your friend."

I tried to choke back my sound of displeasure. In my experience, mothers always had an easier time labeling their daughters' sexuality. Very few fathers had ever acknowledged me as a girlfriend. I was typically introduced as so-and-so's "friend." Mr. Dyson seemed to confirm what was typical.

"Dad, this is my girlfriend Elle," Hunter said, huffing a frustrated sigh. "Elle, meet my dad."

I raised a hand to greet the man, but before I could utter a syllable, Hunter was tugging at my elbow and dragging me down the front walkway towards my car. I let her take the lead; honestly, I had had enough family time for one night. Instead of arguing with her, I turned my head and smiled graciously at the startled man and waved the hand not currently being seized by his daughter.

I unlocked the car and Hunter surprised me by kissing me soundly on the mouth. I was too startled to do anything but stand there while she pressed her lips against mine. I could taste the sweetness of the orange juice she'd had with dinner.

When she pulled away, she smiled wickedly. She grabbed my hand, interlocking our fingers, and spun to face her parents' home. "Bye, Dad!" she chirped. I twisted to look toward the front stoop and saw her startled father, still standing there.

He audibly cleared his throat and tugged at his necktie. "Bye, hun. Drive safe."

Hunter dropped my hand and marched to the passenger side of the car. I fumbled with my keys momentarily and weakly waved once more in the direction of her father. He nodded, still watching us, as I climbed into the car and started the engine before pulling away.

+++++

My car idled at an intersection. I stared at the road directly in front of me. Since we'd left her parents house, neither of us had spoken. I clenched and unclenched my jaw. "Hunter, you know it's not too late."

"For...?" She recognized my serious tone, I'm sure. She looked up and spotted Del Sol's outside the car window. "For coffee?" she guessed. "No. The caffeine will keep me up all night."

I pulled my eyes away from the road just long enough to catch Hunter's attention and frown. "Were you not at that dinner?"

Hunter folded her arms across her chest and looked straight ahead as well. "It could gone worse."

I slapped my palm against the steering wheel in frustration. "I'm not five, Hunter – we've all pretty much establish my age tonight – you don't have to sugarcoat things."

"I'm not sugarcoating anything!" Hunter vehemently insisted. "Look," she stated in a more reasonable tone as she turned slightly in her seat to face me. "My family is very much like a clan. It's hard to break into their inner circle. But you shouldn't let that discourage you. You think my last high school boyfriend got it easy?"

I tightened my grip at the top of the steering wheel. "But at least he was a boy and born in the same decade as you."

Hunter glared at me. "I thought we weren't going to let our age difference get between us anymore."

I stared straight ahead. I knew if I looked at her, my resolve would crumble. "Well, I guess I was wrong. Because it does matter."

In my peripheral vision I saw her wipe at her eyes. "Why are you acting like this?" she asked in a quiet, solemn tone.

I sighed tiredly. "I'm just being reasonable."

"No. You're being fatalistic," she bounced back accusatorily.

"Your family plays board games, Hunter," I tiredly countered. I was honestly exhausted. "You went to church every Sunday until recently. I feel like I'm dirtying your sheets."

She sulked, crossing her arms across her chest. "Isn't that what the laundry is for?"

The rest of the car ride consisted of a tense silence. I ran over a few sentences in my head to apologize or break up with her; I didn't know which to do at this point. I felt like I'd underestimated just how hard this relationship was going to be. Thankfully I didn't need my brain to drive, and my body drove my car back safely to the front of her apartment complex.

When I parked the car in front, but let the engine continue to run, Hunter looked genuinely surprised. The shock shifted to hurt, but she didn't say a word. Instead, she unfastened her seatbelt. "Have a nice night," she said stiffly.

I opened my mouth to say something, anything, but words failed me again. I watched her open the passenger side door, stiffly exit the vehicle, and walk around the front of my car. My headlights illuminated her figure, upright and proud. I waited a few moments, watching to be sure she got inside her apartment building. I sat a few more minutes in my car, just listening to the engine run. Finally, my mind still tormented with indecision, I shifted the car out of park and drove away.

+++++

I drove around town that night with no destination in mind. I just knew that I didn't want to go home. Sylvia would be waiting for me, and she'd warmed up to me a little more, but she still wasn't the cuddly fur ball I'd hoped for when I'd adopted her. She only became that creature when Hunter was near.

I ended up at Troian and Nikole's condo on the other side of town. As soon as Troian answered the door and saw me, she knew something wasn't right. I was quickly ushered inside and seated on a stool at the kitchen island. A variety of bottles of hard liquor appeared, courtesy of Nikole. I poured myself a tumbler full of scotch.

Troian eyeballed my drink choice. I don't think she'd ever seen me drink bourbon before. "I'm guessing dinner with the parents didn't go as planned."

I ran a single finger along the rim of my glass, feeling more than little morose. "Was this relationship doomed from the start?"

Troian exhaled loudly and blew her hair out of her face. "I don't know what to tell you, Bookworm. It certainly wasn't the most ideal situation from the start."

I breathed in sharply through my nose. "I think we broke up." The words felt funny in my mouth.

"What do you mean, you *think*?" Troian asked. She looked as exasperated with me as I felt.

Nikole's features hardened. "What happened?" I knew she felt protective of Hunter, especially after what had happened with Ruby.

"We were having a nice enough time at dinner, but then her mom asked how we met."

"And the shit hit the fan," Troian guessed.

I nodded. "Hunter stormed out, and I followed. And on the drive home I might have suggested her mom was right that we shouldn't be together." I roughly ran my hands through my hair. "I just can't shake the age difference."

"Why are you still hung up on that? Seriously, Elle." Troian shook her head. "Age is just a number. Hunter is probably the most mature girlfriend you've ever had. And it's not like you're the most grownup 30-year-old out there," she pointed out.

I made a frustrated noise. "I know, I know." I pulled at my hair.

"And soon she won't even be a student at your school anymore," Nikole added. "She's graduating in May."

"Then maybe I'll wait a few months and see if she wants to try again." I took a quick slug of my drink and swallowed it down with a grimace. The fiery alcohol burned against the back of my throat and I nearly coughed it back up.

"You're kidding, right?" Nikole looked appalled. "You can't just flit in and out of someone's life when it's convenient for you."

I rested my head in my hands. "I don't know what to do."

"If you really want to be with this girl, you won't let something paltry like 9 years get in the way," Troian said, punctuating her words with a shaking fist. "You make it work."

"You go over to her apartment right now, apologize, and stop screwing up," Nikole added.

Nikole's suggestion sounded horrible. I drained the rest of my drink too quickly. I reached for the bottle again.

Troian gave me a judgmental look. "You sure you want another drink?"

My hand halted and my features pinched together. "Of course I want another one," I said in an annoyed tone.

I knew I was being rude, but my day had soured so much, so quickly, I couldn't wait another moment to get home and crawl into bed. I wanted to bury myself in melancholy and down comforters.

I was screwing everything up. I was self-destructing.

Troian opened her mouth, but stopped when she felt her

girlfriend's hand at her waist.

"Just let her have this," Nikole advised in a low tone. She watched me fumble with the cap on the bottle of scotch as I prepared to serve myself again. "She'll feel like shit in the morning, but that's probably for the best."

Troian frowned. "Fine," she reluctantly conceded.

"I'm sitting right here," I grumbled.

"I reserve the right to talk about you in front of you when you're being an ass," Troian proclaimed.

"When did my life turn into such a drama?" I sighed and rubbed at my face. I abandoned pouring myself a second drink. Nikole was right. Another drink would make me feel worse than I already did.

I'd always thought relationships should be the easiest thing in your life. Whenever they became a complication and not a complement to my life is typically when I ran away. The world of work was supposed to be hard; love was supposed to be easy. But if I continued running when things got tough, I'd be perpetually single.

"That's life," Troian shrugged. "It's not supposed to be easy. If life had no challenges or complications, you'd take for granted the good things in your life."

"So what are you going to do? Walk away or fight for her?" Nikole pressed.

"I wish it were that easy, you guys." I stood up, and I could see the confusion and disappointment on both their faces. I felt it, too. I was confused about what to do and not a little bit disappointed with myself for being such a coward. "Thanks for the drink and the talk," I said, grabbing my jacket. "I've got to get home and feed Sylvia."

Troian gave me an incredulous look. "So that's it? All that obsessing about Hunter for months and months and months, and your answer is to go home and feed your cat?"

I shook my head sadly and started for the front door. "I'm sorry. I just need more time to figure this thing out."

"I'm not going to babysit her for you," I could hear Troian call behind me. "I'm not going to tell you when someone else swoops in and takes your place."

Her words made me pause my exit. "She wouldn't."

Troian didn't look convinced by my weak protest. "She might."

+++++

CHAPTER SIXTEEN

Troian nudged me in the ribs. "What do you think is up with that guy?" She nodded in the direction of a man seated in the exit row. He had the porthole-sized window drawn shut and one hand played solitaire on his phone while the other gripped at the overhead compartment lid. His jaw worked erratically around a piece of gum. He looked the picture of a nervous flyer, except one thing – he wore a commercial pilot uniform.

I gripped onto my armrests tighter; the chair squeaked from the stress. "Oh God," I mumbled forlornly. "We're going to die."

Troian chuckled. She reached in the pouch in front of her knees and pulled out a water bottle. "No. We're fine," she reassured me.

I eyeballed my best friend. "How can you be so sure?"

She uncapped the water bottle and took a small sip. "Because *that* dude's not flying the plane."

The airplane bounced a little with turbulence. I shut my eyes tight and hummed "I Love Paris," beneath my breath.

"Why did you agree to come if you're such a bad flyer?" Troian asked me.

I opened one eye. "And miss your big day? No way."

"It's not that big of a deal."

"No. You're only just a meeting with a major studio who's interested in turning one of your ideas into a television show," I deadpanned. "Not a big deal at all." Troian's modesty was seriously baffling sometimes.

Nikole returned from the airplane bathroom and sat back in her aisle seat. They'd agreed to let me have the window seat so I didn't throw up. It was very admirably, actually. She gave Troian, who sat in the center of the three-seat aisle, a quick kiss before putting her headphones back on and returning to a movie she'd been watching on her tablet.

Troian's hungry gaze on her girlfriend was apparent.

"Hey," I said, garnering her attention. I snapped my fingers in front of her face. "No Mile High Clubbing when I'm around, okay?"

My friend swung her head around to glare at me. "Are you going to cock-block me this entire trip?"

"Maybe," I shrugged. "If I'm not having sex, I don't want anyone else to have any either."

Troian narrowed her eyes at me. "I'm second-guessing inviting you, and we haven't even landed."

Troian and Nikole had advertised the long weekend as the perfect escape. My job was to keep Nikole company while Troian was in meetings pitching her ideas. We were going to go to the beach, drink fruity mixed drinks, and look at girls in bikinis. Normally that would have sounded like the ultimate getaway, but I was still too much in my head about Hunter.

After the disaster that was dinner with Hunter's family, we hadn't completely cut off ties, and it wasn't entirely clear if we'd broken up or if we were just going through a rough patch. Since that night, nearly a week ago, we'd talked a few times on the phone, mostly awkward recountings of how our respective days had been.

I'd been upfront with her about going away with Troian and Nikole for the long weekend. I didn't want her to worry in case she dropped by my house unannounced. She'd offered to feed Sylvia while I was gone because she was the only one the cat liked anyway, but I wouldn't let her. It felt too much like taking advantage of her excessive kindness. I was having Emily, my teacher mentor and co-worker, take care of Sylvia instead.

"When's your meeting with the production company tomorrow?" I asked.

"Bright and early at 10am."

"Are you going to be able to enjoy tonight or are you going to be an anxious mess?"

"Hey," Troian complained. "I'd like to see you have an important meeting and not go a little crazy about it. Just wait until your tenure review meeting comes up."

I'd been trying not to think about that meeting. In less than a month's time, my future with the university would be decided. I would either get a promotion and tenure, or I would be denied tenure and my contract would be terminated. I turned away and stared out the small, oval window to enjoy my view of the tops of clouds. Outside, the sun was hot and it warmed me through the thick Plexiglas. The window was blemished with cloudy water spots; I wondered how often airplanes got washed, if at all. Maybe they just scheduled the particularly dirty planes to fly through Seattle.

Coming on this trip with Troian and Nikole felt like running away, but I'd reasoned it would at least distract me from the chaos that was my romantic life. But maybe it felt a little like running away because that's exactly what I was doing.

+++++

"Hey Bookworm." Nikole nudged my knee with her own. "Don't tell me you brought actual work with you on vacation."

"Sorry," I apologized, "but I've really got to get this done." I looked up from my tablet. "I finally got a publisher for my collection of short stories, so now I've got copyediting to do."

When our plane had landed in Los Angeles the previous night, we'd gone directly to our hotel for an early evening because of Troian's morning meeting. Now, Nikole and I sat poolside in a private cabana at our hotel, soaking in the southern California sun that evaded us so effectively in the Midwest.

Nikole wrinkled her nose. "Sounds thrilling."

I made a humming noise of agreement. "I'm just happy I finally got a publisher for this book. The whole process is ego shattering – one rejection letter after the next. I really needed a win," I noted. "Between that and the Hunter stuff –."

"Take a drink."

I rolled my eyes, but did as she said. I unscrewed the cap on the vodka bottle that was perched on our deck table and poured myself a shot. "Want one?" I offered.

Nikole shook her head. "I'm not the one that broke the rule."

Troian had surprised me the previous night by pulling a bottle of vodka from her luggage. She said the alcohol was to prevent me from being miserable on the weekend trip. The rules were simple: if I mentioned Hunter's name, I had to do a shot. The consequences of breaking that rule didn't make much sense to me though. I would probably bring up her name in conversation a lot more if I was drunk. But maybe that was the whole point – to poison my liver and punish me for being such a coward. At least Nikole couldn't hear my thoughts; I would be passed out by now if she could.

Nikole clucked her tongue against the roof of her mouth. "I don't know how you and Troi do it. Writing. Putting yourself out there just to be critiqued. I don't think I could handle being so vulnerable all the time."

"I wouldn't do it if I didn't have to." I slipped my sunglasses back on so I didn't have to squint into the sun. "But it's publish or perish for me. I need this for my promotion."

"Ah, yes. The highly sought-after security of tenure," Nikole said, nodding. "Then they can't fire you for being a pervert."

"Now you sound like Troi."

Nikole chuckled. "You lack subtlety, Elle. You've been staring at that girl over there for at least 5 minutes." She nodded in the direction of a blonde girl in a bikini sitting at the swim-up bar. "And I haven't seen you blink once."

I shrugged. Maybe I had been staring a little bit. "She's cute."

"And she's totally your type," Nikole added. "Blonde, pale, and long-limbed. I'm sure your staring has *nothing* to do with the fact that she looks like She-Who-Shall-Not-Be-Named."

I frowned. It didn't seem fair to compare Hunter to a Harry Potter villain. I was the one who kept messing up, not her. "Maybe I should try something different from now on," I mused out loud. "Small, short, and exotic."

"Should I be worried?" Nikole looked at me over the top of her sunglasses. "You just described my girlfriend."

"Hah," I snorted. "Don't tell Troian I said that then. She'll never let it drop."

"Your secret is safe with me," she grinned conspiratorially. "Why don't you go talk to that girl?"

"She's not gay." And I still wanted my girlfriend.

"You don't know that. Maybe she's just been waiting for the right girl to come along. You could be that girl."

"I don't want to ditch you."

Nikole threw her arm over the top of the lounge chair and stretched out her legs. "I'm sure I'll manage without you," she said, looking and sounding like she might take a nap in the sun. "If you insist that you're over Hunter, go over there and talk to that girl."

"Take a shot."

"I'm pretty sure the rules don't apply to me," she quipped.

I frowned. "I never said I was over her."

"You know what I mean. Go over there; see if it feels wrong to you. If it does, you know you're an ass who needs to fight for her girl the moment we get back home."

I frowned deeper. "I'm out of excuses."

"Go get her, Tiger."

I eased myself into the pool. The chlorinated water was cold against my sun-warmed skin, but it wasn't entirely unpleasant. I was a strong swimmer, having grown up on the Great Lakes and it took me only a few strokes to reach the poolside bar. Seated at one of the submerged stools was the slender blonde woman Nikole had caught me staring at. Her dark blue bikini looked dynamite against her alabaster skin. Nikole was right. I *did* have a type.

I sat down at the empty stool beside her. A college football game was being broadcast on the flat-screen television above the bar. I didn't recognize either of the teams playing; I was a bad lesbian and knew very little about sports.

I ordered myself a pineapple and Malibu, something I hadn't done since my sorority days as an undergrad. When I got my drink, I fidgeted uneasily. I wanted to be able to talk to the woman seated beside me, but I had no idea what to say. I wondered if Nikole was watching my every move, silently chuckling at my lack of Game. I looked over once in her direction, but I couldn't tell what was going on behind her large sunglasses.

"Goddamn it, White," the blue bikini woman yelled. "Catch the damn ball."

I didn't know how to flirt. I didn't trust myself – I'd probably try to be smooth and end up saying something about guys mishandling balls. But beyond that, I didn't *want* to flirt. I wanted the woman in the blue bikini to be Hunter. Instead of coming up with a line that was sure to fail, I twisted in my seat and faced the woman.

"Hi. I'm Elle."

Something about my awkward introduction seemed to amuse her. "Samantha."

We made small talk under the indirect shade of an oversized thatch roof. She was from the East Coast, vacationing with a group of friends who were currently away getting spa treatments. She didn't like strangers handling her like that, regardless if they were professionals and it was their job, so she'd decided to wait for them at the pool. She wasn't gay, but she still accepted the drink I bought her. Even though I knew I wasn't her type, it felt good to chat without worrying about moral or ethical ramifications. I didn't realize how coiled I had become because of my attraction to Hunter.

About an hour later, after the football game ended, I went back to the poolside bungalow where I'd left Nikole. Troian had returned; she didn't look happy, so I assumed the worst.

"How did the pitch meeting go?" I asked as I sat down in the unoccupied lounge chair next to her.

"Great," she said, tight-lipped. "They loved the idea and they want me to send them a pilot script to look over."

"That's fantastic, Troi!" I cheered. Her body language didn't mirror her news. Something was wrong with my friend. "Are you not happy with how the meeting went?" I guessed.

"The meeting was perfect."

"Then what's with the face?" I asked.

"You ditched my girlfriend to go flirt."

"She told me to," I defended myself. If it hadn't been at her insistence, I would have remained poolside with her. "And I wasn't flirting."

"You left and boys bought her drinks."

"You know you don't have to worry about Nikole," I laughed. "She's as loyal as they come. She just needs to smile less."

"But why don't *I* get free drinks?" Troian pouted.

"Wait. You're upset because you want guys to hit on *you?*" I asked, shaking my head. "Troi, you don't even drink. *And* you don't like boys."

Her bottom lip stuck out even more. "They don't need to know that."

"I'll never understand you."

"Welcome to my world," Nikole quipped. She drank something

pink from a long straw. I would bet my bikini bottoms she hadn't paid for a drink all day. I wondered how many drinks she'd had though. She had a great poker face when it came to alcohol. Her dangerous smile just got a little bit wider.

"I'm getting fried," I announced. "We should go back to the rooms and change so we can celebrate your successful meeting."

"That sounds like a great idea," Troian nodded. Her pout had disappeared. "And I know exactly how we can celebrate."

+++++

"A strip club?" I exclaimed. "Really? *This* is how you want to celebrate?"

Troian nodded furiously. "Dude, this place lets you eat bomb sushi off of naked women. Hello! That sounds like something that should be on everyone's Bucket List."

"Why couldn't we just find a good sushi place to go to instead?" I whined.

"This *is* a good sushi place," Troian exclaimed. "I've read a ton of write-ups about it in like a million blogs and magazines."

Nikole nodded. "She's actually not lying," she confirmed her girlfriend's praise. "Anyway, I've been curious about their food, too."

I sighed despondently. There was no hope for a change in venue if Nikole was siding with Troian. I was outnumbered. I would just have to suck it up.

I looked around at the modest-sized "gentleman's club." I'd never been to a strip club before, and I hadn't known what to expect. Troian had talked up the club the entire cab ride. Apparently the place was supposed to be like an adult Disneyland or something. To me though, it was all a little overwhelming. The club was teeming with crowds, busy I thought even for a Saturday night in Hollywood. The women, the *dancers*, walking around and openly flirting with the club's patrons were pretty, but in a very plastic, uniform way. They all had the same breasts and the same teeth. To make matters worse, I couldn't even order a real drink – some law about nudity and alcohol. I stared down at my glass of plain orange juice and shook my head. What a waste.

"I've got an idea," Troian announced. Her "ideas" always made me nervous.

"What's your idea?" I hesitantly asked.

"I'm buying you a lap dance."

"No you are not."

"It's perfect," she tried to reason. "If you can let a hot, beautiful stranger grind on your unmentionables, then you're over Hunter. No harm. No foul."

I grimaced.

"Just don't let Elle pick the girl," Nikole warned her girlfriend.

"Why not?" Troian asked.

"Because she'll pick that one." She imperceptibly nodded toward one corner of the club where a woman with long hair, the color of corn silk, stood. Her hair was down and slid past her bare shoulders. She was long-limbed with fine bones and small, but natural breasts. I think they were the first real breasts I'd seen since we'd gotten here. I held my breath until I saw her in profile. She had a cute, upturned nose, but it wasn't Hunter's nose. Close. So very close.

"Wow. Doppelganger," Troian openly admired.

I made a face. "Whatever. She looks nothing like her."

"Then you have no reason to reject my offer." Troian's grin was nearly infectious. If I didn't feel so uncomfortable in my surroundings I probably would have smiled as well.

I stared at her incredulously. "You really want to buy me a dance?"

She nodded enthusiastically. "I'm ready to make it rain, but I've got the 'Ol Ball And Chain," she said jerking her thumb in Nikole's direction.

I shook my head. It was cute when Troian insisted she wasn't completely whipped because we all knew the truth.

Despite my protests, Troian and Nikole picked out a stripper for me and pre-paid for the dance so I couldn't back out. The woman never told me her stage name, and I didn't bother to ask. She led me down a short, dark hallway, away from my friends and the main part of the club, and sat me down at a solitary chair. She pulled back a set of thick curtains, partitioning off the space from the rest of the club.

I couldn't deny that she was attractive. Despite their incessant teasing, Nikole and Troian had chosen a tall blonde for me. She

201

wore a matching black bra and panty set that contrasted against her pale skin. The lacy convertible bra struggled to contain the ample breasts that heaved beneath their snug confines and the tiny lace underwear left little to the imagination, doing little more than covering her most intimate parts. She wore a red garter belt slung low on her chiseled hips, and the straps clung to strong thighs and connected to the sheer black thigh-high nylons that covered the expanse of her slender legs.

A song filled the stale air and she began to dance. I didn't recognize the music, but that didn't surprise me; I didn't have a Stripper Billboard Hits playlist. The woman stalked toward me, expertly maneuvering on stiletto heels that would have had me tripping in a few steps. A predatory grin spread across her face as she straddled me, slinging her right leg and then the left over my lap, lightly resting her barely-covered backside on my upper thighs. I could feel her thigh muscles twitch and strain as she hovered there, not wanting to rest her full weight on me.

"Feel free to touch," she said. "I make sure the male clients follow the rules, but I don't mind if the women get a little hands-on." She gave me a conspiratorial wink.

"Oh, uh, I wasn't planning on it," I stammered awkwardly.

She shrugged, noncommittally. "Your loss." She swung her hips from side to side, dipping low every few beats. She ran her hands across her bare torso, the defined curve of her abdominal muscles flexing beneath her own touch. Her hands traveled north, up to her breasts and she squeezed the globes in her palms, the flesh molding and melding between her fingers. Despite the unsettling feeling gnawing at the pit of my stomach, my eyes were transfixed on those hands.

She placed a hand on either side of me, gripping onto the arms of the chair. She leaned forward slightly, and her breasts threatened to spill out of their lacy confines. She snapped her head back, flipping her long, blonde waves and arching her back.

"So what brings you to Hell-A?"

I wasn't expecting the question and it caught me off-guard. I'd never had a lap dance before, and I guess I'd never thought much about what happened behind closed doors. I guess it made sense that the dancers would talk to the client. It normalized it, I suppose.

"What makes you think I'm not from here?"

"Sweetie, no one's actually from Hollywood. We're all transplants looking for a piece of the American Dream."

"I'm just here for a few days with friends. Long weekend vacation," I supplied.

She made an acknowledging humming noise. "Good trip so far?" She laughed before I could respond. "What am I saying? *Of course* you're having a good time. You've got *me* on your lap."

I laughed nervously. I didn't know what to say, what to talk about. I hated small talk and the fact that I was conversing with a half-naked woman who periodically thrust her breasts into my face didn't help matters.

She stood up from my lap and turned to face away, providing me with an eyeful of her pert backside hugged by the thin lace straps of her thong and garter belt. She ran her hands through her hair, continuing to shake her hips to the beat, lifting her locks toward the sky. My eyes traveled north as well, admiring the strong back and shoulder blades that flexed and twitched like the smooth muscles of a panther or jaguar.

She gracefully bent over and ran her hands along the insides of her nylon-encased thighs. She looked back at me with a smirk on her lips. She stood straight again and returned to her position on my lap, this time facing away. She arched her back, her barely-covered chest thrusting out, and she rested her head back against my shoulder. I was rewarded with an unobstructed view of fleshy breasts and a tight abdomen. She ran her fingertips down the exposed flesh spilling over the top of her bra, down her flat stomach, and between her finely muscled thighs.

When she began moving her backside in erotic figure eights on top of my thighs, I couldn't take anymore.

"I'm sorry. I can't do this."

Before she could react to my dismissal, I was out of my chair and out of the private room. The music in the club felt too loud. The bass throbbing from the main stage echoed so much it was making it hard to breathe. I found my friends in the same place where I'd left them. In my absence, they'd ordered sushi.

"Hey, jackweed," Troian called out when she spotted me coming closer. "What are you doing back so soon? I paid for two full songs."

"I know," I sighed. "But it just felt wrong."

Troian sat up straighter, looking alert and ready for action. "Did Blondie suck? I'll go talk to management and we'll get you a different dancer."

"No, no. She was fine," I placated.

Nikole placed her hand over Troian's. "Hun, I think she means it didn't feel right because it wasn't *Hunter* grinding on her lap." She gave me a sympathetic smile.

Troian glared at her girlfriend. "You're lucky there's no alcohol here. You're not supposed to say her name."

A sudden wave of emotion hit me. I felt like I was drowning in guilt and regret. I grabbed my jacket. "I'm gonna grab a cab back to the hotel. You guys should stay though," I insisted. "We're supposed to be celebrating Troi's success, and I'm just being a downer."

"Are you sure?" Nikole asked. "We could come back with you."

"I'm fine, really." I waved her off, urging them to stay. "I just need some fresh air and a soft mattress. You guys have fun."

+++++

The taxi ride back to the hotel was short, but quiet. I was thankful that the driver didn't try to start a conversation with me. I'd had too much small talk with strangers for one day. I got back to my room some time after 2 am. I took a quick shower to rinse the sweat and stripper off before crawling into bed. I was thankful Troian had insisted we stay at a nice hotel so I didn't have to try to sleep while hearing the people in the next room having sex or the sounds of the city still screaming outside.

When I crawled into bed, I lay on my back for a while, still wired from my night out. Normally after a few beers I would have had no problem falling asleep, but juice and Red Bull and naked women were not a cocktail for rest. I grabbed my phone off the bedside table and looked at the time. I was tempted to call Hunter, just to hear her voice before I fell asleep, but I was mindful of the two-hour difference. It would be after 4am back home, and she'd be getting up in a few hours for her internship at the hospital.

I flipped through my contacts until I got to her number. I stared at the picture I'd assigned to her name. It was a black and white close-up of her smiling face. She was holding onto Sylvia, and they were both looking straight into the camera. My thumb hovered over the call button, but I locked my phone instead and returned it to the end table.

+++++

The next morning, after working out for an hour at the hotel's fitness center, I had breakfast poolside. I wasn't alone for long, however, before Troian unceremoniously plopped down in a chair at my table.

"Morning, sunshine," I greeted.

Troian squinted back at me from behind oversized sunglasses and grunted something unintelligible.

"What's wrong?" I laughed. "You look like you're hung-over, but I know you didn't have anything to drink last night."

"Long night," she grumbled. "Didn't sleep." She grabbed my orange juice and smelled it, ascertaining if there was alcohol in it, no doubt. She took an experimental sip.

"Gross," I gagged. "You know I don't need to know about what you and Nik do in your spare time."

"Asshole," she cursed at me while continuing to drink my orange juice. "I was too nervous and excited to sleep so I stayed up working on the pilot."

"Oh. Not as fun." I chuckled at the sour look on her face. I loved how expressive Troian was about everything. She wasn't overly dramatic; she just wore her emotions out loud. "Speaking of Nik," I noted, noticing her absence, "where's your better half this morning?"

Troian pulled her sunglasses off and rubbed the bridge of her nose. "She's still getting ready in the room," she said through a yawn. "You know how she is. She'll be down when she finishes primping."

"What's the plan for the day?" I asked. Troian only had one scheduled meeting this trip, which she'd done yesterday. We had one more full day in California before our flight the next morning. I deferred to Troian's judgment since she was far more familiar with the Los Angeles area than me.

"As soon as Nik gets down here I thought we could go to the beach. I want to get a little color before we return to The Great White North."

I pushed my chair back just enough so I was no longer beneath the protective umbrella. The morning sun was warm on my skin.

"You know," I said as I sipped my coffee, "I could get used to life out here. This weather is amazing," I approved. I slid my sunglasses back over my face. "And the scenery's not too bad either," I murmured as a curvy woman in a bikini walked by.

"You're such a hornball." Troian commandeered the rest of my breakfast and moved on to my bagel. She must really have been stressed out; she was eating carbs.

"I have a healthy sexual appetite," I defended myself. "There's nothing wrong with that."

"Uh huh." Troian finished the last of my Everything bagel. "All I know is that when we get back home you'd better not start crying about how you messed things up with Hunter."

I glanced at my phone, which sat useless on the table. I hadn't received a single call or text from Hunter since we landed. I'd texted to let her know we'd made it to California. She'd responded with a single letter: K.

"I thought about calling her last night."

"Before or after the lap dance?" Troian pointedly asked.

I frowned, feeling instantly guilty. She wasn't really accusing me of anything, but in a way she was. I never should have let Troian buy me a dance if I was still clinging to hope that Hunter and I would reconcile. If I was serious about making it work I shouldn't be ogling girls in bikinis every chance I got. I shouldn't have taken this trip at all. I should have stayed behind and talked, not run away.

"Uh oh," Troian worried out loud. "I broke you, didn't I?"

I looked at my friend through the tears that blurred my vision. "It's really over, isn't it?"

+++++

CHAPTER SEVENTEEN

After the long weekend in California, I threw myself into my work so I didn't have time to think about Hunter. My tenure review was coming up shortly before the end of the semester, so maybe it was fortuitous that I could refocus on my career without the distraction of a significant other. I didn't think we'd broken up, but I knew the longer I waited to talk to her again, the more broken we became. I had expected at least a text message from her, but my phone remained silent beyond the few messages I received from Troian, reminding me of what an asshole I was.

I felt paranoid on campus, sure we'd run into each other walking to and from classes. But since it was her senior year, she had few actual classes and spent the majority of her day at her internship with the local hospital. I thought I saw her everywhere though, but it just turned out my campus was populated with a lot of blonde co-eds.

While I was able to work with relative focus when I was in my faculty office, that all changed when I returned home at the end of the workday. Even though we had been far from living together, my house felt more empty than usual, and I seemed to be surrounded by things that made me think of her. It was especially problematic in my home office, where her light perfume still seemed to cling in the air. And like a masochist, I found myself spending more time in that room than usual. The little red couch where Hunter often did her homework had become my default location in the house.

The significance of the current day wasn't lost on me. It was Hunter's birthday. Her 21st birthday. I wanted to call and wish her a happy birthday, but I didn't want her to think I was checking up on her, keeping tabs, making sure she didn't go overboard. And I worried that talking to me might upset her and lead her to drink even more tonight. And I couldn't just text her. It would have been too flippant and distant. So instead I maintained my radio silence. I had wanted to do something special for her on this day. But instead, I was ignoring her.

Sylvia hopped up on my lap. She was a finicky animal who you could only pet when she wanted it to happen. The rest of the time she'd take a swipe at you if you tried to give her any attention. It made me wonder what her life had been like before I'd adopted her. She was in a rare, affectionate mood this evening, so I put down my book to pay attention to her instead.

Our uncustomary cuddle time was interrupted by my cell phone ringing. I recognized the ringtone and answered the call on the second ring, my chest feeling tight with anticipation.

"Elle?" Even without looking at the phone number, I'd know her voice.

"Hunter." Saying her name was like a prayer. I hadn't allowed myself the indulgence since my California trip and whenever I'd said her name in front of Troian and Nikole, I'd had to drink hard alcohol.

"I was just in a car accident."

"Oh my God. Are you alright, sweetie?" I mentally winced. The endearment felt so natural falling off my tongue.

"I'm okay," she said. She sounded so small on the phone. "Just a little bit shaken up." Her voice wavered with emotion. "I've never been in an accident before. I didn't know who else to call."

"Where are you?" I asked, immediately shooing Sylvia from my lap and grabbing my keys and jacket.

"59th and State."

I mentally pictured the area. It was practically in the heart of campus. "I'll be right there."

"No, Elle, you don't –"

"I'll be right there," I repeated with more force.

Her words were quiet. "Thank you."

+++++

As I jogged the short distance to campus, my mind went back to Hunter's words: *"I didn't know who else to call."* The first time I'd ever gotten into a car accident – an asshole had T-boned me going through a red light – I'd immediately called my dad even though we no longer lived in the same state. It was just my instinctive move. Something goes wrong with the car, call Dad. The fact that Hunter hadn't called her own parents, who only lived a few minutes away, troubled me. Were they punishing her for our relationship or was it the other way around?

In just a few minutes, I was close to the intersection where Hunter had said she was. As I jogged closer, I could see the fire truck and ambulance at the scene. My heart seized in my chest. *You were just on the phone with her,* I reminded myself while my chest felt like it was exploding. *She's fine. She's got to be fine.*

A small crowd had gathered at the scene. It was between afternoon classes and a number of gawkers huddled around the wreck. The two cars had been maneuvered off of the main street and rolled into a student parking lot so traffic could continue. The other car, a charcoal luxury vehicle, had its front end destroyed. I saw Hunter's car, a silver nondescript four-door compact car. The passenger side was smashed in, both doors crumpled up, and the front wheel well was severely bent. My panic deepened.

I scanned the scene frantically until a glimpse of familiar corn-silk blonde caught my eye. I saw Hunter sitting on the back edge of an opened-door ambulance. A paramedic was standing in the way, and from where I was standing, I couldn't see if she'd been injured.

Her name was out of my mouth before I could restrain myself. "Hunter!"

Her grey-blue eyes jerked in the direction of my call. When she looked my way, our eyes met; hers, wide and startled, filled with tears. I wove my way through the ever-growing crowd of onlookers until I erased the distance between us. She threw herself into my arms and buried her face into my shoulder. My arms were only too happy to wrap around her shaking form. We stood there, not speaking. Finally, reluctantly, I pulled back. Her face turned towards mine. On her temple was a butterfly Band-Aid. My fingertips brushed over the small bandage. "You're hurt."

Her hand went to the wound. "It's just a bump."

I searched her face, looking for other signs of injury, but found none – just those wet, grey eyes staring back at me.

"What happened?"

She sucked in a deep breath. "I was leaving campus to go to my internship at the hospital. I guess there was some black ice or something because Professor Drake went through his stop sign and smashed into my passenger side."

I knew Martin Drake. He was an arrogant tenured professor in the Poli-Sci department. Even though he wasn't in my department, it was a small campus and his reputation preceded him. He was one of those Good 'Ol Boys who students often complained to me about, especially the female students who felt overlooked for their male classmates. If it had been another staff member, someone less obnoxious and misogynistic, I might not have snapped.

The man in question was on his cell phone a few yards away. "Hey, Drake!" I hollered. "What the hell were you thinking?" The man in his ugly pleated slacks didn't hear me or was ignoring me.

"Elle," Hunter hushed. "People are looking."

"Let them," I snapped. "Did he even apologize to you?" I asked her.

Her eyes cast down. "He's been on his phone the whole time."

"That son of a bitch," I growled. He probably hadn't even checked in with Hunter to make sure she was okay – just hopped on his phone to call his insurance company.

Hunter's hand at my wrist was the only thing keeping me from going face-to-face with that asshole. It wasn't a particularly tight grasp, and I could have pulled away with little effort, but just her light touch was keeping me from flying off the handle.

"Did you talk to the police already?"

She nodded. "They've come and gone. I'm just waiting for the tow-truck."

A particularly vicious wind chose that moment to whip at my face. "It's freezing out here," I chattered, jerking at the collar of my wool coat. Winter was coming soon. "Why don't you wait at my house? They have your number; they'll call when they get here."

She crossed her arms and her face now looked grave. "That's nice of you to offer, but you don't have to be nice to me anymore."

I opened and shut my mouth a few times, feeling blindsided by her abrupt change in attitude. "Did I do something wrong?"

"No. You freaking out at Professor Drake actually helped calm me down," she said carefully. "But I'm just remembering I'm still supposed to be mad at you."

"If you're still mad, why did you call me?"

"I told you – I didn't know who else to call."

"Not your parents? Or your roommate?"

"I'm not talking to my parents right now. And Sara's in class."

I didn't know what to say. My lips pursed and I nodded. "Okay. Well, if you change your mind, Sylvia and I are just a few minutes away." I couldn't tell if it was the cold chill of the day that was causing tears to prick at the corners of my eyes or the emotion of the moment. Lies. I knew why I felt like crying. She was standing in front of me.

Hunter must have seen the emotion on my face. Her own features softened, and she placed a hand at my wrist. The familiar touch did nothing to help keep my tears under control. "Elle. Thank you for coming. I—."

"Don't worry about it." I tugged again at my jacket collar, pulling it up higher around my face like a shield. It wasn't really that cold; I was used to the weather. But I didn't want her to see my face and know how much I was hurting.

+++++

Early the next morning I found myself standing on the front stoop of her apartment building, flowers in hand. I pressed the button to call up to her apartment and waited. Her voice cut through the eerie silence of that Saturday morning. There seemed to be nobody awake yet, not even the birds. "Hello?"

"Hi," I said, scratching at the back of my neck. I felt vulnerable standing out front even though I knew she couldn't see me. "Can I come in?"

I waited a painful, awkward moment before the front door buzzed and I heard the telltale clicking of the entrance unlocking. I quickly grabbed onto the handle and yanked, gaining entrance and hopefully forgiveness.

I bounded up the quick flight of stairs to her second-floor apartment. I wondered if her roommate was at home. One of these days I'd have to make an effort to get to know her. When I reached Hunter's apartment, the door was open and she was standing in the threshold, looking unhappy.

I thrust the bouquet of flowers out in front of me. I was actually proud of my selection – they weren't the impersonal gas station variety. I'd gone to the flower shop near my house that morning and had handpicked a few wildflowers and some more traditional, recognizable flowers. "Happy belated birthday."

She seemed unimpressed by my efforts, however. "I thought you didn't like cut flowers." She had an uncanny knack for remembering what I considered trivial details. I suppose Nikole might have mentioned something to her about it though. She was always horrified by my dispassionate relationship with cut flowers.

"They aren't for me though," I pointed out. I gave them a little shake, drawing her attention to the bouquet about which I'd been so proud.

She finally took them, her face still unreadable. She took a few steps backwards, back in to her apartment. "Do you want to come in? Sara's at church." My stomach dropped. My Hunter used to go to church with her roommate.

I stepped past the threshold, into her two-bedroom apartment. She wandered away toward the back of the apartment, and rather than hanging out unsure in the front foyer, I followed. The apartment was small and it didn't take long for me to find her. She was in the kitchen, looking through the cabinets until she found a glass vase. Scissors were produced and she began snipping off the ends of the flowers and arranging them in the tall, blue vessel. The bright oranges, reds, and yellows of the wildflowers contrasted nicely with the deep blue hue.

I cleared my throat. "I came to apologize."

"About?"

"Meeting your parents stressed me out a lot more than I thought it was going to."

She nodded serenely, but didn't look up from her task. "I know. And I shouldn't have been so flippant about how badly it went."

"I'm sorry about that, too. I'm just more stressed than usual, I guess." I frowned and looked down at the light-colored linoleum flooring. "I know it's no excuse, but my Tenure Review is coming up, and even though I've been jumping through all the hoops they've asked me to, I'm still nervous about it." I looked up and found her staring intensely at me. "This is the thing I've been working towards all my life, you know?"

"I know, Ellio."

Her use of the nickname tugged at my heart. I braved a step forward her and took the scissors from her hands, just in case. I set them down on the countertop and cautiously wrapped my arms around her waist and pulled her close. "Am I forgiven?" I asked quietly. There seemed a stillness in the room that I dared not disturb.

Her lips quirked, but she nodded. I closed my eyes and let out a deep breath. The tears that tumbled down my cheeks, however, were an unexpected addition to my apology. "I missed you so much."

I felt her fingertips sweep along my cheekbones. "Ellio, it's okay," she hushed as she wiped away the tears. "You don't always have to be the strong, stable one. I can be your rock sometimes, too – if you'll let me."

I breathed noisily out my nose and pressed my forehead against hers. "I have a *really* hard time letting anyone take care of me. It's one of the reasons why I don't let myself get sick."

She pulled back and quirked an eyebrow. "You don't *let* yourself get sick? I didn't realize you had those kind of special powers?"

I smiled cheekily. "It's all mind over matter, baby. I never get a cold."

"You know that's like the Kiss-of-Death, right?" she countered, looking amused. "You just totally jinxed yourself. You'll probably contract the Ebola virus now."

"Stop it," I waved, making a disgruntled face. "Don't distract me. I'm trying to have a serious talk with you."

The smile immediately fell from her lips and her face became somber. "I'm sorry," she said, straight faced, her voice nearly robotic. "I didn't realize we were still having a serious moment."

"Well, we are," I huffed. I didn't want to let her go. Having her let me hold her this close was something I'd missed more than I realized. "After this Tenure Review is over, it'll either be very, very good news or very, very bad news. And either way, I'll need to get out of this town for a little bit to either celebrate or lick my wounds."

Hunter's serious face became a little injured. "Oh." She wet her lips. "For how long?"

I shook my head. "I'm not sure. How long can you get away for? I know your internship still goes over Winter Break."

Hunter blinked once, apparently needing a moment to let my

question register. "Wait." She blinked again. "You want me to come with you?"

"Of course I do." I tightened my grip on her, never wanting to let go. "Did you think I'd just vanish for a couple of weeks and leave you behind to fend for yourself?"

"I'm not a rescue animal," Hunter snorted in protest. "I managed just fine before I met you."

I shook my head and grinned. "Sometimes I wonder."

+++++

CHAPTER EIGHTEEN

Later that evening I returned to Hunter's apartment. I knocked and waited a few moments before the door was abruptly thrown open. The scowl on Hunter's face was quickly replaced with a look of surprise. "You're early," she said in an emotionless voice that would normally make me anxious.

Because of the car accident and our fight she hadn't done anything yesterday to celebrate her 21st birthday. I wanted to make it right, even if it was short notice and the day after her actual birthday. My ability to throw her a proper birthday party was limited though. Her family was out of the question and I still hadn't met Sara, her roommate, or really any of her friends. But I knew that would come in time. She was being mindful of my desire to keep a low-profile, at least until she graduated in May.

"I couldn't wait to see you," I told her truthfully. I wasn't really that early – maybe just half an hour. I wasn't going to let her sour mood ruin our night before it even began. We'd stay in instead until I could turn that frown upside-down. Actually, I kind of preferred that to going out, but it was her birthday, and this is how she wanted to spend it.

I grabbed onto her wrist as she started to turn away. "Hey, are you okay?" I gently asked.

"I'm fine," she insisted. "I just really want this night to go well, you know? I kind of feel like this is the Universe giving us one final chance."

I nodded and leaned in until our foreheads were just barely

touching. It felt so amazing to be this close to her again. It was like my nerve endings were hyper-aware of everything surrounding us, and yet, at the same time, I was completely consumed by her.

"You sure you want to go out tonight?" I asked. I reached up and gently brushed a strand of hair out of her face. "We could always stay in." My thumb stroked along her right cheekbone.

She swallowed hard, her nostrils flared, and the vivid image of taking her, hard, against the kitchen counter suddenly fluttered through my mind. I shuddered and closed my eyes at the intensity. I wondered if it would always be like this between us.

Her voice pulled at me. "We should get going before you make me change my mind."

I couldn't help my smirk. I could make this difficult for her, harder for her to leave this place instead of us tumbling straight into her bed, but I didn't. So instead of lingering any longer, I took her hand and pulled her toward the front door.

+++++

I stared at the nondescript neon sign that announced the name of the club. Peggy's. Hunter's hand was light on my waist, anchoring me when I was more than ready to take flight. "You ready for this, Professor Graft?"

"Let's do it." I turned and gave her a weak smile. "It's not every day that my girlfriend can legally drink."

When we walked inside the bar, I paused long enough to slip out of my jacket. I froze when I recognized the bartender working tonight. Megan, the bartender whom Troian had been convinced was going to be my wife, gave me a smile. I was surprised when she seemed to recognize me.

"Long time no see, Dr. Elle."

"Megan," I greeted, trying to not appear more awkward than I felt. "How have you been?"

"Can't complain," she shrugged, wiping down the bar top. "Went back home to New York for a few months, but Peggy kept my job for me."

"That was nice of her," I said, not really sure what else to say. Apparently Peggy was a real person. I learned something new everyday.

"Yeah. It was." She raised her painted eyebrows. "What can I get for you and your friend?"

"Oh, sorry," I said, turning to Hunter who stood silently beside me. "Megan, this is my girlfriend, Hunter."

Hunter folded her arms across her chest. "Nice to meet you." Her face was impassive, and the warmth of her words didn't reach her tone.

Megan nodded in greeting. "Two beers?" A strange smile passed her lips. "Or maybe shots?"

"Two ambers will be fine," I said in a rush before she could say anything incriminating. "Whatever's on tap." I hoped it was dark enough inside that my red face wasn't visible.

I paid for our drinks and gave Megan a brief wave. When I turned back to Hunter to hand her a beer, her lips were pressed together. Her displeasure was palpable. "Old friend?"

I cleared my throat. "Not really. She's just a girl," I said simply. "At one time Troian tried to set us up."

"Did you sleep with her?" she asked me pointblank.

"I slept in the same bed as her once, but we didn't have sex." *Because I passed out next to her.* I kept that part to myself.

"She's pretty," Hunter observed. She drank from her glass and stared at Megan over the rim.

"Yeah, but you're beautiful."

She turned her eyes to me and clucked her tongue against the roof of her mouth. "Such the charmer, Dr. Elle," she noted, borrowing Megan's nickname for me.

I rested my hand on her hip and toyed with the bottom hem of her shirt. I could feel the heat of her skin through the material. "I like Ellio better."

Her grin widened and any previous annoyance was banished from her face. "Dance with me?"

I couldn't handle how adorable this woman was.

A girl I didn't recognize walked up to us with a wild grin on her face. "Hunter?" she grinned warmly. "I thought that was you." What the hell was up with tonight?

Something about the way this woman was looking at my girlfriend made me feel more than a little territorial. My arm found its way around Hunter's waist.

"Oh, is *this* Elle?" the woman exclaimed as if noticing me standing

217

there for the first time.

Hunter nodded, looking terrified for some reason.

The nameless woman not so subtly raked her eyes over my body. I wasn't a fan of the leer on this woman's face. "Well," she purred, not taking her eyes off me, "now I know why you didn't get back to me," she said, giving me a wink.

I looked at Hunter, hoping she could help me make sense of all this. A pained smile was plastered on her face. The stranger wasn't entirely obtuse, however, and seemed to recognize her uneasiness. "Well, I guess I'll see you around," she chuckled before turning on her heels and sauntering away.

"Who was that?" The slightest bit of heated jealousy stained my tone.

Hunter turned her head from my inquisitive gaze. "Just a girl."

"Uh huh." I wasn't convinced. I knew there was a story here.

She sucked in a sharp breath. "Ok, fine. She's the girl…that I…at Troian and Nikole's party…" She trailed off.

At first I was confused when she didn't finish her sentence. But then I remembered. Hunter's hand was immediately at my elbow, catching me before I could storm off and do something we'd both regret.

"Let me go," I hissed. I tugged with annoyance at her tight hold.

Her grip was unforgiving; I wasn't about to break free. "Stop." Her breath was soft against my ear and she placed a single kiss near my earlobe. My body relaxed without my permission and she released her hold.

Even though I was no longer mad enough to punch a hole through that girl's face, I still continued to glare at her across the slightly crowded bar. "Is that your type?" I asked after a moment of unbroken glaring. My voice sounded like it had come from someplace outside of my body.

"My type?" Her hand found its way into mine. "Honestly?"

I finally turned to look at her. I was filled with nothing but apprehension. "Am I going to like the truth?"

She ducked her head. "Actually, I first noticed her because she kind of reminded me of you." She looked up and gave me a lopsided grin.

I flicked my eyes away from her face and back to where the other girl stood. "No way do I look like that piece of –."

A well-placed finger interrupted my tirade. I crossed my eyes slightly and stared at the finger pressed against my lips. "Don't," she gently chastised. "She's not important. None of that is. You're my type," she said. "Just you."

My eyes uncrossed when I stopped fixating on her finger. My lips curved up, and her hand fell back to her side. "You planning on dancing with me anytime soon?" I challenged, "I'm getting a little antsy."

"I need to go to the bathroom first," she nodded, "and then we can finally have that dance."

I downed the rest of my drink with alarming speed and ease. I wiped at my mouth with the back of my hand and set the empty pint on the bar. "I'll come with."

She quirked an eyebrow. "Don't trust me enough to go to the bathroom by myself?"

Her hand found mine once again. There seemed to be a lot of hand holding going on tonight, but I certainly wasn't complaining. "Oh, I trust you. I just know that trouble has a habit of finding you," I joked.

Her bottom lip stuck out and I leaned in to nip at it. She squeaked and pulled her lip back tight against her mouth. Her grey-blue eyes twinkled under the club lights, making me warm all over.

She pulled on my hand and guided me through the crowds towards the back of the bar where the restrooms were located. I took the opportunity to admire her backside as we made our way closer to the bathroom.

"Like the view?" she called over her shoulder.

Normally getting caught staring at her would have caused me to blush or at least made me tear my eyes away. But tonight was different. Tonight I had nothing to hide.

The women's bathroom was dimly lit, but surprisingly large for such a modest-sized bar. I suppose it made sense that the women's bathroom would be big at a lesbian club, though. The tiled room was narrow with a long line of bathroom stalls along one wall and a string of mirrors and sinks located on the opposite wall.

A thickly built woman with spiky, bleach blonde hair and a lip piercing stood near the front door. "One at a time," she barked out.

She crossed her meaty arms across her ample breasts and glowered at those of us waiting in line, daring us to disobey her rule. When she glared at the girls at the front of the line who were waiting for the next available stall, a few shifted their eyes to the ground.

"Why is there a bouncer in the girl's bathroom?" Hunter covertly whispered to me.

"Probably to make sure there's only one person in a stall at a time," I responded.

"Why would they…" She trailed off and her eyes grew wide when she suddenly answered my own question.

I smirked knowingly. "You can close your mouth now."

Back out in the club, we made our way to the semi-crowded dance floor. It was still early, but the bar had started to fill out since we had gone into the restroom. I could feel eyes on us as we made our way, hand-in-hand, towards the edge of the small dance floor. I felt myself wilting slightly beneath the attention until I felt Hunter squeeze my hand, pulling my attention back to her.

When we found a space on the floor big enough for the two of us, Hunter pulled me close and pressed her mouth solidly against mine. When she pulled away, I was slightly panting. "It's just you and me," she said, her expressive eyes staring hard into my own. I nodded, fixated on the smolder of her gaze.

I took the lead and turned her around, grabbing her hips and pulling her close so my body cradled her backside. I put my arm around her slender waist and pressed the full length of my body against her. We swayed back and forth for a few minutes, our bodies moving as one. The hand that wasn't holding her tightly around the midsection wandered down to the bottom hem of her short skirt. I innocently played with the material, but it felt anything but innocent with her so close, but not close enough.

"I can't wait to get you home," I panted in her ear. My fingers dangerously walked along the tops of her exposed thighs.

"There's always the bathroom," she said.

Without another word and before my brain had time to register what was happening, she clamped her hand around my wrist and dragged me off the dance floor in the direction of the bathroom. She moved with such speed and such purpose that I nearly tripped over my heels trying to keep up with her hurried pace.

She slipped into the women's restroom, pulling me behind her. There was no longer a line for the next stall. Most of the bathroom stalls appeared empty, but a few women stood in front of the sinks and mirrors, washing their hands and fixing hair and makeup. Unlike before, the bouncer stood on the opposite side of the long, narrow bathroom.

The formidable woman knocked hard on one of the closed stalls. "You'd better have four legs," she barked threateningly. The door immediately swung open and two women walked out, both ducking their heads and looking sheepish.

Taking advantage of the distraction, Hunter pulled me into the second empty stall. My heart was pounding in my ears when I closed and locked the stall door behind me.

Her hands immediately circled my waist. "We have to keep quiet," she husked into my ear. "Don't want to get tossed out on our ass by that Big Bertha out there for breaking the rules."

"What about..." I gulped down a mouthful of air. My eyes dropped to the floor. "Two sets of shoes," I pointed out.

She looked down to the floor as well. We might have snuck into the stall undetected, but it was only a matter of time before the burly female bouncer noticed the extra pair of shoes in the single stall.

Her hands crept under the bottom hem of my shirt. "You'll just have to make it look like there's only one person in here." I rose a questioning eyebrow and her smile turned into a leer. "I know you're strong enough to hold me up," was her whispered answer.

Even though I knew we had to be quiet or we'd be discovered, I couldn't help the small, pained whimper that crept out my lips.

She grinned and stepped closer. She grabbed my hand and brought it down to her right thigh. "Hurry up, Ellio," she quietly urged. "We don't have all night."

I worried my bottom lip, but obeyed. I channeled all my energy to my biceps and thighs and with a slight bend of my knees, I lifted her up into my waiting arms. She wrapped her legs around my midsection and my left arm clung around her waist. I placed a solid hand in the center of her back, keeping her steady. I rearranged her weight in my arms and she clung to the back of my neck.

"Don't worry," I said with a small grunt. "I've got you."

I repositioned us so her back was up against one of the stall

221

partitions, practically pinning her body between the wall and me. My free hand, the one not holding her in place, crept up the bottom hem of her skirt. "It's like you planned this or something," I quietly teased.

She bit her bottom lip when my free hand slid further up her muscled thigh beneath her thankfully loose skirt. My fingertips lightly skated over her skin before coming to rest on the elastic of her underwear at her hip. I curled my fingers beneath the waistband, just teasing. "Are these the red ones?" My hand was on the move again as if I would be able to identify her undergarments with just the tips of my fingers.

She shook her head. "They're purple. They're new."

My slightly pursed lips curled up. "Just for me?"

Before I could tease her a little bit more, her mouth was on me. She flicked her tongue against my lower lip and I immediately parted my mouth, allowing her access. I pulled my hand out from beneath her skirt, and she bit back a sudden moan when my hand palmed her breast over her camisole.

My fingers curled over the low neckline of her top, and I gently pulled the stretchy material down, pulling down her bra cup along with it. I cupped her bare breast, urgently kneading the pliable flesh; her nipple immediately responded to my aggressive touch. I knew how sensitive her nipples were, and even though this was just supposed to be a quickie in the women's restroom, I still aimed to be as attentive as ever. My fingers pulled and pinched at a hardened nipple, sending intense shocks of arousal straight to her core.

She clung tighter, squeezing my ribcage between strong thighs and she scratched short, polished nails down my back. I groaned and pressed my full weight against her, pinning her back harder against the bathroom partition. I was a little afraid we were going to destroy the bathroom and cause the stall walls to crash down.

She arched her back, creating more room between our upper torsos. It was just enough room to allow me to slide a free hand between our bodies. My fingers brushed along her panty-covered slit, and I could already feel her arousal through the material. She sucked in a quiet, sharp breath when I started to rub her clit through her underwear. I pressed down with what I hoped was just the right amount of pressure and her hips jerked forward. Even though my view was obscured because of her bunched up skirt, I could feel everything.

I buried my face into her neck. "So warm," I mumbled against her skin. I continued to rub her clit through her underwear in lazy circles, and with her legs spread apart and wantonly wrapped around my torso, she had no choice but to get wetter and wetter. She released a barely contained whimper when I pressed two fingers against her panty-covered hole. I pressed hard, pushing the lace material into her.

I continued those maddening, shallow thrusts until she had no choice but to beg. She gripped the back of my neck harder. "Please," she whimpered.

With anyone else, this was where my taunting, cocky smile would appear. But with her, I had no need to crow. I was tempted to rip off her underwear in my desire to get closer, but instead of destroying her new under-things, I pulled the crotch material out of the way and slid my fingers inside.

I slid into her hard, bottoming out. She gasped, just once, but it was sharp and loud, and my two fingers immediately stilled inside her. We were silent, unmoving, as we both waited to see if we'd been discovered. But after a few tense seconds passed with no one knocking on our stall door, my fingers started to move again. I flexed my digits, curling up into her. Her head fell back, and she banged her head against the metal partition wall.

"Careful," I quietly warned. "Don't give yourself a concussion."

I slid the arm wrapped around her down a little to give my other hand better access. I slowly, deliberately slipped my fingers all the way out. I rubbed her arousal against her clit before sliding back in. She gnashed her teeth when I continued these careful ministrations. It was probably the only thing she could do, short of biting her own tongue off, to keep from crying out.

"I wish I could see you," I panted lowly in her ear. "I want to see you sucking on my fingers."

She closed her eyes tight and released a quiet, yet shuddered breath. She whimpered in agreement. We needed to get home so we could do this the right way.

I widened my stance and shifted her weight in my arm. To keep from falling, she flexed her thighs and pressed her knees into my sides. She grabbed onto my shoulders and started to roll her hips so she was riding my fingers.

I couldn't tear my eyes away from the sight of her grinding her pelvic bone against my hand. "Fuck," I cursed in a pained tone. "You're so fucking sexy, Hunter."

Sweat had started to trickle down the small of my back and a series of quiet grunts were coming from Hunter. I could feel her tightening around my fingers as her orgasm inched closer and my slow, deep thrusts started to quicken. "Elle," she panted. "Don't stop, baby. I'm so close. Please don't stop," she desperately pled.

I thrust harder. "Never gonna stop," I promised.

When her orgasm hit, it was with such force that she threw her head back. Her body went rigid and her biceps eventually relaxed. It was only then that I realized how tired my own arms were. Her eyes fluttered close and her breathing was heavy. I couldn't tell if the sound throbbing in my ears was my rapidly pulsing heart or the echoing bass from the club. Her forehead was pressed against mine, and even though it felt slightly sweaty and sticky, you couldn't pull me away for all the lesbians in the world.

Our moment was broken, however, when a pack of loud, giggly women poured into the restroom. Their voices echoed in the tiled room, and Hunter slowly slid back down so her feet were once again on the floor. Her knees buckled when her shoes touched the ground and my arm was back around her waist to steady her.

"You okay there?" The sound of my voice surprised me. It was strange to hear it echo in my ears after futilely trying to be quiet.

She nodded sheepishly. "Yeah."

"Happy Birthday, baby."

She smiled, in a kind of sleepy, dream-like way. "Elle, can I tell you something without you freaking out?"

I instantly expected the worst. I wondered if it had something to do with the woman from Troian and Nikole's party who I'd met earlier in the bar. "Of course."

"I think I'm in love with you."

It felt right. I felt ready. "I'm so in love with you, Hunter," I returned.

I suddenly heard the booming voice of the bathroom bouncer, and I was struck with a wave of panic. *Oh God.* We were going to get caught. We were going to get dragged out of the bathroom by that woman out there and everyone would know what we had been doing in here.

"I'll go out first, okay?" she said into my ear. Her warm breath tickled me. "Lock the door when I leave, and then you can follow me whenever you're ready. I'll be waiting by the bar."

I gave her a relieved smile. I hope she recognized that my anxiety wasn't about being seen with her or the fact that she'd just said she was in love with me; I was just a little embarrassed that we'd had sex in a public restroom. It was like getting a hickey. I wasn't a teenager anymore.

She leaned in and kissed the tip of my nose. "Don't keep me waiting."

When she left, I refastened the lock on the bathroom stall. I waited a few beats before venturing out myself. She'd gone back out into the club, but I walked straight to the sinks, not making eye contact with anyone.

I stood before the wall-length mirror and appraised my reflection. I straightened the neckline of my camisole and pulled some paper towel off the rack to wipe the smeared lipstick off my mouth. It was Hunter's color, not mine. I tilted my head to the side and continued to inspect my reflection. My hair was slightly wild, but I kind of liked the look.

I smiled broadly at the woman in the mirror. To be honest, I looked like I just had sex in a bathroom stall. And surprisingly, it didn't bother me at all.

+++++

After being out at Peggy's until Last Call, I brought my girlfriend home to her apartment. I could have just as easily brought her back to my house, but I wanted to make an effort to spend more time in her space and in her world. Plus, if she was going to wake up the next morning with a hangover, I figured she'd prefer waking up in her own bed.

I parked my car on the street in front of her apartment. With my arm around Hunter's waist, we made it up the front steps. When we got to the front entrance, I looked through her purse for her keys. "Hey babe, which key is it?"

"I got it," she said, standing up on her own. She pulled the key ring from my hands and promptly threw the keys at the front door. The keys smashed against the entrance and fell noisily to the ground like a wind-chime in a hurricane.

"I don't think that's how keys work, love."

She stooped and picked up the key ring. "I'm not *that* drunk, Elle. I saw a centipede, that's all. Nothing should have that many legs."

"Oh." I shoved my hands into my pockets and waited for her to unlock the front door.

"You coming, Ellio?" She gave me a mischievous grin, and I sucked in a deep breath.

The front door had a tendency to stick. We both put our shoulders against her apartment door and pushed. The door gave way and we unceremoniously stumbled in.

"Shhh…" Hunter hushed me through her giggles. "Sara's sleeping."

As if on cue, a light flicked on in the hallway. "Not anymore."

I'd started to entertain the idea that maybe Hunter's roommate didn't exist, but now I had proof otherwise. A brunette in glasses and a ponytail walked into the hallway, out of room that I assumed was her bedroom. "Hunter," she said crossly, "do you know what time it is?"

Hunter seemed to instantly sober beside me. "Sorry, Sara."

Sara's eyes narrowed behind her thick lenses. "Professor Graft?"

Oh shit. I stared back at the girl. I didn't recognize her, but apparently she knew who *I* was. If I'd had her as a freshman, she could have physically changed, now as a senior; plus, because of the small size of the school, it wasn't unusual for students to know who I was without ever having taken one of my classes.

Hunter grabbed onto my elbow. "We're going to bed," she announced loudly. "See you in the morning."

I gave Sara a weak smile and wave as my girlfriend pulled me past her. I nearly stumbled to keep up as Hunter yanked me into her bedroom and closed the door behind us.

+++++

"I'm never drinking again," Hunter groaned. She rolled over on her side and curled into the fetal position, pulling her knees up to her chin.

After our brief run-in with Sara, the alcohol had really hit Hunter. She'd been putting on a good show up until then, but with her bedroom room closed, her sobriety had fallen apart. I'd helped her into her pajamas and into bed, had positioned a glass of water on her bedside table, and had crawled into bed beside her. Now, the morning after, she was swearing off alcohol entirely.

I sat up and reached for the glass of water I'd had the foresight of putting on her bedside table. "Have some water," I urged.

"No," she stubbornly refused. "It hurts my stomach."

"Drink it," I said more forcefully. "You'll feel better."

"*Nothing* will make me feel better," Hunter dramatically groaned before rolling back over on her back.

I arched an eyebrow. "*Nothing?* That sounds like a challenge to me." I walked my fingertips up the flat plane of her stomach.

"Ellio, I'm *really* not feeling good," she warned.

"Aw, you *must* be feeling bad if you're turning down sex," I teased.

She stuck out her lower lip. "Are you calling me a nympho?"

"Not at all. I just know I'm good at what I do."

"Have you taken a survey?"

"I'm Doctor Elle Graft. I do *everything* to the best of my abilities." I raked my short fingernails down her stomach.

"You're lucky Sara's just in the next room and I don't want to traumatize her."

The mention of her roommate brought back the memory of our brief encounter the previous night. "Sara seems to know who I am."

Hunter blinked up at the ceiling. "I caught that, too."

"I can't remember if I was ever her teacher."

She rolled onto her side and snuggled her head on my lap. I reflexively stroked my fingers through her hair. "She had to take the Writing Seminar – we all did – but I don't ever remember her talking about you. She must not have had you as a professor."

"Or else I didn't make that much of an impression on her," I pointed out.

"I don't see why not," Hunter said, wiggling to get comfortable. "Even straight girls have eyes."

"Do you think..." I paused, a little upset with myself for what I was about to ask my girlfriend to do. "Do you think you could talk to her? Make sure she doesn't say anything to anyone who shouldn't know about us?"

Hunter yawned and looked at her clock radio. "Yeah." She didn't look upset by my continued need for secrecy. "She's actually probably at the Farmer's Market right now, but I'll talk to her when she gets back. Who knows what she even thinks though. It's not like we were making out in front of her or she heard sex noises coming from my room."

I nodded. "I know. But it's also not every day that a professor at your school has a sleepover with your roommate."

Hunter made a humming noise. "True."

I leaned over and kissed her forehead. Even hung-over she still smelled good.

"I need to shower," she announced. "I feel the alcohol oozing out my pores."

"That's hot, baby," I said, wrinkling my nose.

"I know it's not. But what *would* be hot is my gorgeous girlfriend joining me in the shower. You know," she said, batting her long eyelashes up at me, "doing our part to save the environment, one shower at a time."

I made a disgruntled noise. God it was tempting. Oh-so-tempting. But I also knew I would be paranoid the entire time, wondering when her roommate would be coming home.

"I'm going to pass this time," I reluctantly said.

"No fun." She raked her fingers across my abdomen. "Are you *sure* I can't change your mind? Think about that carbon footprint."

This woman was going to be the death of me.

CHAPTER NINETEEN

The Monday after Hunter's birthday weekend, I sat at my faculty desk, browsing through the pictures on my phone. I stopped on an image of Hunter smiling, proud, holding up her first legal shot of alcohol. The aftereffects of the pint-sized drink were in the next photo with the most ridiculous, disgusted look captured on her face forever.

The night out at Peggy's, even though I had been originally reticent about showing my face at that bar again, had actually been really fun. Troian and Nikole had shown up later that evening – late as usual – but for once their tardiness had been to my advantage. Troian, of course, instantly suspicious whenever I looked remotely too happy, had concluded that I was either drunk or that Hunter had, in her words, "fucked me within an inch of my life." I had just serenely smiled and denied my friend the satisfaction of knowing the source of my happiness. It was true though – I was happy. Happier than I had been in a very long time. Little more than a week ago I had been miserable, running away to California with my friends, and running away from lap dances and blue bikinis. But now I was feeling secure and in love. I had the best girlfriend, the best of friends, and the career I'd always dreamed about.

A knock at my faculty office door pulled me out of my Hunter-induced trance. "Hey, Elle?"

"Yeah?" I looked up and saw my mentor, Emily, standing in the doorway. "Oh hey, Em. What's up?"

"I don't know if it's my place to say anything, but there's a rumor going around that I thought you should be made aware of."

One of the challenges of working for such a small school with such a small student population was the rumor mill. Even amongst the faculty members it could feel more like high school than a professional work environment sometimes. It wasn't a typical week at this university without some minor "scandal" making waves amongst the students, faculty, and staff.

"Oh, I hope it's a juicy one," I said, picking up my cup of tea.

"Juicy enough," she confirmed with a smug smile. "Apparently you're dating a student."

I nearly choked on my hot tea. "What?" I set my ceramic mug down; it felt like I couldn't catch my breath – like someone had punched me in the gut.

I must have worn my emotions on my face because Emily quietly cursed. I don't think I'd ever heard her swear before. She shut my office door and sat down in the spare chair. "What are you thinking, Elle?!" she hissed. Her face had taken on an unimpressed, pinched look, and I anticipated the worst from my teacher mentor.

I sucked in a deep breath. "She's not my student anymore," I defended myself, "and we didn't do *anything* while she was my student." My voice sounded a lot calmer than I actually felt. "Nothing unethical happened."

"Thank goodness," Emily breathed. "Because that's the *one* thing that will definitely get you canned, regardless of how good a teacher or scholar you are." She sighed and rubbed at her face. "You know this is probably going to come up in your review, right?"

I swallowed hard and nodded. "Am I in trouble, Em?"

She shook her head, looking remorseful. "I don't know, Elle. I honestly don't know how the members of your committee are going to take this."

I chewed on the inside of my cheek. "Do you know if it's gotten to Bob yet?"

"Don't worry about Bob. Worry about the other dinosaurs. Although they're probably wildly jealous you snagged a student," she joked with a tight smile.

Thad and I were the only really young faculty members in the department. The rest were mostly grey-haired men with great beards and hiked up pants that should have retired years ago. But with the state of the economy, they clung to their endowed chairs until they died. Because of the poor job market, I had been fortunate to be hired right out of graduate school. I had a lot of other friends still looking for jobs, adjuncting or doing something completely outside of academia – working at libraries, writing centers, or trying their own hand at being independent authors.

"Where did you hear the rumor?" I tentatively asked.

"One of the mail clerks at the Student Center," she said. "I was picking up mail and one of the little old ladies who works there saw I was in the English Department with you. She asked me if it was true."

"What did you say?"

Emily's face looked stonily serious. "That you're a grown-ass woman and that it's not anyone's business who you are or aren't dating."

"Thanks, Emily." I didn't know how this could have happened. Had someone seen us together at Peggy's? Was Hunter's roommate, Sara, responsible? Had it been the scene I had made at the site of the car accident and people assumed? Or had it been something else altogether? I thought I'd been so careful, but ever since getting back from California and I'd gotten my second chance with Hunter, I'd been a little bolder, a little more reckless. This was the worst timing ever. My tenure review was at the end of the week. I didn't have time for damage control.

"Listen, try not to worry about it, Elle," Emily advised me. "It's out of your hands now."

Easy for her to say.

+++++

That panicked look still hadn't left my face when I escaped to Troian and Nikole's condo soon after Emily left. I cancelled the rest of my classes and meetings for the day, knowing there was no way I'd be able to concentrate. I knocked loudly and with purpose on my best friends' front door. I could hear music coming from the other side, so I knew at least one of them was home. As a writer, Troian generally worked from home and could be found in her condo during the weekday unless Nikole was shorthanded and needed the extra help. I knocked again.

"Keep your shirt on," came Troian's voice. "I'm coming."

Normally her disgruntled attitude would have made me laugh, but I was too distracted for that today. The door swung open and she stood there, scowling. "What? Are you checking in on me? Couldn't be bothered to call in advance?"

"They know about Hunter and me."

The sour look on Troian's face faltered. "Who?"

"My university."

Troian's face visibly blanched and she stepped backwards. "Come in."

I paced the carpet in the living room while my friend watched from her seat on the couch. "How did they find out?"

I shook my head. "I have no idea. My teacher mentor, Emily – I think I've told you about her before – she told me she'd heard it from the mail ladies at the Student Union."

"Shit. That means it's *everywhere*." Troian had gone to my university as an undergrad years ago and she knew how vicious and unforgiving the small school's rumor-mill could be. She herself had remained closeted until after graduation to avoid it.

"What's the worst thing that could happen?" Troian asked reasonably.

I slowed my perpetual back and forth. "I could get fired."

"Would they really do that?"

I shrugged. I honestly didn't know.

"This is perfect. This is just the push you needed."

I stopped pacing altogether. "What are you talking about?"

"Now you can come work for me on this new TV show. The Studio loved the pilot script I sent them last week and they've ordered a half-season run of scripts."

"That's great news, Troi. Congratulations." I was genuinely happy for my friend even with my troubling issue. "But I'm not a screenwriter. I'm an English teacher."

"You're a writer – and a talented one at that. This could be really good for you."

I raised an eyebrow at my friend. "*You* didn't start the rumor on campus, did you?"

Troian laughed at my suggestion. "God, I'm almost mad at myself for *not* coming up with that idea."

I sat down heavily next to Troian on the couch and released a deep sigh. I rested my head in my hands.

"So now what?" Troian asked. "Are you still having your tenure review at the end of the week?"

I kept my head in my heads. "I haven't heard otherwise, so I'm assuming it's still on. They probably have to still meet with me as a formality. Then they'll deny me tenure on some technicality to avoid a teacher-student sex scandal, and then I'll get fired."

"That's not fair though," Troian said, raising her voice. "You didn't do anything wrong. You haven't broken any laws. If they fire you, we'll sue them."

"They can do whatever they want, Troi," I sighed miserably, looking up. "It's a private school and my sexuality doesn't prevent me from getting fired in this state."

Troian was quiet for a moment, no doubt letting my words sink in.

"Hey, if it gets bad, you know you're going to be okay, right?" She placed a reassuring hand on my shoulder. "Even if you get, I don't know, banned from teaching for the rest of your life, you've still got Nik and me. We'll totally hook you up with something, even if it's not writing with me. Gardening. Fast food. You'll be okay."

"I know." I nodded wetly and wiped at my nose. "Troian to the rescue."

+++++

I was cutting up vegetables for stir-fry when Hunter came over later that night. She tossed her bag on one of the kitchen countertops and gave me a quick peck on the cheek.

"Good day?" she asked me as she stole a piece of red bell pepper. She popped it into her mouth and smiled.

"It was okay," I replied, not looking up from the cutting board.

"Just okay?" she clucked. "Well, I'll have to see what I can do to make it better then." Her arms slipped around my waist, and I felt her press the full length of her body against my back. I closed my eyes and just enjoyed the feeling.

"Well, apparently there's a rumor going around campus that I'm dating a student."

I felt her body immediately stiffen. "You're dating a student? Do I know her?" I knew she was trying to make a joke and keep the mood light, but her voice sounded too high and tight. Regrettably, her arms fell away from my waist. "How did you find out?"

"Emily Sullivan. She's a professor in my department." I finished cutting up bell peppers and moved on to scallions.

"And how did she know?"

"Campus mailroom rumor-mill." My responses came out as terse, bulleted bursts, but it was the best that I could do without breaking down. I feared that if I elaborated too much that I might break down and cry. Since leaving Troian's house I'd done my best to keep my brain busy.

"Did they say my name specifically?"

"No. Just that I'm dating a student."

"Ellio," Hunter said experimentally, "are you alright?"

I kept my eyes trained on the cutting board, not wanting to slice off a finger. It also helped me maintain my calm exterior. I worried if I looked at her concerned visage, I might lose it. "Do I not look alright?"

"You look fine. And that's the part that's worrying me." Her hands fell on top of mine, stopping me from continuing cutting up vegetables. "Just stop for a second, okay?" She turned me around to face her and continued holding onto both of my hands. "What does this mean for us? Do I have to go into hiding? Can we not see each other until after graduation? Because I'll do it; just tell me what you need me to do."

"No," I said emphatically. "Nothing changes."

"You've got your review in a few days," she unnecessarily reminded me. "I don't want to be the reason they don't award you tenure."

She looked so concerned, it made my heart flutter. "Nothing changes," I said again. I pulled her to me. "My stupidity has caused too much drama between us, and I'm sorry for that. I'm not going to let myself be ruled by fear anymore. I want to be with you, Hunter. And if this is what gets me fired, then I wasn't meant to work at this school."

Her wide eyes blinked. "Just like that?" she asked. "You'd risk your job to stay with me?"

"It's just a job," I shrugged. After leaving Troian's house, I'd had more time to think about my situation. "There'll be others."

"I could say the same thing about me," she countered. "I'm just a girl. There'll be others."

I shook my head. "But you're *my* girl; I don't want anyone else."

Her eyes looked a little wet. "Can I help you with dinner?"

I smiled. "Why don't you pick out a bottle of wine from the rack for tonight?"

She nodded and tucked a lock of hair behind her ear. "I don't want to keep bringing this up, but how do you think the rumor started? I mean, I haven't told *anyone*. And Sara promised me she'd be discrete."

"I've been thinking about that, too." In truth the person culpable was limited. I hated thinking over the short list of people who knew that my girlfriend was a former student. I hated to think that anyone could betray me like that.

I mentally shook myself. It was done. The University knew. Emily was right. I needed to stop worrying; it was out of my hands now. The only thing I could do was wait. Wait until my tenure review.

+++++

I stood at the lavatory mirror and stared at my reflection. I hadn't felt like this in years – not since just before my presentation in front of the faculty when I was a job candidate for the position I currently held. I pulled my hair back into a tight bun. It was my lucky hairstyle. I wore it like this whenever I needed to feel professional. It was a little like Dumbo and his magic feather, but I'd take whatever edge I could, regardless if it was just psychosomatic.

A toilet flushed and my teaching mentor, Emily, appeared when one of the stall doors opened. Our eyes met through the vanity mirror and she gave me a tight smile. She stood next to me and began to wash her hands. "You'll be fine in there," she said, working up a sudsy lather.

"How can you be so sure?" I responded. We were the only ones in the bathroom and my voice echoed against the tile, sounding hollow to my ears.

She turned off the faucets and shook her hands. "You're too good of a teacher, colleague, and scholar for them to deny you tenure. They've invested too much in you to just let you go."

I couldn't meet her eyes directly, so I continued looking at her reflection. "I want to thank you for giving me the heads up about the rumor."

Emily pulled paper towel from the machine. "Is she worth it?"

I bit my lower lip. That Emily knew what pronoun to use shouldn't have come as a shock, but it was still a little jarring. "Yeah," I said with a nod. "She is."

Emily rested her hand on my shoulder and gave it a squeeze. "I hope so." She let go and offered me a final, encouraging smile. "Good luck in there, Dr. Graft."

I left the restrooms shortly after Emily's pep talk. I couldn't continue to hide and I couldn't delay this meeting any longer. As I stood in the hallway, just outside the conference room where my future would soon be decided, I could hear the quiet din coming from inside the room. I straightened the hem of my pencil skirt, and I straightened my shoulders. I pulled the door open and the chatter immediately quieted. I tried to not let that unsettle me. It happened nearly everyday I taught. I strode into the room with my chin elevated, mustering as much confidence as I could.

I took my seat at the center of a conference table that normally sat three or four. I hadn't sat in a conference room with so many of my faculty peers since my on-campus interview years ago. I took my time, arranging my things, unzipping my workbag, and pulling out a legal pad and pen. I snapped the pen to life and scrawled my name and the date in the right-hand corner of the top sheet. It was unnecessary. This wasn't a written test. There were no notes I needed to take. But, like my lucky hairstyle, writing my name and the date on that piece of paper was familiar and comforting.

Across the room, seated facing me, were the members of my tenure committee. My Department Chair, Bob Birken, was in the center flanked on either side by two full-ranking professors. I thought back to what Emily had referred to them as – dinosaurs. I recognized and knew them all because of the small size of our department, but I wasn't close to any of them. There were nearly 20 of us between the full-time tenure track and part-time adjuncts. Besides my Chair, Bob, the other four members had been chosen because our work rarely gave us an opportunity to become friendly. They were all white men, all full-ranking professors, and all grey haired or balding. One of the men, Thomas Dosey, was a Jesuit priest. I was worried the most about him. I had been to other tenure-track reviews before, to kind of get an indication of what I'd be subject to since every department at every university did theirs differently. The atmosphere in the room felt tense to me, but maybe I was just projecting.

Seated in the perimeter of the room was other faculty from the department. I gave Emily a smile as she sat down in an empty seat next to Thad. I smiled in his direction as well, but he didn't return the greeting. I wondered if he had on his Game-Face because of the serious nature of this meeting or if his stony exterior was in response to having heard that I was gay and taken.

The semester had been filled with one-on-one meetings with the Department Chair, getting colleagues to write letters of recommendation for me, and having other faculty observe my teaching on unannounced classroom visits. I thought I had built a solid relationship with Bob and that he would have given me some kind of warning or heads up that the review wasn't going in my favor. I had been publishing since my original hire date, so that wasn't anything to worry about. I always got excellent end-of-semester student reviews, too. The only thing that could get in my way of the promotion would have been choosing a faculty peer with a vendetta against me to write me a letter of recommendation. And now the Hunter thing.

Bob took a sip of water before beginning. It all felt very much like I was on trial. In a way, I suppose, I was. The questions that followed from each member of the tenure committee were mundane and unthreatening. Emily had prepared me well, and I was ready for everything they threw at me. Time passed quickly, and with each new question that wasn't the Question-I-Dreaded, I started to relax. Maybe this was it. Maybe they didn't care. Maybe I was actually going to get this promotion.

Bob adjusted his reading glasses on his nose and coughed, sounding uncomfortable. "Um, just one final question before we adjourn to make our decision, Dr. Graft."

My pulse throbbed a little faster. Oh no. *This was it.* "Yes?"

He shuffled his papers around. "Uh, what is the nature of your relationship with Hunter Dyson?"

I didn't blink. "She's my partner."

A few members of the committee looked startled and a spattering of hushed murmurs followed my answer. I didn't know what kind of response they'd been expecting from me, but I had been prepared for this. I wasn't going to sputter, or make excuses, or look weak. I was stronger than that. I wasn't going to deny my relationship, either. We had done nothing wrong. I wasn't going to let myself be bullied by fear anymore.

Bob nodded solidly. "Thank you, Elle," he said with a brief smile. "I think we have all we need."

I rose from the table and smiled mildly at each member of the tenure committee. "Thank you all for your time today," I said in the most civil tone I could muster. "I look forward to hearing your decision."

My hands shook a little and it took me a moment to collect my workbag and the legal pad that was still blank except for my name and the date. When I finally gathered my things, I strode out of the conference room and didn't look back.

I took the elevator down without bothering to stop at my office first. When the doors opened again on the ground level, I exited the lift. There, sitting nervously in the building lobby like it was a hospital waiting room, was Hunter. I hadn't known she would be waiting for me. I thought she was at the hospital today.

She spotted me and immediately stood up. She looked so perfect, even in jeans and a t-shirt. Her winter jacket was left, forgotten for the moment, on the chair in which she'd previously sat.

I could see the concern etched across her beautiful face. "So?" she asked me, wringing her hands in front of her body. "How did it go?"

Instead of finding my words, I burst into tears, and for the first time in recent memory, I wanted someone to take care of me. She threw her arms around me, and I let myself be weak.

+++++

EPILOGUE

I leaned against the balcony and breathed in. The air felt a little crisp and smelled of salt and seaweed. The sun, burning through a morning fog, already felt warm on my skin. It was mid-December, but you'd never know it. Malibu was beautiful around Christmas time.

I watched her wade on the shoreline. From the anonymity of my balcony perch, I watched Hunter kick at the crashing whitecaps as they crested and slammed against the sandy shoreline, slowly eating away at the solid land mass. One day the ocean would reclaim the rest of the world.

She seemed to me a piece of beach glass, sharp around the edges and unremarkable until years of being thrown against the sandy shore had worn down her sharpness and polished her smooth. She kicked her long legs, timing each lift of her limbs perfectly with the rolling waves. Something about it struck me – like she was fighting against something so massive, despite knowing the impossibility of ever winning.

I turned from the balcony and wandered downstairs to the kitchen, with its magnificent views of the ocean, and began gathering the materials I'd need to make us breakfast. The Malibu condo on the beach was a bit of an indulgence, but I'd promised myself that when I had my tenure review, regardless of the outcome, I'd rent a beachfront property for as long as I could and spoil myself for all my hard work. Troian, with her influential Hollywood connections, had gotten me a good price on the rental property and I had it through the end of the month. Hunter had flown to California with me after her last final of Fall semester was complete, but would be returning home for Christmas to spend the holiday with her parents. I thought that maybe she might return to Malibu with Troian and Nikole for New Years, but for now I was thankful for the time we had together.

Not long after I started on the waffles, fruit, and bacon, Hunter came bouncing into the kitchen like an over-exuberant puppy. "How's my Associate Professor girlfriend doing this morning?"

"That's a mouthful."

"That's what she said," Hunter retorted. She picked up a blueberry from the bowl of fruit salad and popped it into my mouth.

"I would be doing even better if you hadn't snuck out on me this morning. I woke up to an empty bed," I pouted around the piece of fruit.

"But this weather is just too perfect," she remarked, sneaking a piece of bacon off the paper towel where it cooled. "I couldn't *not* take advantage of it."

"Have a nice run?" I asked.

"Mmhmm," Hunter confirmed, resting her chin on my shoulder. "The best. I love running on packed sand."

"You're ridiculous," I remarked. "No one actually *likes* running, do they?"

"Just you wait, babe. I'm going to get you into running one of these days. It's addictive," she added, "like sex."

I cleared my throat. It still made me blush to hear her talk like that even though I should know better by now. "Well in the meantime, why don't you hop in the shower, and by the time you get out, I'll have breakfast ready."

"You. Are. Amazing." Her arms tightened around my waist and she punctuated each word with a nuzzle of her nose against the back of my neck. "How did I get so lucky?" She stood on her tiptoes to kiss my cheek and then spun away to skip down the hallway in the direction of the bathroom.

I continued stirring the waffle batter. "I guess you can thank your winter jacket," I mumbled under my breath.

"What'd you say, Ellio?" Hunter's voice filtered down the hallway. "I didn't hear you."

"Nothing, love," I said, raising the volume of my voice. "Don't take too long in there or the waffles will get soggy."

"You could always join me," she sing-songed as she made her way to the bathroom attached to the master bedroom. I'd already fallen in love with that bathroom – a massive Kohler shower and a tub that put most backyard pools to shame. "That's why God invented microwaves."

I bit my bottom lip to keep from laughing out loud. How had *I* gotten so lucky? I wasn't quite sure the answer to that question, but I knew I owed someone from the University Physical Plant at least a fruit basket for that damn broken classroom heater.

When my tenure committee had called me with the results of my review, just hours after the public meeting, I'd honestly been flabbergasted to hear their news. They wanted to promote me from an Assistant to Associate Professor – I'd achieved that long-awaited tenured status.

Troian seemed to be the only one disappointed by the news. I still could have resigned and joined her new television-series venture, but I'd meant what I'd told her before – I was an educator, not a scriptwriter. Writing screenplays would have been the easy route. I wouldn't have to apologize for my sexuality. I wouldn't have to continually deal with the knowing smirks from faculty and staff. But in a few years all of the current students would have graduated, and in time another "scandal" would distract the university employees from my own personal drama.

When the new contract had been signed, and I was sure they couldn't retract the recent appointment, I'd approached the Chair of my Department, Bob Birken, to find out how they'd known about my relationship with Hunter. He revealed that the Dean's Office of the College of Arts & Sciences had received an anonymous phone call regarding the matter. From there, they'd taken the time to look over Hunter's records, looking for grade discrepancies to see if she'd received any special treatment from me while in my class. I was offended they'd gone through Hunter's student records, but I'd bit back my indigent retort, knowing it was just standard procedure for these kinds of things.

Finding nothing incriminating, since there *was* nothing to find, they'd determined that no ethical breaches had been made and that as long as Hunter didn't enroll in any of my other classes in the future, we were free to continue dating without university interference. The latter wasn't going to be an issue since she was graduating in a semester.

I was still bothered by not knowing who had betrayed my confidences. I'd contacted Ruby not long after my tenure meeting. She'd insisted she hadn't called the Dean, staying loyal to her promise to me. I believed her, but that unfortunately meant that one of Hunter's parents had probably made the call, hoping to get me fired.

Maybe I'd been too careless at Peggy's on Hunter's birthday night, or maybe my outburst at the scene of her car accident had drawn unwanted attention to our relationship. But my gut told me that Hunter's parents had something to do with it. I hadn't approached the topic with Hunter yet though. She'd told me she and her mom were just starting to rebuild their relationship. We'd get to that bridge eventually.

Down the hallway I could hear the shower turning on followed by the sound of Hunter's melodic voice singing a song I didn't immediately recognize. I stared at the plate of fleshly-made waffles. Hunter's words echoed in my head: *That's why God invented microwaves.*

I pulled the plug on the waffle maker and tossed the bowl of extra batter into the sink. We had plenty of time to have breakfast later. But for now, I had a carbon footprint to whittle away at with my girlfriend.

+++++

ABOUT THE AUTHOR

Eliza Lentzski is the author of lesbian fiction, romance, and erotica novels including *Second Chances, Date Night, Diary of a Human, Love, Lust, & Other Mistakes*, and the forthcoming *All That Is Gold* (Fall 2013). Although a historian by day, Eliza is passionate about fiction. She calls the Midwest her home along with her partner and their cat and turtle.

Follow her on Twitter, @ElizaLentzski, and Like her on Facebook (http://www.facebook.com/elizalentzski) for updates and exclusive previews of future original releases.

Made in the USA
Lexington, KY
25 September 2013